THE MOTHER MURDERS

THE
MOTHER
MURDERS

Dale L. Gilbert

St. Martin's Press
New York

Library of Congress Cataloging-in-Publication Data

   Gilbert, Dale L.
     The mother murders.
     I. Title.
PS3557.I338M6   1989   813'.54   88–29813
ISBN 0–312–02613–7

First Edition

10 9 8 7 6 5 4 3 2 1

THE
MOTHER
MURDERS

CHAPTER 1

*T*he earth had nearly stopped bucking and rolling beneath my feet. An acquaintance from the marina where my boat was moored had conned me into signing on as a foredeck ape for that raucous, downhill slide known as the Acapulco Race. His outdated Columbia 50 had finished well back in class B. My equilibrium finished two days later. My digestion was lost at sea, and yet to be heard from. I'd flown home the night before and was enjoying an early morning romp on the beach with Dirk for the first time in more than two weeks.

Dirk is a real clam, but often gets chatty as an old maid around the end of the second mile. It's simply another form of intimidation—gives him a chance to show you he's not the least bit winded.

"You'll never guess who called me while you were gone, Matt," he told me.

"Who?" My answers tended to be brief. After all, I was lugging around maybe thirty pounds more beef than he was. Besides, he was right—I couldn't begin to guess. Nobody ever called Dirk.

"Marlee Reynaud—my stepmother." He stated it rather diffidently, as if uncertain of an appropriate emotion. Dirk wasn't on intimate terms with emotions.

It's a good thing he'd thrown in the identification, or I'd never have known who he was talking about. "I never knew you two kept in touch."

"We haven't; she just happened to read one of those articles the papers are always running about the boss, and it gave our names, too. Turns out she works right up the road in Solana Beach, so she gave me a call."

"That's terrific—what's she like?"

"She's okay, I guess; we didn't talk too much. Guess she left that backwater parish in Louisiana after I . . . what happened to my father. Went to Baton Rouge, and picked up enough secretarial skills to land a job. Marlee was always quick—and ambitious. Couple of months ago, she came out here just like she always dreamed. Got a pretty good job as a secretary for some builder."

He spoke as effortlessly as if we were parked on a bench, even as we thrashed our way through soft, ankle-deep sand at a good clip. Sand running is easily the toughest kind of jogging, but it really installs overload springs in the legs. And it requires only a fraction of the time and distance of hard-surface running. Best of all, it doesn't damage the musculoskeletal system, as jogging often can.

I lumbered beside him, gasping like a beached whale. "How old's this stepmother of yours?"

Dirk frowned in concentration. "Let's see—she was sixteen when my father married her, I think. I was seven. That makes her forty-three now. She invited me over to her place for dinner last night."

"Forty-three, huh? Hell, she's still on the right side of the hill. If she's cute, I might even take her out to dinner myself."

For an instant his thin, lynx-like face hardened into an ugly mask. Then he saw the goofy grin on my face and actually blushed. "She's not your type; she's a real lady."

"It's just as well. Judging by that look on your face, dating your stepmother would be a risky proposition."

It was coming up on nine o'clock on a Monday morning in April. By the time we'd backtracked, some early bird sun worshipers were already arriving. The typical coastal overcast wouldn't burn off much before eleven, but there they were, staggering under armloads of beach furniture, coolers, even DC TVs. One guy was busy setting up his portable computer. With any luck, they'd never even notice they'd left home.

Louis—our beloved dimwit, who keeps the house shining and pretends he can cook—hadn't had a chance to launch an assault on my stomach in two weeks, so I knew I was in for the Prodigal Son treatment. Later, I'd sneak out and have breakfast at a coffee shop in La Jolla.

Randy was glad to see me back. Dr. Randolph Bruckner is our resident whiz kid. His elaborate lab takes up the entire basement of the huge, old Spanish-style house, belching forth such diverse items of interest as miracle elixirs for my boss and exotic weaponry for me.

My boss, of course, you know. Carter Winfield is the oldest living former secretary of state, and easily the most revered. Everybody also knows he had the presidency handed to him on a platter, but he handed it back. The press likes to refer to him as a national treasure. I wouldn't know about that; they never had to live with him. The truth is, we all treasure him, too, except when he's so stubborn, unreasonable, or pompous we'd like to boot his bony behind. Which is frequently. He answers to the name Win as the result of a long-ago proposed campaign slogan: Win with Winfield. The memory of it appalls him to this day. I suspect it may have been one of the reasons he refused to run. But then, he'd never run for any elective office. If there were a way to become president by demanding it, he probably would have done so. Anyway, Randy and I are about the only ones alive who can get away with calling him Win.

I was busy describing the delights of changing headsails on a bow that was underwater half the time—this was on the dog watch during an icy gale—when Win entered the room. He's my height—six foot even—but I'd make two of him. Except between the ears. There may not be much spring in his step, but he doesn't shuffle like an old man either. His face hasn't shown up on any stamps yet, but it's going to look just fine when they get around to it. He has one of those faces women envy—the older he gets, the better it looks. The hair, though pale silver now, is still a lush crop. With the possible exception of a mite too much patrician nose, everything else is standard issue. Everything except the eyes. The only pair I've ever seen like them was owned by a hawk in a cage in the San Diego Zoo.

"Good morning, group," he greeted us. The vibrant baritone that had once swayed recalcitrant heads of state was still intact. His appearance at breakfast was not unheard of, but rare.

I responded with a "Morning, Win." Randy managed a muffled sound around a mouthful of food. Dirk, suffering from a severe case of hero worship, insisted on a "Good morning, Mr. Winfield."

Win settled gracefully into his chair at the head of the big oak table, hooking his ever-present cane over the back. He never seemed to utilize the wide-grained beauty, which he insisted was English oak, but I figure that was because of pride, of which he had enough for an army. I suspected maybe he leaned on it pretty good when he was sure no one was watching.

Favoring me with those incredibly intense gray eyes, he said: "I see the intrepid sailor is home from the deeps. How was your voyage, Matt? Must I anticipate enduring more such absences in the future, or have my predictions come to pass?"

That explained his unusual appearance at breakfast—he'd come to gloat. "They have—as usual. I believe you described it as 'a puerile sport, measuring little more than a man's wealth, without even the redeeming factor of being enjoyable.' What can I say? You hit it on the head. If I ever get that particular wild hair again—which I sincerely doubt—I'll stand under an ice-cold shower, and tear up hundred-dollar bills until it goes away. The principle's about the same."

"An excellent analogy. I once made the same mistake. My best friend badgered me into crewing on his schooner in the Bermuda Race. Lovely vessel! I'd day-sailed aboard her any number of times, and enjoyed his companionship enormously. But the moment that starter's gun sounded, I found myself trapped at sea in close company with an absolute tyrant. It was unbelievable. There must be some atavistic potential still deep in the hearts of men, able to be triggered by the primitive factors of sea, sails, and competition."

He was feeling expansive, and with good reason. He'd just verified that I'd been as miserable as he'd hoped I'd be, and I wouldn't be deserting him again just to get blown somewhere on a boat.

Louis shuffled in bearing a big covered silver platter. He grinned when he saw Win. Setting it down, he lifted the lid with a flourish. Something over half a dozen eggs—it was impossible to get an exact count—were revealed swimming in an oily yellow sea. My stomach knotted at the sight, and I looked at Win in dismay. He smiled back. Win was immune to such mundane considerations as food, and Louis could do no wrong in his eyes. Some day I'll find out why.

I refilled my coffee cup and tried not to watch Randy and Dirk transferring some of the runny hen fruit to their plates. Desperately hungry, I scraped most of the black off a couple of slices of toast and layered them half an inch thick with jam. You never knew with Louis. Sometimes the eggs came out with the same plastic consistency as the trick ones you find in novelty shops. Occasionally, they were even edible. He had a short attention span, was the problem.

"Dirk, how was your evening?" Win inquired. "How long since you'd seen your stepmother?" Small talk from Win was another rarity. Especially with Dirk.

Dirk shifted uncomfortably. He'd gladly have taken on tigers if Win asked, but when it came to table talk he came all over shy. "About sixteen years, I guess. She still fries everything, but it was all right. Sounds as if she likes it here, and her job is okay, too. It was good seeing her." That was quite a speech, for Dirk.

"I'm pleased to hear it. Though you share no actual consanguinity, I'm sure her propinquity will provide you with many satisfactions."

I made a mental note to see Dirk after breakfast and translate consanguinity and propinquity. Win liked using words he was afraid were being neglected or in danger of being lost. If you didn't happen to understand, that was your tough luck. He figured there were plenty of dictionaries in the house. The thought of Dirk looking up a word in a dictionary made me smile.

Randy took over the conversation, beginning a detailed explanation of his current project. It apparently involved delivering drugs like antibiotics by aerosol directly into the cardiovascular system via the lungs. When I asked what the point was, he told us the digestive process altered, and even destroyed, many medicines that were swallowed.

It was quite a show to watch him when he got excited. His Coke-bottle-bottom glasses transformed his small brown eyes into huge, superanimated orbs. Trickles of local clover honey, to which Randy was sorely addicted, dripped down his pudgy chins. It's always been a toss-up which he loved most—talking or eating. It only figured he was happiest while doing both.

Since I was faking it with nothing but coffee and toast, I finished ahead of the pack and was nursing my third cup when the doorbell rang. Fortunately, the one skill Louis had somehow mastered was making a decent cup of coffee. He came blasting out of the kitchen, his bare feet slapping across the tiled floor. We'd tried getting him to wear shoes, but he liked the feel of the cool tile underfoot. But he hated interruptions during meals. You'd have thought he was a four-star chef. Hell, maybe he thought he was.

"I'll get it," I told him, holding my hand up. "I'm finished anyway."

"Thank you, Matt." A look of relief appeared on his face, and he about-faced and hurried back into the sanctuary of his kitchen. One of his duties he hated most was answering the door. Strangers were difficult for him. I imagined it was mutual, when callers found themselves faced with a barefoot guy in wrinkled clothes, usually in need of a shave and very likely a bath as well. Whenever possible, I intercepted him, especially if we were expecting a client. As far as I knew, that was not the case this morning. I took my time strolling down the long hall and opening the massive, hand-carved door. It swung in on its hinges like a dream.

I had to fight to resist a powerful urge to slam it back shut. Inspector Dixon, together with two other plainclothes types, was standing outside waiting ominously. The smug look on Dixon's fat face worried me. He'd assumed the job of being the bane of our existence ever since Win and I had gotten our P.I. licenses. You'd have to ask him why. He looked like Oliver Hardy, except he wasn't funny. They say he was a top-notch lab man—criminalist—before he transferred to Homicide. Guys I know at the SDPD swear he used to talk like a college professor, but now he came on like one of the Bowery Boys. I guess he thought it fitted his new tough-guy image. Picture Stan Laurel's buddy, Ollie, trying to play a tough guy, and you'll understand why I had a hard time keeping a straight face.

"Let me guess," I told him. "You sell enough subscriptions and you get to go to camp this summer."

"Dunno who ever said you were cute, Doyle. Take it from me—they lied!" He bulled his way in, with the others right on his heels. Those two were tense, eyes probing everywhere, jackets open, hands restless, hovering. They all but had their guns drawn.

It made no sense to me. "If you want to see Mr. Winfield it's a little early. We're all still at breakfast. I'll let you wait in the office if you promise not to swipe any paper clips."

"Never mind the office, and the hell with your boss. All I want to know is where's that murdering little playmate of yours?"

"If you mean Dirk," I told him evenly, "I suggest you mind

your mouth. You can practice doing it on the way out." I re-opened the door and waited.

Without accepting my invitation, he reached inside his rumpled jacket and extracted a couple of folded forms I imme-diately recognized as warrants. "Close the door, Junior," he ad-vised me rudely. "I've got two, see? One for him, and another to search the house. I'd just as soon serve them both; no telling what a search of this joint would turn up. Your choice!"

I held out my hand and accepted them, examining each carefully, stunned to silence for once in my life. It wasn't that I really thought he'd try to slip one by me with a phony warrant, but my mind was in high gear and I was buying time to see what it came up with. Frantically, I juggled all the options. There were very damn few. Turning Dixon loose in the place was entirely out of the question, and served no purpose. If he had a warrant for Dirk, best to let him serve it, and then proceed to make him live to regret it.

"Spelled his name right, so I guess it's official. What'd he do? Forget to pay a traffic ticket?"

"When it's your name on the warrant, that's when I'll tell you, Doyle. It doesn't figure to be too long. Now quit stalling and produce Dirk Bomande—now!"

I motioned for them to follow and headed back toward the dining room. Randy was still chattering away, and continued to do so even as Win and Dirk froze, eyes fixed upon the trio behind me. I think Randy's peripheral vision must be lousy, but he fi-nally followed the others' gaze and shut up.

"Mr. Doyle," Win said gravely, "you should have invited these gentlemen to wait in the office. Please do so now. Though they haven't an appointment, I'll do them the courtesy of seeing them after breakfast."

Even as Win spoke, Dixon pointed at Dirk, and the pair of detectives circled the table from opposing sides. Dirk rose to his feet, stretched like a cat, forcing himself to relax, preparing him-self, I knew, for mayhem. Unless I moved quickly, there were two cops I knew of who were about to die with their boots on.

"Win, order Dirk to stay cool—they've got a proper warrant. Whatever this is about, let's not compound it."

Win broke off glaring at Dixon and faced Dirk. "Sit down and compose yourself, Mr. Bomande." That settled it—Dirk calmly obeyed the only man in the world whose commands were sacrosanct to him. "Don't touch him," he charged the two men bracketing Dirk. Then he shifted back to Dixon, eyes blazing fire. "This is intolerable, Inspector. How dare you intrude upon my household like this?"

Dixon's voice always betrayed his dilemma concerning Win until he got wound up. He hated him on general principles—as he did all private cops—and he hated him for making a monkey out of him in the past, but he still couldn't quite get over the fact that he was dealing with one of the most revered men in the country. So a note of deference snuck in on him every time, he knew it, and he hated it.

"I wouldn't call it an intrusion, Mr. Winfield. This . . . Mr. Bomande is a murder suspect. We're going to have to take him downtown and book him. And I'll give you some good advice— you'd better start looking for another chauffeur," he added smugly, just to show he wasn't cowed by Win.

"A suspect in the murder of whom?" demanded Win.

"I don't mind telling you," Dixon allowed expansively. "The victim's name was Marlee Reynaud."

Dirk's normally stoic face registered first confusion, then shock, and finally horror. The kitchen door opened a crack, and I caught a glimpse of Louis's nose. Win appeared absorbed in thought, puzzled. "Marlee Reynaud?"

"Dirk's stepmother," I prompted him.

Win looked over at Dirk. "I'm sorry. To have barely re- discovered her after so many years, then learn of her demise in this brutal fashion—it's unspeakable!" He reached over and gripped Dirk's rocklike forearm. It was a remarkable gesture for a man who often went to extraordinary lengths to avoid physical contact with his fellow men.

"Okay, Bomande; let's get it over with," Dixon snapped.

Win snapped right back. "Ask your infernal questions here—use my office if you must. I accept all responsibility for the actions of this man. Your past harrying of me and my staff has been only a minor annoyance, but this . . . ."

"I'm not here to harry anybody," Dixon broke in. He'd gotten over the hump, now, and was willing to swap verbal brickbats with my boss all day. "And I'm not the least bit interested in hearing him answer any questions. It's all sewed up—he did it. So you might reconsider that remark about accepting all responsibility." He nodded at the nearest of his men and told him, "Bundle him up and let's get out of here."

Win looked angrier than I'd ever seen him before. "You are not to touch this man in my house," he stated matter-of-factly. "And beyond its walls, you will treat him properly, within the letter of the law, extending him every right and privilege to which he's due."

He pushed himself erect, making a bit of a production of it, I thought, grabbed his cane, and said, "Come, Dirk; walk with me to the door." Placing his hand on Dirk's shoulders, they walked slowly in tandem down the long hall. Another unprecedented physical gesture on Win's part. Then I saw the reason for it—Win was talking a mile a minute into Dirk's ear. I couldn't make out what Win was telling him, but I hoped he was ordering him to refrain from killing off any of his captors before we could bail him out.

I got the door, and they went out on the red tile porch. Win stepped back, grimacing in real pain at the sight of them cuffing Dirk. That done, they led him over to the back seat of the unmarked black car at the foot of the steps. The four of us—Win, Randy, Louis, and me—stood silent vigil until the vehicle was completely out of sight.

Win preceded me into the office, where I folded myself into my favorite chair in the world and waited. Win's door-sized desk was in front and to the right of my smaller one. Once he got settled, I had him in three-quarter profile. I could gauge his agitation level by the way his jaw muscles worked. He doesn't know it, but he grinds his teeth when he's upset. He was upset now.

"That man is an insupportable ass, Matt. Did you know he tried to stop me from obtaining my private investigator's license? On the basis of both age and my having a convicted felon, Dirk, in my employ."

"Dixon? Yeah, he doesn't approve of private enterprise—especially ours. But he's no fool; better figure he's got a pretty strong case against Dirk, or he'd never have pulled this stunt. Of course he managed it to humiliate you, that's just like him, but he didn't get those warrants on charm alone." I reached under my desk for my North San Diego County phone directory. "We're in luck! Marlee's listed in the new phone book. Not even ten minutes north of here, in Solana Beach. I'm going up there and nose around a little. Any instructions?"

"No," he replied angrily. "Circumstances will dictate. Be circumspect. I can't afford having you run afoul of that vexatious cossack as well."

"Cheer up! By the look on your face you'd think you were half convinced he's guilty. We both know damn well he's not, and even Dixon wouldn't manufacture evidence to convict an innocent man."

An expression of grave concern remained deeply etched on Win's narrow face. "I'm afraid I've seen too much during my lifetime to share your touchingly naive belief in unerring justice. And have you forgotten the fact that Dirk killed her husband—his own father?"

CHAPTER 2

I hadn't forgotten. As I rolled north along Pacific Coast Highway, I remembered the bizarre tale of Dirk's early life Win had told me when I first came to the big hacienda-style house to live and work. At the tender age of seven, Dirk had witnessed his father, in the throes of a drunken rage, murder his mother and hide her weighted body in the deepest waters of the bayou bordering their crude home. She'd been the sum total of everything worthwhile in the boy's lonely life in the wild. Withdrawing into himself, the child dedicated his life to one goal. He became nearly as one with the beasts of the surrounding marsh and forest. The few hours a day spent at the tiny school nearly ten miles away were only a nuisance to be endured until he could resume his true education alone and unfettered by convention. Every day he trained: running, swimming, hunting, fishing, exercising; driving his small body into a bone-weary state of fatigue that would enable him to sleep beneath the same roof as his hated father one more night.

A few months after his mother's "disappearance," Marlee

moved in. She'd apparently tried to establish some rapport with the wildly independent child, but such a hope was forlorn. She sometimes managed to slip him enough food to sustain him, together with what he harvested from woods and stream as a result of his ever-increasing skills. The only regular meal of the day, supper, was often denied him on the basis of some real or imagined transgression. He was as likely to find a beating waiting when he returned home as a meal. Little did the man realize that even this outrage was utilized by the boy as a part of his training regimen.

Dirk was just thirteen the night things reached a climax. Again in a colossal drunken rage, his father greeted him on his return with the pronouncement he was going to give the boy the beating of his life. When he selected a fireplace poker as his weapon, Dirk knew he would have to fight for his very life.

The battle stacked up badly for the adolescent. Though nearly six years of intensive effort had molded his slender physique to the strength and suppleness of a sapling, he faced a man more than a head taller, nearly a hundred pounds heavier, and not yet too far from his prime. The fight was joined. The boy sustained many a punishing blow, yet fought on tenaciously. Marlee, perhaps sensing the seriousness of the confrontation—or maybe out of personal fear—ran screaming into the night.

As the gruesome struggle wore on, the man found himself becoming spent, yet the boy seemed to grow only stronger. Soon, it was the smaller combatant who scored more often, and his opponent hadn't the ability to absorb as much punishment. Ultimately, the boy rendered him senseless with a powerful kick directly to the solar plexus. When he regained his senses, the dazed father found himself lying trussed in the bottom of the fish-foul punt normally found tied to his dock. He must have been horrified to discover the homemade concrete anchor that was fastened to his belt. Surely he realized it was no coincidence, when the boat stopped at the precise spot where he'd disposed of his wife so many years before. Dirk had never said whether or not words were exchanged before he rolled the hated man over the

gunnel, to disappear forever, but it's inconceivable the man went
to his horrid death in silence.

When it was done, Dirk had rowed north as far as navigable
waters existed, then discarded the boat and never looked back.
He'd never actually known whether or not the authorities were
even looking for him. In 1971 he'd enlisted in the army, and
spent two tours of duty in Vietnam. Then, nearly eight years after
the fact, as he stepped off the ship from Southeast Asia to a
supposed hero's welcome, they were waiting for him. By
guilelessly enlisting under his true name, he'd ultimately pro-
grammed his own capture. And there is no statute of limitations
on murder.

He might have gotten away with his self-defense plea had his
court-provided lawyer been even marginally skilled, or had Dirk
bothered to present himself more sympathetically to the jury. He
had not; his ability to relate to his peers was severely stunted as a
result of his lonely habits. Even his superb combat record became
a two-edged sword. On the one hand, it colored him as a loyal,
fiercely dedicated citizen. On the other, it profiled him as an
unusually willing and efficient slayer of men. Such men are
priceless on the front lines, but back home on the streets they
tend to make people uneasy.

The verdict was manslaughter, and Dirk served seven years.
It would have been longer if Win hadn't somehow heard about the
case and ultimately arranged Dirk's parole. It had worked out
well for both parties. Dirk was whole again, as near as he'd ever
be. He suffered from severe aversion to confined spaces. More
than once, I'd watched him jump to his feet inside the house and
run outdoors for a while. It was going to be hard time for him
until we got him free again. I swore it wouldn't take one minute
longer than necessary, if I could help it. Dirk had been my strong
right arm on many a case and had almost certainly saved my life
on one occasion. I'd get him out if I had to use dynamite.

The address in the tiny beach community north of Del Mar
turned out to be one of those sterile-looking buildings that seem

to sprout throughout Southern California after every good rain. It stood six stories and featured a phony-looking split rail fence around a shallow lawn of ivy. Beyond that it had all the charm of the black obelisk in *2001*.

As I neared the glass door, I saw an old guy in a screaming Hawaiian shirt giving me the eye. He didn't move to open the door for me, and when I pushed against it I found it was locked. It was a situation that was becoming increasingly common in the new buildings. We used to lock up the bad guys and the rest of us were left free. It was a nice setup while it lasted. But now there are too many bad guys and too many lawyers, so we lock ourselves in little people boxes and the crooks are allowed to roam free.

"May I help you?" he grunted through a hole only the size of a mail slot high up on the door. From his petulant tone of voice, it was obvious helping me wasn't really all that high on his list of priorities.

"Detective Doyle," I told him sternly, slowly reaching for my wallet. The impression was designed to show I was perfectly willing to fish out my badge, but it was up to him to ask. It was one of the many things about me that drove Inspector Dixon nuts. He was constantly accusing me of impersonating a police officer. My contention was always that it was perfectly proper, since my name is Doyle, and I'm a bona fide detective. It was a gap we'd never bridge.

The old man pulled the door open; I helped, which gave my hands something else to do, thus preventing me from showing my badge. There was a glass-fronted black felt board on the wall showing the names of the tenants in small, white plastic letters. I spotted Reynaud.

"Some of the lab boys are still up in 28, aren't they?" I asked.

"A couple," he bobbed his hairless round head. "There was a whole gang up there half the night, but most of them left just after I came on."

"Point me toward it; I haven't been up yet."

He told me one flight up and turn left. "You must be forensic," he added knowingly.

So he read detective stories and felt like showing off. We were going to be friends yet. "Naw, staring into those damn microscopes makes you bug-eyed. My job is to just hang around until they pin it on somebody, and then I plug 'em. It's part of a new austerity drive. Only costs eight cents for a slug, and the slate's wiped clean."

"If only it were true," he grinned wistfully.

The door to 28 was closed. I stood there in the cheaply carpeted hall and held a debate with myself. Odds were long, whoever was in there wasn't about to open up to me so I decided to save it for later. The doors were staggered so that 27 was five yards back down the hall. I guess the idea was that if both tenants ever happened to open their doors simultaneously, they couldn't get a peek inside each other's private cell.

I worked the buzzer until I decided it must be dead, then began rapping on the door. That got immediate results. The door flew open, and a stubby harridan stood glaring daggers at me. Her curlered hair looked like the interior of an old tube-type TV set, and her cheeks and forehead were plastered with hardened mud.

"This is really too much! You promised me you'd leave me alone." She spoke to me through clenched teeth, I guess because her face was set in concrete.

"Sorry; nobody told me. But now the damage is done, we may as well get it over with." I smiled at her disarmingly; it was like looking eyeball to eyeball with the Creature from the Black Lagoon.

She stepped aside with an exaggerated sigh of resignation. Closing the door, she turned and told me: "Look, I had to take off a sick day because this horrible thing across the hall kept me up all night. What do I have to do to get some rest—check into a hotel?"

"This really will be the end of it—I promise. It's just that memory fades so quickly, these first few hours are so vital to an investigation. Please try and understand."

"I would have thought you people had arrested that man by now. Her stepson. You don't mean to tell me you're letting a killer like that walk the streets?"

It rocked me. It wasn't like the police to volunteer information, especially that kind. "Who told you her stepson was a killer?"

"She told me herself. Told me the whole gruesome story about how that maniac killed his very own father—imagine!"

"You must have been very close to Mrs. Reynaud."

"Not really—hadn't spoken to her a dozen times all told, I'm sure."

"Really? Well, about last night: Go over all of it, beginning with the first thing you saw or heard having any connection with either the deceased or the suspect."

She shook her head in obvious disgust, and proceeded to rattle it off as if it were a lesson learned by rote. "Her stepson arrived just as '60 Minutes' was beginning—seven o'clock—and he left the first time at ten-thirty. She was dead by then, of course."

She'd stated it as a simple, irrefutable absolute. It was a little chilling, even though I didn't believe her for a moment. "Let's back up here a minute. . . . I'm sorry but I've forgotten your name."

"You don't seem to know much," she commented dryly. "Madge Burman."

"Matt Doyle, Madge. Now how did it happen you saw Dirk . . . ah, Mrs. Reynaud's stepson, both arrive and leave?"

"I explained all that before. This place must be built out of cardboard. Five hundred a month for a one-bedroom, and you get paper walls. I didn't have to see him. I heard her answer the door and let him in. She yelled, 'Oh, it's so nice to see you again,' or something just like it."

Today was supposed to have been a day off, so it's possible my brain wasn't in high gear, but somehow I knew I'd missed something. "Okay, then you say you heard him leave at around ten-thirty—fine—but where do you get it she was dead then?"

"Simple! I heard him at the door saying, 'Good night and thanks for dinner,' or thereabouts, but I didn't hear her. That's the point, see? She never let anyone leave her apartment without standing in the door and chatting at the top of her lungs for another five minutes. Never! Used to drive me to distraction. Couldn't hear a word of dialogue on the show I was watching until she shut up. I'm sure it struck me funny at the time, not hearing her say a word, but it just didn't register until later. Of course, it wouldn't have helped the poor soul anyway; she was stone dead by then."

I wished she'd quit saying that. "That's all you actually heard then?"

"That's all. There's no decent news on Sundays at eleven, so I went to bed. My bedroom is removed from the hall—thank God—so I never heard him when he came back. The next thing I knew was when you people started banging on my door around three-thirty this morning."

Just when I thought I'd caught up with her, she'd thrown me good. "Run that by me again, Madge? If you couldn't hear anything from your bedroom, why do you keep saying he came back? And why would he do that?"

Her answer was to roll her protuberant eyes heavenward. "Why?" she shouted at me. "How else do you think he got the body away from here? Carried the poor soul out with him the first time—right by the night man?"

I was totally stunned. There wasn't even a corpse. It took me a minute to regroup. "So who called the police, Madge?"

"The Holmes's down in 26. It's nothing for those two to stagger in around two or after. But they weren't too bombed to notice Marlee's door wide open, and the blood everywhere."

It was getting curiouser and curiouser. I needed time to do some digesting. After assuring the woman she could sleep the clock around without fear of interruption, I fled back down to the foyer. I asked my buddy in the gaudy shirt: "You say you came on at seven this morning?"

"Yup, same as always."

"So who let all the troops in and out until seven?"

His eyes acquired a gleam of absolute pleasure. "Night man—George. He got the duty on account of they wanted him for questioning anyway."

"What are George's normal hours?"

"Comes to relieve me at three every afternoon. Supposed to; he's usually a few minutes late. Locks her up at eleven sharp every night, except they hauled him back out of bed at about three this morning. Boy, I'm here to tell you he was some mad."

"I'll bet, especially since he didn't have a single thing to tell them . . . us. Isn't that right?"

"Yup, but you fellas got to remember, negative evidence is just as important as . . . the other kind."

He definitely read mysteries. "I'll try and remember. What's the drill here when someone wants to get in after eleven?"

"Nobody's got no business coming in here after eleven except the tenants, and they got keys. If one of them wants to let somebody in that late, they got to arrange to be here to let them in."

I thanked my would-be mentor and decided to go back upstairs. Passing on the elevator, I trudged up a flight of cement steps and made my way down to number 28. Apparently the prevailing theory was that Dirk had killed her, left with her key, then came back after the night man had retired and removed the body. I was beginning to cheer up a little. It didn't sound like much of a case to me.

I rang the bell beside the Reynaud apartment, hoping Madge had gone back to bed and wasn't awake to hear me trying to talk my way in.

The lab cop who opened the door looked vaguely familiar. "Hi, I'm Matt Doyle," I told him in my chummiest tone. "Don't I know you?"

Ignoring me, he turned and yelled over his shoulder. "Hey, Ernie! Dixon was right. Doyle just showed up."

The voice settled it. "Roger . . . Turner. Now I remember. You were there the time Dixon arrested me for withholding evidence in the Herbert murder. You got quite a chuckle out of it, as I recall."

Roger's eyes twinkled behind a pair of rimless glasses as he rubbed his hand over the stubble sprouting from his chin. "Yeah, but no handouts today, Doyle. Sorry. I got nothing against you personally but the Inspector left specific orders about you. It would cost me my next promotion to tell you what time it is."

A jug-eared man emerged from somewhere in the back of the apartment. "I've gone through every page of every damn book. Nothing! I'm ready to pack it in if you are."

"What are you looking for in books, Ernie?" I asked politely. "I thought you guys already had the can tied securely to somebody's tail."

"We sure do, don't you worry. We got motive. We got the murder weapon with the suspect's prints all over it. And we can definitely place that suspect here at the time of the murder. And just for an added bonus, he's already a convicted murderer. Patricide, no less. I understand he's a buddy of yours, Doyle. You aren't exactly choosy who you hang out with, are you?"

Without conscious thought, my feet were moving, and my hands were making fists, but Roger stepped in and formed a human roadblock between us. He glanced over his shoulder at Ernie and shook his head in disgust. "This is the guy we were ordered not to so much as sneeze in front of, remember? What are you planning to do next—mail him a copy of the lab report?"

Ernie gave me a quick sneer, shrugged, and left the room with his fists clenched, too. He wasn't mad at me; he was pissed at himself for letting me finesse him into running off at the mouth. From where I was standing, I could see plenty of rust-colored stains on the beige carpet near the center of the living room, and an eighteen-inch length of white tape where the location of something vital had been marked.

"I don't suppose you'd care to tell me what the weapon was?" I inquired of Roger politely.

"You're one hell of a fine supposer," Roger complimented me.

"Thank you. Now what kind of a guesser would I be if I guessed it was a carving knife about a foot and a half long?"

Roger's tight little smile dissolved into a look of utter contempt. "Since when do you have to guess? Chances are the bastard who did this told you all about it. For all I know, he got you to come back here with him to help lug her out. Inspector Dixon is going to find it very interesting that you were able to describe the murder weapon accurately, when nobody outside the department knows anything about it. We were sitting on that fact, Doyle. This is one time that big mouth of yours is going to get you in deep trouble."

I was too mad to tell him that anyone with the brains God gave a mule could figure out what that eighteen-inch strip of tape signified. My adrenaline was sending hostile messages out, so I decided to leave before things got out of hand. It's okay to make monkeys out of cops, but it's not all right to slug them.

Ten minutes later I was slowing to turn in the drive. The sun was beginning to burn its way through the morning haze and it hurt my eyes to look directly at the white stucco walls of the oversized house I had called home for over four years. The red tile roof even gleamed under the burnished rays, though Win assured me they were the original tiles laid nearly seventy years ago when the mansion was built. The not-so-small sea of grass surrounding the house was as trim as a putting green. That reflected the dedication Dirk devoted to one of his jobs—gardening. It suddenly occurred to me that if he weren't returned to duty promptly, it was certain to become one of mine. I looked over my right shoulder at the strip of beach below, where we'd run together only a few hours earlier. The memory was already taking on the half-remembered, half-imagined patina of time. I wondered how long it would be before our next run, and for the first time I was worried.

When I rounded the curve of the drive, which opened up a view of the garages, I saw two SDPD vehicles. And when I climbed out of my car I heard sounds—voices and the banging of drawers maybe—coming from Dirk's apartment over the garages. Rushing up the worn stone steps, I found Dixon himself standing just inside the door, watching as four men searched the place. They worked methodically and with great enthusiasm, no doubt doubly so under the stern eye of their department head. They certainly weren't showing much concern over leaving the place as they'd found it. A wave of nausea hit me in the pit of the stomach, seeing them pawing over Dirk's few pitiful possessions, disturbing the precise orderliness I'd kidded him about so often.

Dixon turned to survey me through a cloud of smoke. Ashes were scattered about his feet, disgustingly reflected in the high gloss of the hardwood floor I knew Dirk buffed marine-style, on his hands and knees with a blanket. Two dead butts lay nearby as well. "Good thing you're around," he growled. "Might save you a trip downtown. At least it will if you cooperate. I want some answers—straight for once—without any of your cracks."

"First you clean this up!" My voice sounded ragged; I would have barely recognized it as my own.

"What? What the hell are you mumbling about?"

"I'll keep it simple for you. I realize you have a warrant, but it doesn't give you the right to damage a man's home or make it unlivable for him. Dirk's home is not an ashtray. He sanded these floors himself—by hand—and waxes them the same way every week. The place will reek of cigarette smoke for days. Clean it up. And don't light up another one in here. You know damn well he's a nut about it."

"Excuse me all to hell," he sneered, "but I wouldn't worry too much about it bothering him if I were you. He's being held without bail. And considering the evidence, there's no possible way he'll ever see this place again."

"How much?" I demanded coldly.

"How much what?" He started to drop the stub of his lit cigarette, caught himself, walked over to the door, and flicked it into a high arc out over the drive.

"How much do you want to bet we won't have Dirk home again very soon?"

He laughed. It wasn't a pleasant, joyous laugh; it was more like the laugh the neighborhood bully might give, just before he beats up some kid half his size. "I don't take candy from babies. Trust me—if you knew how it really stacked up, you'd dummy up and start running ads for a replacement. Now, for the record, did you hear him come home last night? Stop and think before you answer. Accessory after the fact in a capital offense is a lot more than a slap on the wrist."

"Not until after you clean it up," I told him again.

His big face reddened. "Don't push it too hard, kid. You've been downtown with me before, and you can be again if you push. There are even those who think you maybe should be in adjoining cells with your buddy. But I told them no. I told them if you were in on it, it would have been clean, not with evidence to convict lying around like pine needles under a Christmas tree. Don't make me change my mind, Doyle."

"I wouldn't pull this if it was me, but this is for Dirk. If I were you, I'd remember you're in the private home of one of the most respected public figures in the history of this country. One word from me, and he'll pick up the phone and make a call that could put you back in a black and white, patrolling the fence along the Mexican border. Don't ask me who he'll call, that's not my department, but he's an expert. Whoever it is, I guarantee you they'll hear him out. He doesn't think much more of Dirk than you do your right arm. I've never held this sword over your head before, though there've been times I was tempted, and I doubt I ever will again. But right now I am. Do I go tell him to make the call, or do you act civilized and clean up your own mess?"

Dixon's fat face was crimson now, but we both knew how it was going to end. You couldn't budge him with a tank when he was in the right, but he knew his ass was hanging out on this one. He tried to outglare me for a ten count, then snapped at the nearest of his crew. "Duggan, grab a broom and get rid of those butts." Then he stomped out onto the landing before lighting another one. "Same question; I'm waiting," he snarled, then gratefully drew in a lungful of acrid smoke.

"I didn't hear him—I wish I had. These walls are over a foot thick, and the house and garages are detached, as you can see. I might have heard the car, but I went to bed early—around nine. I'd just flown in from Acapulco last evening, after nearly a week getting my brains battered on a racing yacht, and I was completely beat."

Mumbling something I'm sure was not complimentary about "smart-assed jet-setters," he scribbled in his pocket memo pad. I beat it down the steps and into the house. Win was sitting at his desk, watching the tail end of the noon news on the TV built into the wall of bookcases opposite his desk. He immediately hit the remote button on the underside of his desk and killed it.

"Is that insufferable dullard still befouling my home?" he demanded.

"Still at it, but I made them promise to leave things as they found them or we'd send them a bill. How come you're watching the news in the middle of the day? You know damn well it always turns you into a bear. This is no time to go curmudgeonly on me."

It was true. It wasn't all the bad news, he was used to that. What drove him wild was the full ration of grammatical errors and mispronounced words from the perfect plastic faces on the screen. He often told me he still remembered when newscasters had to have something between their ears besides pretty hair, some faint notion of what they were talking about. He'd point out that Edward R. Murrow—the acknowledged best ever—was not much for looks. I'd argue television was strictly a visual medium, and appearance counted for plenty now. He'd always end it by insisting it was not unreasonable to expect a major market commentator to possess a working knowledge of the English language and the ability to pronounce correctly the names of the world's nations and their leaders.

"I confess it was a mistake, Matt. A futile attempt to distract my benumbed brain until we could discover the extent of Dirk's jeopardy."

"Did you get hold of Hoffman?" Hoffman Price was his attorney. Mine too, whenever someone thought I'd stepped over the line. I'd had occasion to use him more than once, since it was Dixon's contention I was over the line the moment I got out of bed in the morning.

"Mr. Price should be calling at any time. Before I speak to him it would be helpful to have your report. Can you tell me the unfortunate set of circumstances that have led to this sorry plight?"

I gave it to him as always, complete with quotation marks around it. I've even been known to include facial expressions and body language, if I thought it altered the true meaning of the words.

He took it all in, leaning his head back and staring up, as if checking for cracks in the ceiling. He may have been, because the instant one appeared, he'd frown and order it repaired. The phone rang within a few minutes of my finishing. Hoffman asked for Win. I stayed on, too.

"Yes, Mr. Price," Win greeted him hopefully. "I trust you have good news for me?"

"Not really, Mr. Winfield. I've seen him. He hasn't been formally charged yet, but my sources in the D.A.'s office tell me the way the case is stacking up, he will be any minute. They tell me it's very tight, the case against him. You asked me to report on his frame of mind. Mr. Bomande seems all right to me. Of course he's withdrawn, uncommunicative, but as far as we're concerned, that's all for the best. I'll admit it would be nice if he'd at least talk to me, though.

"They'll likely attempt to have the judge waive bail, and quite frankly, they'll almost certainly succeed. I'll fight it; quite a bit will depend on who the sitting judge is. Right now I'm going to stage a commando raid on the D.A.'s office and try getting a peek at their hole cards. I'll keep you posted."

"By all means do so. Tell Mr. Bomande to remain steadfast, and that Mr. Doyle and I are taking all possible steps to remedy the situation. Thank you."

We hung up simultaneously. Our eyes met and I told him, "So, we're taking steps, huh?"

"Certainly. It appears to be a simple, straightforward matter.

Some person or persons unknown murdered Mrs. Reynaud. The police are convinced it was Dirk, since by unhappy coincidence, he was there last evening. We have a considerable advantage, since we know better. It may be possible to commit a murder spontaneously, and leave no incriminating evidence, but not so when the crime is premeditated, as this one most certainly was. You realize, of course, the most interesting aspect of this homicide?"

"Yeah—I'm not blind either. Dirk was set up to take the fall for it."

"Precisely. It remains for us to utilize our advantage and find out why the poor woman was killed. This shouldn't pose any great difficulties; inevitably the solution will lead us to the culprit." Whereupon he folded his arms, tilted his fine old head back, and looked at me as if he'd already done everything but give the killer a ride to headquarters, and what was I waiting for?

"Neat! Very neat. Nobody appreciates a positive thinker any more than I do, but do you mind if I point something out to you?"

"Please do," he allowed graciously.

"You say it's an advantage for us to know Dirk's innocent because the cops are out of it. An advantage for who? Certainly not Dirk. I'd love to have the cops working on this. The marines too, if I could swing it. I've heard you say plenty of times the police are better equipped to solve the vast majority of crimes. As I see it, we're in one hell of a mess. We've got one man in the field—me—to do a job Homicide would no doubt assign to at least a platoon, if they weren't so stuck on Dirk. And in case you haven't yet registered the fact, this is beginning to shape up as a pretty slick operation. Whoever pulled it off did a disgustingly fine job of it."

"Good, solid observations, Matt; you do well to expound them. But don't despair. The scoundrel we seek has already committed an irreparable error. One which will certainly bring about his downfall."

"Which is?"

"He selected as his scapegoat a man we are both determined to defend and exonerate. How intelligent was that, I ask you?"

The guy made Norman Vincent Peale look like a pessimist.

CHAPTER 3

At breakfast the next morning, we were all uncomfortably aware of Dirk's vacant chair. I don't think we'd realized fully until then how much like a family we'd become. I'd spent Monday afternoon and evening back at Marlee's building calling on more of her neighbors in an attempt to find out who she was close to, as well as anything else helpful. It had been a bust. The profile I'd come away with was one of a loner whose life centered around her job and the firm determination to acquire the world's best suntan.

I'd actually only found half a dozen tenants who'd even admit recognizing her on sight. None qualified as friends. Or enemies, as far as I'd been able to tell. I'd even tackled Madge again in the evening, knowing it was safe because I could hear her TV from the hall. And there was nothing wrong with her hearing, I could hear everybody's TV from the hall. From her listening post, given her natural inclination to snoop, I figured she could give me a fair assessment of gentlemen callers, and maybe even supply some names. But according to her, there hadn't been any.

"He was arraigned at four o'clock yesterday afternoon," Win

was explaining darkly to Randy. "To be held without bond, this decision predicated upon his previous conviction for felony manslaughter, only after fleeing the scene and remaining at large for over eight years. I suppose one may hardly blame the court; it sounds damning enough stated in those terms."

Randy blinked sadly. "After all he's been through, being confined again is sure to be extremely tough on him. I can't help thinking how he was when you first brought him here. He even slept outside on the lawn for the first couple of months."

Win nodded absently, no doubt remembering too. He snapped out of it, and turned his attention to me. "That Burman woman—is she unimpeachable? She appears to be the nearest thing to a main character thus far in this dreary scenario. She goes miles out of her way to indict Dirk—why? Some of her statements ring false somehow. She alludes to Mrs. Reynaud tarrying at her door to chatter with callers; others state the victim seldom even exchanged civil greetings with her neighbors. Is it possible this woman is somehow involved?"

I didn't have to agonize over that very long. "If she is she's a better actress than I ever heard of. I'd say no—but with a condition."

"What condition?"

"The condition being if events should prove me wrong I get to change my vote."

Win chuckled dryly. "Your instincts are extraordinarily acute, except where younger and more winsome lasses are involved, so let us accept as a working hypothesis that she is nothing other than what she appears to be. Having so accredited her, we are forced to believe Mrs. Reynaud had established no liaisons beyond those inherent in her work. Does this suggest an itinerary for you today?"

I played with my second cup of coffee and planned to stop off for breakfast as soon as I left the house. If I didn't have a mission afterwards, I would have invited Randy along. Even he hadn't been able to stomach the morning fodder today. "I think I can guess, Win. Shouldn't be too hard to get her employer's address from the manager of that rabbit warren she lived in. But there's something else; I know where there's a completely reliable witness who was at the scene and should be able to tell us one hell of a lot."

Win's face registered surprise. "Then drop all else and interview that person at once, by all means."

"I can't—not until you get your brain in overdrive and figure out a way. I'm talking about Dirk. He was the last one to see her alive, not counting the killer. They'd just spent an entire evening together. He must know things. He's just the kind of witness you dream about. Maybe he doesn't realize he has facts and details that would help, but they have to be there and we need them desperately. Example: Was she expecting anyone else after he left? Was she upset, nervous-acting, scared? I've got a hundred others and nobody else can answer them but Dirk. You've got to set it up for me to see him. I don't care how you engineer it but it isn't optional."

Win inclined his head fractionally, a mannerism acknowledging his complete agreement. "You are using your faculties to good advantage. As it happens, I stole a march on you and instructed Mr. Price to make the arrangements last evening, but no matter. You weren't far behind, and I commend you."

It was so typical. Maybe he had, but on the other hand, maybe it wouldn't get done until he arrived at the office in another few minutes. It did explain why he'd shown the necessary drive to go as far as he had in government service. He suffered from the worst case of one-upmanship I'd ever heard of.

I gave him my best grin as I got up to leave the table. "Give my regards to Hoffman when you talk to him within the next ten minutes." The remark would be innocuous enough, unless he really hadn't already talked to the lawyer about setting me up to see Dirk. If that were the case, it would serve as a clear message that I was on to him. His may be the worst recorded case of one-upmanship, but I freely admit to having a touch of it myself.

"Matt has a remarkable gift," I could hear him telling Randy, as I left the room. "It's quite impossible for him to spend any length of time in the presence of a dissembler and fail to sense it."

Yeah, I thought, and I can spot a fibber, too.

＊　　＊　　＊

I elected to return to Marlee's building and get the information in person; people have gotten too used to saying no over the phone these days. It proved simple enough. The middle-aged woman who peered out from behind bizarre bat-wing glasses promptly extracted a file card from the metal box on her desk, and even donated a piece of scratch paper for me to write on.

My destination turned out to be within a mile, which probably explained Marlee's selection of her apartment. Blaise Construction was perched on a bluff overlooking the Pacific. According to the sign in front, twenty-four luxury condos were being built for an equal number of fortunate buyers and investors. The name of the project was—appropriately enough—Sea View. Prices from one hundred and twenty-five thousand. The key word was *from*.

The project appeared to be well along. A third of the units were completed outside and the rest were roughed in enough to be receiving unlikely looking thick, blue Spanish tiles set at a rakish angle along the roofs' leading edges. They were obviously just for effect, because the actual roofs were absolutely flat. Surprisingly few workers were on the site. I counted only three. In addition to the condos, a forty-foot house trailer occupied the center of the lot, and there was a large storage shed sheathed in corrugated metal about twenty feet away from the trailer.

Parking just off the road, I went up to the door marked *Office* at the forward end of the trailer and knocked.

The inner door opened. A pair of bored black eyes pointed down at me. They belonged to a guy with a hard, dark face, and all the humanity of a marble bust. "Who're you?" he asked.

"Matt Doyle—detective. I have a question or two about your former employee, Marlee Reynaud."

The eyes finally blinked, as if reluctant to show even a trace of humanity. It was like watching shutters close on a pair of old cameras. Every alarm bell, siren, and warning flag I had was in full cry. "Hold it." He closed the door in my face and left me standing there like an idiot.

A half minute later the door flew open. He was back again,

now sporting a yellow hardhat over his black locks. "Come on in," he told me. The words were accompanied by a sorry excuse for a smile; the antediluvian eyes weren't having any part of it.

I peeled back the screen door, and stepped up into the trailer. Inside was nothing fancy, just a small desk and a few beat-up folding chairs. My guide motioned me to follow him to the rear of the coach. The scanty galley we passed midway was intact, as was the minuscule bath, but a bulkhead had been removed to open up the entire aft end into one decent-sized office. The desk was nearly the size of mine. The chairs were comfortable looking, and a handsome couch hugged one wall. The couch was held down by two men who might have been related to my guide.

Upon closer inspection, their similarity became more of an impression than a fact. They all had different features, but the overall effect was still striking. All three had similar coloring, clothing, body type, and facial expression—blank.

They were in sharp contrast to the man behind the desk. He rose, extended his hand, and beamed at me. "I'm Roscoe Blaise, Officer; what can I do for you today?" His bonhomie suggested nothing would please him more than to be able to do something for me every day. Roscoe was under medium height and almost unbelievably fat. His head was mostly skin except for a tonsure running from ear to ear. There was power in the square, calloused paw I grasped.

"It's not Officer, Mr. Blaise. It's just Matt." I used the excuse of going for my wallet and license to stop letting him continue pulverizing my hand. "I work for Carter Winfield; he's taken an active interest in the death of your employee, Marlee Reynaud."

"Carter Winfield—imagine that! You mean he actually does still work? And as a detective? Just imagine that." He lowered his impressive beam back onto his chair and leaned back. His hard little eyes appeared friendly but watchful.

"He certainly does, especially in this particular case."

"I've read about it in the papers," he nodded in understanding. "How does it happen a man like Carter Winfield had a killer like that in his employment?"

"It's a long story. So just say we think the police have acted hastily. What exactly was Mrs. Reynaud's job here?" I was forced by the layout to sit facing Roscoe, which left me with my back to the trio on the sofa. It felt a lot like crossing Broadway downtown during rush hour with my back to the traffic.

"Poor, dear Marlee. Incredible how I'd come to value and depend on her in just two short months. She was basically a secretary, but we didn't have enough correspondence to keep her busy so she also assumed the bookkeeping duties. She was a great one for work, always willing to go that extra mile. I'm afraid I'd made quite a mess of the books. Tried to do everything all myself here from the start. Big mistake; I've got no gift for it. Then Marlee came along and in no time at all she had everything shaped up in here. God knows what I'll do now." His tone matched the doleful expression on his face. I'd have believed he was genuinely saddened if not for the big happy grin on his face when I first walked in, before he'd realized my commitment to Dirk.

"You could start by helping me find out who actually killed her."

"I only wish I could. Ask me anything you want, but I honestly can't imagine what I could tell you that would help."

"So nothing obvious comes to mind, Mr. Blaise? No angry boyfriend? What about her motive for moving here all the way from Louisiana? Any hint she might have been running from someone or something back there? These are pretty close quarters. It seems to me even in only two months you would have gotten to know one another pretty well."

Roscoe waited fifteen or twenty seconds, giving at least a fair impersonation of a man thinking hard, before wagging his huge head, alternately pulling taut and forming big folds of the flesh hanging from his chins. "You'd have to have known her—Marlee wasn't the gregarious type. We never exchanged confidences. Perhaps we might have in time but it hadn't happened yet. I don't believe there was any man in her life; I don't see how there could have been, frankly. She nearly always took work home with her; that's how she got the books caught up. As for why she moved here, I'd guess it was the same reason as the rest of us: weather, the beaches, more opportunity, money—you know."

"How did she seem to you the last time you saw her . . . Friday?"

"Yes, it was on Friday. Nothing the least bit out of the ordinary happened that I can recall. I do remember asking her if she'd like to go for a boat ride Sunday. I really wanted to do something nice for her, to kind of make up for all that extra work she'd done in the evenings. I've got a forty-seven-foot Pacemaker Coho, so I offered to take her out for the day, but she didn't seem the least bit interested."

It was the opening I'd been waiting for. Now I could slip in the one question that counted. "Of course she wasn't—that was the night she'd already invited her stepson over for dinner. It was to be their first meeting in twenty-one years. Surely she explained that was why she couldn't go?"

"No, as a matter of fact, she merely told me she didn't care for boats. First I heard of a stepson was when I read about it in the papers."

I hadn't expected him to admit knowing Dirk was due at her apartment Sunday, but I had counted on picking up some impression about whether or not he was lying. It was a bust; not only didn't he give the slightest sign of prevaricating, I got the strong impression he was telling the truth about Marlee's rejection of his offer to go boating.

There still remained the pair and a spare lined up behind me. Frustrated, I stood up and turned around. "How about you guys? She must have had someone around here she could talk to." The thought of anyone being able to confide in any of that trio of stumps was laughable, but I was fresh out of good ideas and was stalling, waiting for a fresh delivery of inspiration.

Meantime, they sat there giving me three identical vacant looks, as if I'd spoken Serbo-Croatian.

"Forgive me," Roscoe spoke up. "Rude of me not to have introduced my foremen to you. The one on the right is Danny, the middle one is Joe, and then Tommy. Gentlemen, please give serious consideration to Mr. Doyle's questions."

Him they understood, though I could have sworn my English was every bit as good as his.

Tommy shrugged and stared out the filthy window.

Joe shook his head.

Danny, the one who'd let me in, managed to mumble, "She never said nothing much around me."

With that show of wholehearted cooperation over, Roscoe waddled from behind his desk, apparently to award me the courtesy of showing me to the door. "Sorry we couldn't be of more assistance, Mr. Doyle."

"Thanks for trying," I told him, lying. "But tell me something. How come three foremen on a job this size? You've got as many chiefs as you do Indians."

"It's very true," he admitted ruefully. "To be honest, it's a matter of funding. We're a small project, and we've had problems. Weather has delayed us almost from the beginning. Until I can find buyers for at least four of the finished units, I'm in a real bind. I don't suppose you'd be interested in a nice condo overlooking the sea?" he grinned up at me.

"No, sorry. But if things are so tough I still don't see why you don't shuck at least two of them, rather than cutting back on productive workers."

"I guess I didn't make myself clear; they're not actually employees—they're partners. Each of them holds shares in the company, and they don't affect the payroll because they draw no salaries."

Roscoe stood framed in the doorway and watched me trudge through the dust to my car. Once I glanced back and he waved. The azure-colored roofing tiles were forming a skirting around the south end of the building at a turtle's pace.

An old man sprawled in a cheap lawn chair in the mobile home park across the road peered at me. When I saw him, he called out to me. "Ain't figurin' on buying one of them damn turkeys, are you?"

"Nope!" I called back. "I would have, except for all that ugly blue tile around the roof. Makes it look like a savings and loan."

"I'm telling ya," he warned me ominously, "them fellas don't have no idea what they're doin'."

I climbed behind the wheel and drove away. It occurred to me that Roscoe might have a hard time finding buyers until he finds a way to muzzle his critic across the street.

I got home just in time to watch Hoffman Price unfold himself from the driver's seat of his Ferrari. It was always good for a chuckle. He was one of the few men I had to look up to, to talk with. His corn-colored hair never seemed on intimate terms with a comb, and from his pasty complexion you'd think he lived in Greenland instead of Southern California.

He waited for me at the front door. "Hello, Matt; still driving that old ladies' car, I see."

"Try tailing somebody in that red bomb of yours some day, and see how far you get. My goal is to blend into traffic, not stop it. So when do I get to see Dirk?"

"That's why I'm here." His bantering tone suddenly became somber. "They've plugged up every hole; I'm afraid it can't be done. The other side is playing this one very tough, Matt."

"Come on into the office. I've got a guy in there who specializes in tough."

We marched down the short stretch of hall and into the office. Win looked up from his ever-present book, pleased to see us. Hoffman was the only lawyer I knew of whose name didn't bring a scowl to the old man's face. I'd once heard Win say that the single most productive thing that could possibly be done to shape up the Congress would be to bar all attorneys from holding office in either the House or the Senate.

"Sit down, Mr. Price. May I assume you've concluded making the arrangements we discussed?"

Hoffman shifted uneasily—he hated to let Win down as much as any of the rest of us. "I'm afraid not. The rules are being strictly enforced this time. Attorney of record and immediate family only. I can't prove it's been made a directive, but I've gotten the distinct impression Matt's been barred specifically."

Win's incredibly expressive face hardened into a mask of icy fury. "Being a thorough man, I assume you've exhausted every conceivable avenue."

Hoffman nodded miserably. "I'm afraid so, sir."

"How about me doing a little alteration job?" I suggested. "Palm me off as Dirk's long-lost cousin or whatever."

"Superb, Matt! Not only would you certainly join Dirk in jail, you'd cause Mr. Price's disbarment. Rein in your impetuosity for the time being—what's needed is guile."

"Okay, guile is your department—guile away."

"There's really only one alternative," Hoffman told us. "Make up a list of whatever questions you want answered and I'll take care of it."

Win rejected that notion with a shake of his head. "Dirk is an unusually private person. I can only surmise how much more withdrawn he's become as a result of this latest assault on his freedom. You've already reported his reluctance—more correctly, his total inability—to communicate with you. Even if you came back with monosyllabic replies to a list of likely questions, it would be of very little value. The data I require is as subtle as a snowflake, if indeed it even exists. It certainly cannot be relegated to a written exam, to be administered by a stranger."

"That brings us right back to square one," I said. "I'm the only one he'll open up to. Say Hoffman sets it up by phone. He never has to lay eyes on me. I go in alone, talk to Dirk, and then beat it."

Win gave me one of his patented looks of utter dismay. "You are determined to desert me—leaving me to solve this puzzle alone— aren't you? Unfortunately, the notoriety that attends our activities has made you nearly as recognizable as me. And you're quite mistaken; there's another with whom Dirk would be entirely candid."

"And who the hell's that?"

"Me," he replied grimly.

CHAPTER 4

The thing was, with Win you never really knew where the man stopped and the legend began. I've seen him fluttering in his chair, looking all papery and frail, barely able to speak above a whisper. This usually means he's trapped in the presence of someone he doesn't want hanging around, or maybe he wants something he just can't get through normal channels. If the sympathy angle fails to fly, I've also seen him suddenly take on excellent color, stop fluttering, and roar like a lion.

This time there was no mistake; it was ladled on pretty damn thick. All the way downtown he'd been busy lecturing me. As we pulled up in front of the federal holding tank on F Street I told him, "Relax, Win; I promise to bite my tongue and be cool. Remember me? I'm the half of this team that does all the fieldwork. At least up until now. And what makes you think you're another Olivier anyway?"

He grunted, as if in disgust. "I spent most of my adult life in politics, as a so-called public servant, God forgive me. Translate that as being 'on' almost every single minute of every day. I even played the role of secretary of state for eight seemingly endless years. My audience was comprised largely of intransigent and inimical antagonists from every corner of the globe. I'd like to see Lord Laurence pull that one off."

So much for false modesty. Hoffman was waiting in front of the tall, sinister-looking federal detention center. I pulled up, jumped out, and came around to open the right rear door. It was amazing! Win was nearly a deadweight in my hands as I helped him out. In the half hour since he'd gotten into the car, his face had paled to the point where you'd swear you could see the bones beneath.

Gripping his cane tightly in his right hand, he left it to me to support most of his weight from the port side. As we crabbed our slow way across the wide sidewalk, reporters converged on us from all directions. Cameras clicked, microphones stabbed at us, a dizzying cacophony of questions inundated us. I had to fight to keep from grinning.

Hoffman ran interference, telling them, "Secretary Winfield will make a statement inside. Please let him through. As you can see, this is all very difficult for him, so please don't expect him to stand out here and conduct a press conference."

The results of my "leak" to every network affiliate and independent with a market share of one or more was most gratifying, even though it was all Win's idea. The marble steps were wide and not at all steep, but he made heavy going of it. A lot of footage was shot, capturing the struggle in all its pathos. At last we entered the high double doors and approached the visitors' information counter. The gaggle of press was quiet now, loath to miss a single word of what was coming.

A fat clerk regarded us, along with the small mob around us, with a look of utter confusion. Finally he picked us out as the nucleus of the cell, and his furtive eyes settled on Win. "It's you!" he gasped, as he finally recognized him.

Win braced himself against the bar-high counter directly in front of the awestruck clerk and spoke into the silence. "I've come to see my son," he said in a voice quavering with apparent fatigue but that easily carried to the farthest reporter in the group. "His name is Dirk Bomande. I'll ask that you make the arrangements as quickly as possible. I'm really not feeling very well right now."

The clerk had to swallow twice before he managed to get out: "Son? But, sir, he couldn't possibly be your . . ."

"Certainly he is!" Win insisted, rapping the counter with his cane for emphasis. "Arrange it at once."

I swear the poor guy jumped four inches when the cane hit. Nodding agreeably, he fumbled for the phone, managed to punch a three digit number successfully on only the third try, then mumbled something plaintive sounding.

In less than a minute a stern-looking character in a dark gray suit came charging down the hall with clenched fists. He faltered and lost some of his steam when he saw the size and composition of our group, but it was clear he meant to make a stand. Ignoring us, he addressed himself only to Win. "Mr. Secretary Winfield, I'm Harold Masters, the director here. I'm terribly sorry you've gone to all this trouble for nothing, but my orders are quite specific concerning the prisoner, Dirk Bomande."

Win contrived to have to look up at Masters—I don't know how, since Win was the taller of the two—and fixed him with his patented basset hound look. The cameras went nuts—they were eating it with a spoon. "Are you a patriot, son?" Win asked softly.

"I'd certainly like to think so, sir."

"Good! I guess you know I am, too. Here's the situation: I can't stand here and debate with you for long so let's make it quick. As you may be aware, I almost never leave my home for reasons of age and health, but my son's peril has forced me to come here today in spite of the considerable personal cost. You were a very young man, probably still in high school, when I left public office. Strange, isn't it, that of all the people who are kind enough to remember me fondly, and have wanted to do things for me over the years, you and only you stand in a position to grant me the one thing I desire in these last days of my life—to spend a few moments with my son for what may well be the final time." I half expected to hear the muted sounds of bugles and drums in the distance, he was that convincing.

"Your son, Mr. Secretary? I'm afraid I don't understand."

"Mr. Bomande is my ward. Some years ago I interceded for his parole and assumed full and complete responsibility for his care and custody. Other than through accident of birth, I consider him my son in every sense of the word. Most of my life was given to public office, asking nothing in return but the privilege of serving. There are those who might tell you that I performed my duties well. Then is this too much to ask? A few brief moments in return for all the years?"

Unnoticed, Win jabbed Hoffman in the foot with his cane. The lawyer took his cue. "Mr. Secretary, I'm concerned about all these reporters and television cameras. They make this a touchy situation. Without meaning to, I'm very much afraid we've put Mr. Masters here in an untenable position."

"Not at all," Harold assured us. "I'm merely following instructions."

"That's the point I was about to make," Hoffman went on sympathetically. "You're only doing what the local authorities have told you to do. It's not your fault everyone from the attorney general, who is a dear friend of Secretary Winfield, down to your immediate superior will be extraordinarily upset with you if we're thrown out of here. Notwithstanding your instructions from the locals, people all across this country are going to want to know why you weren't capable of making such an obvious judgment call."

Sweat had suddenly materialized at Masters's temples and all across his forehead. "Stay right here; I have to make a quick phone call."

"I'm afraid I'll never make it," Win stopped him in his tracks. "My heart is becoming most irregular and, like an old fool, I've forgotten my pills. I had no intention of placing you in such a potentially dangerous situation, but I must ask you to make a decision."

Harold was teetering on the brink, but still he hedged. "I'd really give anything to be able to . . ." he started to say, obviously meaning it.

"Forgive me," Win interrupted. "I was under the mistaken impression you were in charge here."

"I am in complete charge of this facility."

"Then why not act as if you are?" Win needled him.

"Wait a minute!" I figured it was time for my speaking part. "I think there's an easy solution to this whole mess, Mr. Masters. The no-visitors rule was imposed strictly to keep me out—never mind why—but that's the truth. It was never meant to exclude Secretary Winfield; you think for one moment anyone in authority anywhere would want that? It's just that no one ever expected him to make this difficult effort and come down here. So why don't you make a big deal of refusing me visiting rights with the cameras rolling—that will get you off the hook—and let Secretary Winfield go along with Dirk's attorney for a brief visit. Mr. Price will be going in to see Dirk in any event. Then everybody's happy."

Harold was so confused by then he grasped gladly at the imaginary victory. Hoffman took my place as Win's brace. As soon as a form was produced and signed, they were gone. Win even signed his name old and shaky; this in spite of the fact that his handwriting was as flawless as the examples in the penmanship books. I had to admit I was impressed.

Half an hour later they were back, Harold tagging along like a pup, lapping up Win's every word. The news hounds closed ranks, and I saw Win make a face, but they'd served us well, so he gave them some of what they'd been waiting for. He passed on all questions pertaining to his visit, or Dirk's case, but gave them an earful otherwise. They finally left, happy with fodder for half a dozen headlines and editorials unlikely to thrill the current administration. It wasn't that Win had anything against the administration—he just knew what reporters liked.

He developed a sudden burst of energy as we hit the sidewalk, ducking into the back seat quickly under his own steam. "Home, Matt—flank speed!" he ordered.

"Yeah, I know; it's your heart. You should never go out without your pills." Waving jauntily at the minicams, I took off.

"My stomach, not my heart," he growled.

"Well, I have to admit it. Olivier could stand a few lessons from you. How'd it go with Dirk?"

"The trip was worthwhile, unpleasant as it was. I believe it gave Dirk a considerable boost. You can't imagine what it's like in there, Matt—the stench!"

"I don't have to imagine. You forget, Dixon made me an overnight guest last year on that trumped-up withholding charge. And that was city jail, which makes this place seem like a Ramada Inn. By the time I got home you wouldn't even talk to me until I took two showers and burned my clothes."

"Yes, we served the inspector an ample portion of crow, with dessert of humble pie, on that occasion and we'll do so again. I gave Dirk my word on it."

"Since he thinks everything you say is carved in stone somewhere, that must have cheered him up. Did you manage to see him in his cell?"

"We did. Mr. Masters became quite accommodating, once he was out of camera range."

Getting information out of Win was like panning for gold; I had to beg for every little nugget. "What do I have to do, call Hoffman to find out what you learned?"

"Forgive me; I was attempting to examine every nuance of Dirk's statement while it was still vivid in my mind. The facts are these: He received a call from his stepmother, Mrs. Reynaud, Wednesday last, inviting him to dinner at her home Sunday evening. After his initial shock, he accepted willingly. Though she'd failed to prevent his father's brutality, and done a meager job of feeding and clothing him as a boy, still she was the nearest thing to family he'd ever have and time heals all wounds. He arrived promptly at 7 P.M., spending a pleasant, if somewhat uneasy, evening. And it seems Dirk lied to us during breakfast Sunday morning, just prior to his arrest."

The words *lie* and *Dirk* used in conjunction like that were so incongruous it took me a few seconds to recover. "Dirk would be more likely to jump out of an airplane than to lie to you—explain!"

"Perhaps *lie* was too strong a word. He told us his stepmother still fries everything. This statement caused me a great deal of concern and confusion, but now my mind's at rest on an important point. The principal entrée served by his stepmother was a baked ham. Dirk was asked to carve, as would be customary. He described the knife as a new-looking one with a sharp blade and cheap plastic handle. Ideal for taking prints, I should imagine. Presumably this later became the murder weapon, which explains the damning presence of Dirk's prints.

"Mrs. Reynaud spent much of the time telling Dirk about her second husband, who was apparently killed in a fall. Dirk left her at ten-thirty. No future meetings were mentioned, and he was left with the distinct impression none would be forthcoming. He couldn't explain it, but he sensed she was ill at ease and seemed distracted, especially toward the end of the evening."

"Surely you got more than that out of him?"

"I'm afraid not, with one insignificant exception. After dinner, the dishes were left undone; you can well imagine how that disturbed Dirk's obsession for order. When, after excusing herself for a minute or two, she returned to find him preparing to do the dishes, she became inappropriately agitated."

"Sure; that's normal. Lots of women would be if a guest just took it on themselves to do the dishes. So all we've got is a long-lost stepmother who really didn't seem all that thrilled to see Dirk, and his notion she may have been a little antsy by the time he left. Wonderful! And you promised Dirk we'd get him out, huh? I hope you didn't set a time limit."

"The trouble with you, Matt, is you equate progress with heavy breathing and the flow of adrenaline. It so happens I find something highly suggestive amid this apparent paucity of data."

"I couldn't be more pleased; all I find is absolute proof of his guilt." The stark solemnity of my statement was all but lost to him, since he reads faces and the backs of my ears don't reveal all that much.

"Mrs. Reynaud's increasing disquiet as the evening progressed might well indicate the approach of another, less pleasant appointment. One in which she may have even anticipated an element of danger. It occurs to me the original motive for inviting Dirk might have been to have him there as protection during the upcoming confrontation. If so, what made her change. . . ?"

There followed an ominous ten seconds of silence while he scrambled to rerun our current conversation in his mind. "You just said I'd given you absolute proof of his guilt. Please explain," he demanded stiffly.

"His prints on the carving knife. We know that's a major factor in the case against him. A new knife with a cheap plastic handle and his prints identifiable—it's conclusive! If it was the murder weapon—we have to assume it was, the cops aren't baboons—no one else could have handled it after Dirk, or his prints would've been superimposed over Dirk's. Considering the force necessary to grip a knife hard enough to kill someone, Dirk's prints wouldn't have even been traceable."

Win fought to deny the cold, brutal fact. "Of course there's a way. Rubber gloves, perhaps?"

"The things you don't know about your job. Rubber gloves would both eliminate Dirk's prints and leave a clear pattern the lab boys would recognize like their mothers' faces."

There wasn't a sound out of the back seat until we left the freeway north of La Jolla. "Are you telling me you're seriously courting the idea of Dirk's actual guilt?" Win finally asked me.

"Hell no! I just wanted you to hear it from me first. You can bet that's going to be the crux of the D.A.'s case."

"I've told you before, the district attorney is laboring under a severe disadvantage. No doubt he believes in Dirk's guilt without reservation." He stated it as if it were a serious character defect, like necrophilia.

"What a break!" I muttered softly, as I pulled off Torrey Pines Road and headed into the home stretch. When we were still over a hundred yards from our turn-in I noticed the men and then the vehicles. The men were working in pairs, spread out all over the big lawn. I stared at the duet nearest the drive; one guy wore earphones and carried something that looked like a cheap vacuum cleaner. His partner lugged a long piece of one-inch steel rod over his shoulder. It had a short crossbar at one end.

Win was the first to find his voice. "Matt," he whispered, dumbfounded, "what on earth are they doing?"

"What they are doing," I replied in the same library-soft voice, "is they are getting ready to tear up your yard to find Marlee Reynaud's corpse."

CHAPTER 5

*F*or a few dreadful moments when I pulled up in front of the house and saw Dixon's face wreathed in smiles, I thought they'd already found something. Randy sat on a step, glaring at the inspector's back, and Louis stood planted firmly in the doorway, as if daring them to make a try for his kitchen.

I raced around to open Win's door—fully expecting him to carry on with the doddering act—but he sprang out, brushed me aside, and stalked directly up to Dixon. The two of them stood there glaring at one another. There was barely eighteen inches between them, but they were worlds apart.

"This is outrageous!" Win shouted. I stood close, ready to go for the English oak cane if it showed signs of becoming a deadly weapon. "Of all the asinine, imbecilic intrusions upon private property I've ever heard of, none approaches this."

"Save it." Dixon told him. "The good doctor there has the proper paperwork, and there's not a damn thing you can do about it." He rocked back on his heels, feeling cocky and loving it.

Win looked over to see Randy morosely wave the warrant he

was holding. "Complete, utter lackwit," he told the policeman's big, red face, then spun on his heel and tramped up the steps.

I followed, keeping my jaw clamped, but Dixon had to give me the needle. "If you don't want the entire place excavated, why don't you tell us where to look? You're his buddy—didn't he tell you?"

Before I could shout a proper retort, Win turned to ask me, "Matt, why on earth didn't we think to ask that of Dirk just now. So foolish of us. There we were, having that nice long chat with him in private right there in his cell, and it never occurred to either of us."

Dixon's face was a study; it went from smug to horrified in only three seconds, but didn't miss a single expression in the entire spectrum between. It was beautiful to see. His face had all the charming characteristics of the most perfect soufflé ever baked. I wouldn't have thought it capable of so much subtlety, but it turned out to be a veritable kaleidoscope. "They let you in to see Bomande?" he finally managed to rasp.

"Check the six o'clock news," I grinned.

As I ducked inside chuckling, Louis offered to bring me something to make up for having missed lunch. I was so desperate—even Louis can manage a sandwich—I took him up on it. Win was sitting hunched forward, apparently studying the steeple he'd made with his fingers. It was an unusual posture—he usually sat very erect. I'd seen him slump like that before; it wasn't a good sign.

"You sure scored a direct hit on our friend out there," I congratulated him, trying to cheer him up.

"Trading insults with a ninny is surely the height of inanity," he muttered sourly. "I suggest we address ourselves to more profitable endeavors from now on. This entire situation is becoming more odious by the hour. Dirk is enslaved, my home is under constant violation, my tranquility forfeit—it's beyond all endurance."

"I know something else that's driving both of us nuts. We don't even have a client we can soak."

"Aye, there's another rub," he groused, too depressed to bother denying it.

Louis entered bearing a tray. I was glad to see a steaming cup of coffee. There was also a pair of man-sized sandwiches, about which the less said the better. I carefully wrapped the second one in a big manila envelope in my trash basket, so he wouldn't spot it when he emptied the wicker basket. The truth probably was, we threw away more food than we ate in that house, but nobody wanted to hurt Louis's feelings.

Win watched me morosely, then said: "Unlike the ambivalent Melancholy Dane, Matt, I've never had trouble deciding between suffering slings and arrows or taking direct action. We must put this affair behind us as quickly as possible."

"Hear, hear," I seconded, wishing I had another cup of coffee to sluice away the dust-dry taste of the sandwich.

"As you know, I normally prefer to proceed using logic when solving a case. In this instance, I feel compelled to skip ahead a few spaces, and hope to find the verification needed at the other end."

"Sounds like a crooked game of hopscotch to me."

"It is, at that."

"Let me guess: You want me to check over Marlee's apartment one square inch at a time. It's risky, you know. It'll have an official seal on it, and if I get caught you'll have to bluff your way in to see me, too."

"You've guessed incorrectly; that's one of the steps we are going to skip over. As you say, the risk outweighs the potential for reward, so let's postulate that any evidence therein extant has been uncovered by the police. Inspector Dixon enjoys all the powers of creative reasoning of a tree sloth, but he's competent enough at basic procedural work. And I think we may assume a maximum effort was expended in this case," he added in a bitter tone.

"Okay, so we've leapt right over that little item—the hell with clues, we're in a hurry—but where did we land?"

"Squarely on Roscoe Blaise's construction site—Sea View."

"That's what I figured, but I thought I'd give you the satisfaction of telling me. I agree it's a good percentage play. Cheaper than backtracking Marlee to Baton Rouge, and safer than breaking into her apartment. I wouldn't put it past Dixon to have her place under surveillance, just hoping for me to show. By the way, what am I looking for?"

"Propinquity will dictate, I should imagine. We are now proceeding on the premise Mrs. Reynaud was killed because she stumbled upon something incriminating during the course of her work at Sea View. It only remains for you to stumble upon it as well."

"That's my specialty all right—stumbling!" I stood up, stretched, and picked up the tray with the coffee cup on it. "Looks as though I'm in for a long night, so I guess I'd better try and catch a nap."

As I headed for the door, Win cautioned me. "You will remember to take Mr. Smith along?"

Mr. Smith was his euphemism for my Smith and Wesson .38. He hated guns and couldn't bring himself to refer to them directly. It was one of his blind spots. He was like a repressed mother who could only speak in terms of "poo-poo" when referring to her child's bodily functions. Sometimes I found it amusing, and other times it drove me wild. "Not to worry—he'll be along. Right now I'm going to check with Dixon and see whether anybody's struck oil out there."

"Ignore him," Win commanded sternly. "You'll only serve to aggravate him into increased effort. It was a mistake for me to tweak his self-esteem on the way in earlier; leave him strictly alone."

What was this? Since when was it a mistake to kid Dixon? "So what if he gets aggravated? All they're doing after all is running around with their metal detectors and sticking steel probes into the ground. Hell, we're getting our lawn aerated free."

Win frowned up at me. "I see it hasn't occurred to you, Matt. If someone has seriously set out to indict Dirk for murder—we agree it looks as if that's the case—and given he's as clever as

I fear him to be, I have every expectation that Marlee Reynaud's corpse is indeed somewhere out there, just waiting to be found."

His somber announcement rocked me. It made sense. "I see what you mean. In that case, I'll leave him alone. See you in the morning." After taking the tray out to the kitchen and thanking Louis for the fodder, I went upstairs. As I set about darkening the room for sleep, I resisted the urge to look out the windows to check on the search team's progress. Half the time I resented Win's penchant for keeping things to himself; the other half I wished he'd keep his maudlin thoughts quiet. This was an example of the latter. His parting remark pretty well obliterated any chance I'd had of getting to sleep.

CHAPTER 6

Several slow passes by the condo site revealed no signs of activity and no lights. The big double gates were closed, securing the whole area within the heavy hurricane fencing. I'd expected the site to be brightly illuminated by several mercury vapor security lights but such was not the case. All the better for me. I was a little concerned about the dark sedan parked between the trailer-office and the storage building, but I could think of plenty of reasons for its presence, and the total lack of lights cinched it. Parking a quarter-mile away, I worked my way back through the scrub manzanita south of the condos. The nighttime coastal haze had begun unrolling over the land on schedule, diffusing the early morning moonlight high overhead.

I was wearing my James Bond outfit—black slacks, black turtleneck, ditto shoes and socks. Mr. Smith rested in a belt holster, heavy but comforting. Technically, I should have rubbed mud—or was it soot?—over my face and hands, but that's where I drew the line. It would have been a dead giveaway at any rate—people would've heard me laughing a mile away.

Climbing the security fence was a breeze. So easy that it
worried me. How much could they have to hide? The car still
made me extra cautious, so I circled the trailer completely,
checking for sounds or lights that may have been well shaded.
Nothing!

I'd developed the habit of noticing locks years ago, especially when there was any chance I'd be paying a return visit after
hours. The modest fencing and the original cheesy look caused
me to doubt the importance of my current mission. I'd looked up
the lock in my collection of catalogues at home and brought the
three most likely keys. The first one worked. It was ridiculous; I
had a feeling any of the three would have worked.

The shades were up, so the interior was dimly visible. I
strained to catch any sound of someone sleeping. The likely spot
would be the couch in the rear office, so I decided to settle my
mind on that first. It was impossible to move without hearing eerie
complaints from the thin plywood flooring beneath the carpet, but
I was beginning to relax now. The couch was empty. The entire
coach was empty. And so was the entire compound, obviously.

I spent the next half hour scanning every document, bill,
and piece of correspondence in the place. There were surprisingly
few. The truly discouraging thing was, neither the file cabinet nor
any of the desk drawers was locked. I still made a point of being
thorough. Being a firm believer in Murphy's Law, I knew sure as
hell if I skipped a single document, it would be the one that
would have broken the case.

The kitchen and bathroom even got a good going-over. I'd
started in Roscoe's office—where any really important material
figured to be—and was just finishing up the small desk in front—
Marlee's—when I was startled into immobility by a shaft of blazing light. It had come from the storage shed. It lasted no more
than two seconds, then disappeared. I knew exactly what it was.
Someone had either entered or left the brightly lighted building.
The fact amazed me; the rough-looking structure should have
leaked light like a sieve.

My next shock came in the form of the ghostly crunch of

footsteps approaching the trailer. I quickly scuttled back into the cover of the tiny kitchen, keeping low, out of line with the windows. The sound of a key in the lock gave me a sick feeling in the pit of my stomach. I'd left it unlocked. I may as well have brought a brass band and fired off some rockets announcing my presence.

Indirect fluorescent lighting blazed into life overhead, blinding me temporarily. The cheap flooring announced the steady progress of someone approaching my cul-de-sac. I started to reach for my gun but checked. It was bad enough I was about to be caught red-handed for breaking and entering, without adding a charge of assault with a deadly weapon. It was my fervent hope I wasn't about to frighten some poor old codger of a night watchman right into a coronary.

That fear was laid to rest forever as soon as my stalker arrived in the galley. When we'd met the day before, I'd thought his eyes were a little hostile, but I was changing my mind. I had a perfect view of the business end of the revolver he was aiming at the center of my chest. Compared with it, his eyes were absolutely benign. A smile of self-satisfaction played with the corners of his pencil-thin mouth.

"I had a feeling about you. Up!"

I obliged, busily calculating odds. There are things you look for. People are usually as terrified to find themselves behind a gun as they would be in front of it. They grip it too tightly—it trembles, wavering back and forth over maybe a thirty-degree arc. Their eyes are irresistibly drawn to the gun. But not this one. His eyes locked onto mine, and the barrel tracked the middle of my chest as if it were radar-controlled.

"You're Danny, aren't you?" I asked him as casually as possible.

No response, other than an inclination of the head, ordering me to come around the counter into the front room.

"You want to know why I'm here, it's the same as before. Except now I'm convinced none of you had anything to do with Marlee's death, so you can put away the cannon."

The idea seemed to amuse him. I didn't like what I was

reading in his face. Here was a man, I suddenly realized, who was totally capable of killing me with neither reason nor remorse. I began hyperventilating deliberately, forcing myself to gear down until the time came. Lousy as the odds were, I'd decided they were only going to get worse.

Danny maintained the distance between us as I followed his mute command and came forward into the hall. He was discouragingly professional, and smart enough to credit me with being the same. There wasn't about to be an opportunity for me to strike out with either foot or fist.

A few feet into the front room I stopped, leaving Danny bracketed in the narrow bottleneck between the kitchen and office. "I guess you'll want this," I said glumly, slowly removing my own pistol, careful to pinch-grip it harmlessly between thumb and forefinger. The last thing I wanted to do was make him feel threatened. "Take it—I want you to rest easy." I held it straight-armed toward him, allowing it to dangle impotently.

He reached out with his left hand, forced to glance down once to align his probing fingers with the gun. The instant his eyes broke contact with mine, I moved. I'd tucked my right shoulder back as much as possible and suckered him into getting too close. Just as I'd hoped, when he swiveled his left shoulder forward to receive my weapon, it had left his gun pointing diagonally across his body for an instant. As his fingers closed over Mr. Smith's cylinder, I snaked out with my hidden reserve of reach, seized his wrist, and at the same instant yanked as hard as I could—falling backwards hard and fast. The idea was to spin him sideways so quickly that his shot would go wide.

It was a qualified success at best. Even as I planted my foot in his armpit—and did my level best to tear his arm out of its socket—there was a roar, and somebody set off a bomb in my left side. I ended up flat on my back, with Danny sailing not so serenely overhead. I held on grimly, determined to deny the huge pain for the moment. He landed beyond me, still clutching his gun in his right hand. I had to admire his tenacity, if not his judgment. Since I still had firm control of his left hand, he should have utilized his right to break his fall. He'd retained the gun instead.

Danny landing full tilt on the plywood flooring sounded like a huge base drum. I let go my death grip on his wrist, recovered my gun, then risked a three-second delay while I checked something intriguing about his fingers. After that I came out of the blocks fast, and ran out the door, still deliberately ignoring the spreading, wet, burning sensation in my side. At that stage I simply didn't want to know.

I hit the ground running. My night vision was poor after adjusting to the lights of the trailer, but not so bad that I didn't spot the wide band of light coming from the storage shed. A pair of dark silhouettes exited together just as I ducked behind the shelter of the trailer.

"Check inside, Joe—I'm going after him."

I didn't recognize the voice because Tommy hadn't spoken the day before, but it figured to be him. So that put all of Roscoe Blaise's three so-called foremen inside the shed in the middle of the night. I didn't have to guess what they were doing—I knew! Now the trick was going to be to live long enough to tell somebody.

I was pounding the ground for all I was worth, but at over two hundred pounds I am something less than a world-class sprinter. My head was spinning; either that or the landscape was. The wire fence lay dead ahead. Suddenly it looked twenty feet high. I realized that even if I managed to negotiate it, Tommy would be right on top of me by then. And a wire fence between us wouldn't be much help; all he'd have to do was stand there and pot me right through it. It never occurred to me to doubt that he would be armed and willing.

Snatching a six-foot length of board stacked away from the fence, I leaned it against the wire, while making as much noise about it as possible. It was my earnest hope he'd buy it as my route of departure. In the meantime, I turned right and headed for the only segment of the site that wasn't ringed by the fence. There was no need for a fence on the west side. It was protected by something much better—the sheer cliffs overlooking the sea.

My reasoning—admittedly becoming a little vague by then—was that even though I wasn't up to climbing a fence I was certainly capable of falling over a cliff. When I reached the lip I crouched and surveyed the scarred face of the sandstone bluff. As I'd expected, it wasn't materially different from the one in front of Win's house. Dirk and I had scaled that one a couple of times out of sheer boredom. It was tricky, because you could never be sure that the place where you put your weight wouldn't crumble beneath you; but there were always plenty of nooks and crannies gouged out from the effects of wind, sea, and rain. The San Diego Police Department had a special rescue squad, used mostly to pluck tourists from these cliffs after they'd panicked and gotten stuck halfway. The squad was kept busy, especially in the summer, and a few tourists died each year from falling before the rescuers got to them. I was counting on my experience with the treacherous sandstone to prevent me from being terrorized by fear of the unknown. The cliff looked formidable, more precipitous than it actually was in the unreliable moonlight. With any luck at all they'd buy the fence gambit, and all I'd have to do would be to get out of sight over the edge.

As I gritted my teeth and lowered myself over, I could hear Tommy climbing over the fence. It was music. It looked to be about a hundred and fifty feet to the beach below. I didn't linger, just in case. And it was a damn good thing. In less than a minute, I heard Joe somewhere near the fence yelling, "Tommy, where the hell are you?"

I managed to work my way down another six feet before I heard him again. "What makes you so damn sure he went over the fence?"

I held my breath, but Tommy's end of the exchanges were indistinguishable.

"I don't think so. Danny's out like a light, but it was his gun that was fired, and there's blood all over the place."

All I could make out was a distant mumble in reply.

"No, it's not his. Look! I followed a trail of blood to here with this flashlight. See? It turns here and goes toward the cliff. Get your tail back over here, and let's nail the son of a bitch, whoever he is."

I thanked the gods that at least Joe knew how to speak up. My mind raced, busy discarding unworkable plans. A race down the face of the bluff would be foolish; they wouldn't have to even catch me. All they'd have to do would be shoot me, or just force me to fall. There remained only one option that made any sense to me at all. Peeling off my bloody sweater, I flung it as far out away from the hillside as possible. It fluttered below, arranging itself quite nicely on the sand a few feet from the base of the sandstone wall. Then I scrabbled to my left, searching wildly for the one thing I hoped might save me now.

Knowing time was running short, I leaned out as far as I dared. I thought I saw what I was looking for ten feet farther along and a few feet lower. It appeared to be one of those deep holes scoured into the soft stone. I hoped to reach it in time and find it deep enough to swallow me.

There was no time to test each hand- and foothold, so I trusted the fates and hurried toward it. The stretching effort necessary to remove my sweater had cost me; it felt as if something had torn inside. I was aware of a renewed flow of sticky dampness streaming down my left leg.

"See! There's a couple of drops right there. It proves he went down this way, like I figured."

The nearness of Joe's voice galvanized me into action. I hit the hole and rolled inside, but yet taking great care not to dislodge a single grain of sand. It was scarcely a comfortable perch. I had to draw my knees up to my chin, and the floor was angled downward a good twenty degrees. I was freezing cold without my sweater, and it was a struggle to keep my teeth from becoming castanets.

The broad beam of a flashlight played across the opening to my tiny nook.

"Look! There's something—right straight down on the beach." Joe's voice was quite close and very excited.

"Maybe it's his and maybe not," mumbled Tommy. "Either way, he's long gone now."

"Look! The blood leads right to here. We gotta go down and get him. We know he's hurt pretty bad. How far away can he be?"

"You nuts? I'm not going down this cliff in the middle of the night. Maybe he's Spiderman, but I'd break my fucking neck."

"The hell you're not. You know what's at stake up here. Until now we've had it soft; here's where we earn our keep. If you don't move it, I'll personally guarantee you a busted neck."

Grumbling remarks about never claiming to be a human fly, Tommy, as I pictured him, turned to begin backing down the precipice. Soundlessly, I breathed through my wide-open mouth. From their noises I could tell they were making their descent right where I had. It meant they'd pass within fifteen feet of my mole hole. To my relief, I heard no more discussion of tracking blood spoor; they'd bought the idea of my having somehow made the full descent.

Time dragged agonizingly. The pain in my left side began emerging in earnest from behind its curtain of shock and adrenaline. My enforced fetal position wasn't helping. It pulled the muscles of my left side just at a time they wanted to be left alone and allowed to contract. There were a couple of times I felt my consciousness slipping and I really had to concentrate to keep from passing out and tumbling out of my hole and rolling one hundred and twenty-five feet to the beach below.

I'd monitored their progress by snatches of my enemy's conversation. Tommy was mostly lost to me, but Joe's hearty encouragement and advice on where to place hands and feet was clear proof he was descending first. After some minutes of complete silence I took the risk of poking my head out to see where they were. It wasn't until one of them turned on a flash that I was able to place them. The very lowest sandy portion of the cliff was a more gradual slope. They were facing away from the cliff and quickly butt-scooting down the last fifteen or twenty feet.

It was time. Even those two clowns would soon figure out I'd never made the trip along with my sweater when they found no tracks in the virgin sand below. I took a breath, bit my lip, and flexed my half-numbed fingers, summoning up whatever hidden reserves I had left.

Ascent was easier because I could see what I was doing. I only had twenty-five feet to go, and I soon scrambled gratefully over the top. I'd have given plenty to spend just five minutes inside that storage shed, but that was out of the question. I was long overdue to pass out and that would have been a poor spot to do it. For all I knew, Danny was up and around by now—or even Roscoe was on the scene—and I was still far from clear.

A quick scan of the area showed no movement, so I took the chance and got to my feet shakily. Backtracking the fence to the pile of lumber, I began lugging boards over and stacking them right up against the wire barrier. When the pile was about five feet high, I held onto the fence and walked up the irregular butts projecting from the end of the stack. I straddled the top, clenched my teeth, and heaved my other leg over the top.

It took me a while to make it back to my feet, using the fence for handholds. The only thing that kept me going was the certain knowledge Joe and Tommy were well on their way back up the cliff by now and probably somewhat irritated with me. I walked stilt-legged away from the fence, blinking my eyes furiously, tricking them into focusing clearly for increasingly shorter periods of time.

The quarter-mile to my car became a ten-mile hike with full field pack. When I arrived at last, I did so with my revolver in my hand. No way had I gone through all that to be suckered by someone smart enough to just wait for me. There was no one, which was fortunate. By then I was seeing double, and the way things were going, I'd have probably shot the wrong one.

I have absolutely no memory of the drive home, no doubt a considerable blessing. The strange alchemy that enables people to drive on auto pilot must have successfully assumed command. And welcome to it. Unlock the door, go up the stairs, and flop on the couch, but only after spreading several layers of thick towels over it. I'd have opted for the bed, but the phone was next to the couch and there was no question of putting off the call. I picked up the receiver and punched the button designated station 5.

It took a very long time to answer. Randy's sleep-weary voice finally came on and said, "Huh?"

"It's me, Matt."

"Jesus, Matt—it's three-thirty in the morning."

"Yeah, I heard. Lousy thing to do, get myself shot at such an inconvenient time. What can I say? If I live, I'll apologize."

"Shot! Where are you?"

"My room."

"On my way!" He sounded wide awake now.

I couldn't think of any more pressing business, so I stopped gritting my teeth and tried finding a comfortable position. When Randy found me a few minutes later, I was unconscious. And a girl once told me I didn't know how to relax.

CHAPTER 7

It's more than a little sobering to realize how quickly you can lose it. One little bullet hole and some lost blood, and I felt as if I'd be overmatched if I had to wrestle a toy poodle pup. I finally broke through the surface about noon. There remained a faint memory of swimming forever upward through a sea of molasses. Though I hurt like hell, I was oriented, and content to lie there feeling secure, admiring the swirls of the plaster work on the coved ceiling overhead.

The shroud of sleep continued sloughing away. Eventually I became truly aware of my surroundings and sensed I was not alone. Turning my head slightly, I found Win sitting beside my bed, regarding me with grave concern.

"Are you cogent?" he inquired doubtfully.

"That's never been officially settled, but he didn't plug me in the head, so I should be reasonably intact between the ears."

The handsome old face softened into a familiar smile. "I'm pleased to hear it. Randy tells me you've been shot through the left oblique muscle. More to the point, you've suffered considerable blood loss. If you think you're capable of sitting partially upright, I'll ring Louis to bring you a meal of tea and toast."

I braced my arms and levered myself up enough so he could jam a couple of pillows under my shoulders. Somebody heaved a javelin into my lower left side but I did my best to ignore it. "Tea and toast? Be serious—let's talk steak. And I guarantee I'll eat it, no matter what Louis does to it."

"Not today, I'm afraid, Matt. Randy will explain; it has something to do with mild shock and possible renal failure. Not a happy prospect, is it?" He got to his feet, gave me an avuncular look, and left the room. A few seconds later I could hear him talking on my phone.

All this fussing made me angry; when he returned, it was to find me glaring up at him. "Let's don't get all carried away with this Nursey-Jane routine, Win. I've been hit a lot worse than a .32 through the love handle, and I know what I need to get back on my feet. And it's not tea and toast—it's steak!"

Win calmly resumed his seat and frowned. "Love handle?"

"That's what they called the obliques when . . ." I saw his eyes twinkling, and realized I wasn't playing with a full deck quite yet. "Listen!" I grumped, "are you interested in hearing how I have practically solved the case, or have you decided to devote the rest of your life to nursing?"

I could see the flare of excitement behind his eyes. It made it all worth the price just to see that flash of pleasure. "I would indeed, Matt. You have my full and undivided attention."

I gave him all of it, which didn't take too long. I was finished by the time Louis arrived with my geriatric repast. That poor little guy had such an anguished look on his pinched face I kidded him plenty just to cheer him up. By the time I finished that miserable excuse for a meal I was stuffed, and my eyelids weighed roughly ten pounds apiece.

"You're to be commended for successfully extricating yourself from a very difficult situation," Win told me. "I note that you refrained from using your gun in spite of grave provocation. While it's true I abhor the use of firearms, I want it clearly understood

between us, this does not mean you are to risk your life un-
necessarily out of respect for my personal beliefs."

"Don't give it another thought. I've used my gun in the past
and I would have last night if it had been appropriate. It wouldn't
have helped. I was too far gone to hold them all for the police and
I would have had a hard time explaining it if I shot them all.
What I had to do was get away, and a gun wouldn't have helped."

"I just wanted to be certain you understood. You didn't
make it clear to me whether the one you call Danny was killed or
not. If so, I assume we may anticipate a visit from our erstwhile
tormentor, Inspector Dixon."

"No, Danny's not dead; but it wouldn't surprise me any to
see him wearing one of those foam rubber neck braces. And don't
worry about Dixon—these guys are hardly in any position to start
filing formal charges."

"That's comforting. But I fail to see how it is you've practically solved the case, as you put it. At most you've established
the strong possibility of culpability. Your reception could scarcely
be ascribed to normal security procedures. But beyond that . . ."
He paused, noting the smirk on my face. "Unless of course you've
omitted a point or two. Is that possible?"

"Does a bear shit in the woods?" I said, feeling giddy. "I
noticed Danny's fingers were coated with some sort of white pow-
der when he had me covered. Later, when he was out, I took a
closer look. It was coke! I'm sure of it. There was plenty of it
packed under his nails, too."

A smile composed of equal parts relief and satisfaction split
Win's face. "Now that *is* interesting," he agreed. "No wonder they
were so determined to see that you extended your stay on the
premises. It validates every one of our hypotheses. It is no longer
mere wishful thinking to assume Mrs. Reynaud made a similar
discovery and died for it."

I contributed something brilliant—I forget what.

"Stop mumbling, Matt, and go back to sleep. We mustn't
overreach your capacities like this. Forgive me. And well done."

I let loose and slipped back down below the molasses sea, pleased as a kid with straight A's on his report card.

The next time I surfaced, it was to find Randy sitting forward in the chair, peering at me intently. "What are you doing, looking for bugs?" I asked.

He blinked his owl-looking eyes, came over, and peeled back the covers. "Not really; I just came up to change your dressing and didn't want to wake you." His pudgy little fingers went to work on my middle.

"What time is it?"

"Shortly after six," he told me distractedly.

"How's everything look?"

"Fine, Matt; just fine. Vital signs are all good. I'm repacking the wound with sulfas—no sign of any infection yet."

"What do you mean, yet? You sound as if you haven't given up hope."

"No, there's really no reason to anticipate problems. Still, it was close, you know. Your left kidney would have been involved if the bullet had struck about two inches interior."

"Close only counts in horseshoes and hand grenades. Tell me I can have some real food tonight, or prepare to defend yourself."

He pulled the bedclothes back up over me. "I guess it will be all right, Matt. Kidney output appears to be about normal. If you'll promise to really force the liquids, I'll let you try a moderate meal."

"I'll promise anything; go tell Louis to broil me a cow." He was halfway to the door before I processed what he'd said. "How the hell do you know whether my kidney output's normal or not?"

Randy leered back at me, chuckling with absolute delight. "How do you think? Check and see for yourself—some detective you are. And by the way," he added seriously, "I'd suggest you take it easy on that candy for a while. A couple of pieces won't hurt—in fact it will make you want to drink more fluids—but hold it down to, say, no more than three during the evening."

For a man who prided himself on an ability to observe and correlate data, it was something of a shock to realize I'd been catheterized for half a day without even being aware of it. My hands sought out the obscene plastic tubing violating the sanctity of my body. Of course, all my receptors were busy with the pain in my side, but still it was quite a blow. For some reason, it bothered me more than the hole in my flesh. Then I idly wondered what Randy'd been blathering about candy until I spotted the big box of Whitman Samplers on my bedside table. Apparently I was somebody's valentine.

When Louis entered bearing a tray an hour later, Win was with him. Louis was grinning from ear to ear; serving me tea and toast had probably hurt him more than it had me. I was suddenly hesitant to see what was on the tray, knowing what he could do to a perfectly fine cut of meat on an off day.

"I see you've managed to browbeat Randy into letting you have your way, as usual," Win commented, nodding at the T-bone steak on my plate. By some miracle, it appeared to be only slightly incinerated.

"Yeah, I can eat as many cows as I want, but only three chocolates. Hell of a deal, since I don't like candy anyway." I was sitting more or less upright, braced against some pillows and ready for action. My salivary glands were threatening to drown me.

Win regarded me quizzically, then he saw the box of candy sitting on my little bedside table. "Where did this come from?" he demanded sharply.

"I put it there, sir," Louis piped up. "It was delivered this afternoon. It's for Matt, from that lawyer, Mr. Price." He recited the details proudly, obviously happy to have remembered them. Louis usually forgot things pretty quickly.

"How can you be sure it's from Mr. Price?" demanded Win angrily. Louis looked as if he'd been kicked, and I was astonished at Win's harsh tone. We were all careful in our expectations of Louis, but none more so than Win.

"There is a note—here!" Louis told him defensively, remov-

ing the lid and handing him a small folded card. It made me feel
bad to see how his hands shook. It also didn't thrill me that they
were none too clean.

I looked at the exposed candies with little interest. But they
were tempting, each virginal looking in their own personal paper
boat. I spotted a caramel that would do nicely for dessert.

"'Dear Matt,'" Win read aloud, "'sorry to hear about your
ordeal. Last time I was laid up I found these comforting. I'll be by
to see you soon. All best wishes for a speedy recovery, Hoffman
Price.'"

"Nice of him," I commented, focusing most of my attention
on my scalpel work over the steak. "Have some of those if you
want, guys. I hate to eat alone, but I'm sure not going to share
this steak with anybody."

"Mr. Price didn't send this," Win said grimly.

I froze with a forkful of the delectable meat halfway home.
"Huh?"

"We should be extremely grateful you don't have a sweet
tooth, Matt. I'm all but certain there's an added deadly ingredient
in these familiar, innocuous-looking delicacies."

"I'll be damned! You mean you recognize Hoffman's handwriting?"

"I don't have to—I recognize his style. So would you if you
were fully alert. If he were to send you anything, it would more
likely be a bottle of fine brandy, a liqueur—never candy. And
the accompanying note would reflect his acerbic wit—never this
sort of pallid sentiment." He carefully replaced the lid on the box
and handed it to Louis.

"Take this down to Dr. Bruckner at once. Tell him I want it
analyzed for noxious additives. You do understand these candies
are almost certainly lethal?" He wanted to make darn sure Louis
didn't decide to sample along the way.

He understood all right: Louis was shaking as if he were on
the verge of a fit. "I brought them into the house," he wailed. "I
laid them here—open—right at Matt's bedside while he slept. So
he could reach . . . For anyone to . . ."

"Stop that!" Win commanded. "If anyone here is subject to indictment it's me. Your job is to keep the house clean and prepare meals. My job is outmaneuvering felons. At the moment, you are certainly doing a better job than I. This falls within my job description, not yours. Were there any other unusual deliveries today? No, disregard unusual—was there anything whatever delivered to this house today, in addition to these chocolates?"

Louis scrunched up his face in an obvious effort to think. "No, sir! Not another thing," he finally swore.

"Good! You are to alert me immediately upon the arrival of any and all deliveries, beginning now. I don't care what it is or how it comes—everything! Go now, and tell Dr. Bruckner I'll be waiting for the results here."

Louis hurried off, holding the box of candy rigidly, away from his body, as if it were full of snakes.

"Unspeakable knavery!" Win growled. "I hold a particular aversion to poisoners; they are among the most ignoble of all would-be murderers. And to attempt to strike within these very walls? It would seem we have inadvertently become pitted against an exceedingly cunning and ruthless adversary."

"Be funny if they were nothing but chocolates," I warned him.

"Not funny—miraculous!" he replied darkly. "Hoffman Price is totally unaware of your incapacitation."

Now I was beginning to share his somber mood. "I guess that settles it then. Wonder what's next. Bombs? Paratroopers?"

"Eat your steak," he advised grimly. "With Dirk incarcerated, we're at sufficient disadvantage. The sooner you're fit the better. I have a feeling this time we've engaged in mortal combat with a particularly sanguinary foe."

"Anyone ever tell you you're a charming dinner companion? A real aid to digestion you are, yes sir." I forked a big chunk of T-bone into my mouth and chewed furiously. I was half amused and half angry when I found myself analyzing the taste, checking for any trace of bitter almonds.

"How long do you think Louis will remember about the deliveries?" I asked.

"He'll be reminded sufficiently often so that he won't forget. Randy and I will be vigilant."

Silence reigned in the room, except for the clink of my knife and fork. The overdone meat was losing its appeal now.

Win sat uncomfortably in the too-low bedroom chair, gazing dreamily at his tented fingers. "It's times like these when I think perhaps I should have been content to sit back and write my memoirs like all the rest of them," he told me sourly.

"So why didn't you?"

"The world of letters scarcely needed another study in self-aggrandizement. Of course, I could have done mine differently— I could have told the truth. No, that would never do. To slay an entire herd of sacred cows—most of whom are dead now anyway—what would be the point? Do you know the real reason I decided to become a detective, Matt?"

"You always told me it was because you got tired of doing the *Times* crossword puzzle."

"That too; but the truth is I need the money. Does that shock you?"

"It would if I believed it. How hard up can you be? This place? Louis? Randy? Between those two it must cost more to run this place than some small towns. Your retirement benefits from the consular service and Department of State wouldn't begin to cover it, I know, but obviously you've got other sources?"

He said: "Don't forget, I spent most of my life in public office, Matt. And I didn't come from a moneyed family. There's only one way to get rich in public office, and I elected not to avail myself of that infamous route. My highest salary in office was less than the mayor of San Diego currently earns. The only reason I have this house is I happened to fall in love with it and buy it before World War II, when this entire area was nothing more than inexpensive pasture land for the stable horses at Del Mar Race Track. Now the property taxes are equal to half my government retirement income. Add my Social Security income—which wouldn't even buy the groceries around here—and that's it. Then we've got Randy, bless him, who's forever dunning me for some piece of exotic equipment I never heard of, and which invariably costs about as much as an automobile.

"So it was hardly just a whim when I decided to become a working detective. I needed income badly and it was the only career I could imagine in which the intellectual challenge attracted me. Think about it: even with my background, there aren't a lot of career opportunities available to a man my age. I suppose I could have sold insurance or real estate or sat on some board of directors just so they could put my name on their letterhead. But all these things were repugnant to me. You see, I've long since reached an age where I value my privacy. Though I lay claim to as much love of my fellow man as anyone else, I prefer not to have to spend the time I have left rubbing elbows with him. And so I chose to become a detective and I hired you to be my alter ego beyond the walls of this house."

I sat there stunned. "How come you never told me this before? And why are you telling me now?"

"Matt, seeing you in the condition you were in last night and now finding that damnable box of death at your bedside, it suddenly occurs to me it's one thing for me to accept the cerebral challenges of what we do, but it's quite another to keep putting your life at risk time and time again. Until now, I actually believe I had some kind of abstracted and naive image of our work. Now I'm faced with the grim reality of having death a resident in my own home. Don't misunderstand; I don't believe I'm a physical coward—at my age it's easy not to be a coward—but I'm having a difficult time facing the fact that my avocation places everyone in this house under a very real threat of violence. You most of all. What if that bullet had been two inches over? And Randy says he has no idea how you stayed on your feet long enough to elude your pursuers and drive back here."

I put down my knife and fork with a vast sigh. "Why not take the blame for world hunger and bad weather while you're at it? Personally I feel pretty great about what we do, and I always thought you did too. This crazy world of ours is full of incredibly nasty folks, and I really like getting the chance to put a few of them out of commission. I was doing it long before we met, don't forget. And when I get racked up, it's usually because I deserve to. It means I made a mistake. I certainly made one last night. Because I'd drawn a blank on my search and there didn't appear to be any security I allowed someone to walk right up and take me. I'm not proud of myself, but in spite of all Dirk's training I'm only human, and mistakes will be made. The point is, I'd prefer to make them here, working for you. It beats mucking around back in Chicago, getting shot by a lower class of criminal.

"What are you thinking? That we should surrender our licenses just because we had a close call? So someone sent us a box of lethal candy—big deal! You want to leave Dirk parked in a concrete box for the next twenty-five years? Hell, Win, there isn't a soul in this house who wouldn't walk through fire for you and thank you for the privilege. Now may I respectfully suggest we cut the crap and get around to something constructive?"

The old boy seemed to have something caught in his throat when he tried to reply, so he merely nodded agreement. Then the phone rang, and he went into my small front room and answered it. I heard him tell whoever it was that something wouldn't be necessary. When he came back there was a glint of anger in his eyes. "Randy reports each of the first three chocolates he examined contained a lethal dose of potassium cyanide. Death would have followed ingestion within five minutes."

"When you're right, you're right, Win. God bless those marvelous instincts of yours. I'd already picked out one of the caramels for dessert. I suggest we send it back to Roscoe and the boys with an appropriate message."

He gave me a horrified look. "We couldn't think of that. There's the chance they might fall into the hands of some innocent bystander. No, Matt—I'll see that they're destroyed properly. But I do have a course of action in mind."

"Let's hear the battle plan."

"After our conference—based upon your report—I had a

talk with the local director of the Bureau of Narcotics. I have every reason to believe his agency has already staged a raid on Sea View by now. It will at least be a start if we can get them indicted for their narcotics violations. From there, it should be a simple matter to prove motive and opportunity for the murder of Marlee Reynaud. Not only will an atmosphere of strong suspicion be created, their arrest will render them *hors de combat* and give us time to prove a connection."

"Once we manage to spring Dirk, will that be the end?"

He shook his head soberly. "I shouldn't think so. We'd do well to assume we're bound in mortal combat."

"I think you're dead right," I yawned. "If nothing else, we owe it to Dirk to nail them for the murder they tried to hang on him. We can't just leave it an open question, floating over his head like . . ."

Win got to his feet and began removing the pillows from behind my shoulders. Somehow I'd lost my train of thought. "Surrender yourself to the arms of Morpheus," he told me gently. "I'll be back in the morning. Good night, Matt."

"Night, Boss." I was asleep before he reached the door.

There was enough diffused light leaking through the drawn drapes when I woke up to tip me that it was morning. Or afternoon for all I knew. Someone had removed my clock radio to make room for a carafe of water and a glass on my bedside table. I lay there and took a vote of all the medical experts present concerning the advisability of my getting out of bed. The motion carried by a one vote margin.

Bracing my elbows, I edged back against the headboard and swung my legs over the side. Something fouled my right leg and I was painfully reminded of my umbilicus. I took a deep breath and removed my catheter. The sensation was roughly equivalent to peeing molten lead. Examining it objectively now that it was no longer a part of me, I wondered whether Randy was all that competent after all. Surely the clear plastic tube in my hand was meant for watering gardens.

My feet fished for the floor and found it. I eased myself erect—almost. Actually, the best I could manage was a hunched posture, but at least I was mobile. It didn't take much more than five minutes to mince my way across the room and into the bath. When I opened the door I was confronted by the sight of myself in the full-length mirror. A seedy-looking character leered back at me. I winked, told him, "Looking good, Gramps," and quickly looked away.

I found out how difficult it is to wash your face with only one hand. It did unpleasant things to my side when I tried to raise my left arm, so I was working solo. Brushing my teeth was okay, but shaving presented a minor problem. It's tough looking in my medicine cabinet mirror while stooped over.

Inordinately pleased with myself after completing my rituals, I eased my way over to the dresser and retrieved my watch. It was absolutely amazing how lost I'd felt without that familiar reference around my wrist.

Halfway to the chair where I'd planned to await visitors, the room began tilting erratically. Either the long overdue California earthquake had finally arrived or I'd shot my wad. I stilt-walked the final eight feet—legs wide—and gratefully collapsed back onto my bed.

Ten minutes later, Randy came rushing in like a flustered penguin. "How're we feeling today, Matt?"

"Who's 'we'? You got a turd in your pocket?" I replied sourly.

"My, my, getting fed up with the program already, are we? I know it must be tough for you, but it's likely to be only another couple of days." He reached under my bed and retrieved a shiny stainless pan with a curiously familiar rim around most of the edge.

"What the hell's that?"

"You know very well: it's commonly called a bedpan. I should think some use for it would have occurred to you by now."

I noted the impish look of delight on his chubby cherubic face. It made all my efforts worth the price. "Use it for a hat, pal—I don't need it."

"You will! I'll just leave it here where you can get to it." He reached over and nestled it beside my legs on top of the bed.

"I'm telling you one more time: Either get that obscenity out of here or I'll feed it to you. I just checked—mine is still in the bathroom where it belongs. It's bigger and better, makes soothing noises like a waterfall, and washes itself. And it's never shown the poor taste of getting into bed with me. Altogether one of man's finest achievements. Let's hear it for Sir John Crapper."

Randy's jaw dropped. He jerked away my covers to confirm the worst. The look of shock on his face made my maiden voyage a real bargain at twice the price. "You damned idiot! Let's see what new damage you've managed to inflict on yourself." His deft fingers began stripping away the tape around my side.

"Good thing you're the doctor and I'm the detective. I don't think it would have worked very well the other way around. You're not observant enough. Didn't even notice my clean shave or my wristwatch. And if I had to go around sticking my fingers into other people's juices I'd be a flop, too."

After admitting nothing too terrible had resulted from my brief foray into normalcy, Randy gathered his pans, tubes, and bottles and left, promising to hustle Louis up with vast amounts of breakfast. He refused to commit himself concerning the likely quality.

It was nearly noon by the time Win made it to my room. His grim look told the story I'd been afraid of. "What'd you expect?" I asked grumpily. "They'd have the evidence all labeled neatly and on display?"

"I see you've anticipated events correctly," he grumbled right back at me.

"What the hell, Win; we gave them thirty hours to clean house."

"True," he sighed, "but I still retained hope because they had no way of knowing you'd observed cocaine on Danny's fingers. What really surprises me is the officers' inability to discover even the slightest trace. Armed with the foreknowledge that the drug had been there, you'd think they'd have sophisticated methods of manifesting evidence."

"They do—almost as sophisticated as the crooks have of disposing of it. So you're telling me they came up completely empty?"

"They found one thing of more than passing interest: That storage building was completely soundproofed and blacked out for night work. It's extremely inappropriate and suggestive, of course, but hardly actionable. Your friend, Mr. Roscoe Blaise, explained it away by attempting to tell the officers it was an experiment into the feasibility of soundproofing the units under construction. He went on to say the cost proved prohibitive in the end, and the feature was discarded. No one believed him—I'm certain—but neither can he be impeached."

"Cheer up! Remember, if it was easy everybody'd be doing it." It gave me a lift to see he hadn't slipped back into the funk he'd been in the night before. In spite of the bad news he appeared to be the old Win—pedantic and optimistic.

He responded with a grim smile. "I'm pleased to hear of your progress, though Randy thinks you're behaving foolishly by rushing things. Have you any suggestions?" He sat and looked at me expectantly, letting me know we couldn't afford to just sit around and wait for developments.

"Matter of fact, I have. I'd give plenty to find out who Roscoe and the three stooges really are. Where they're from. And I've given some thought to how we might find out. Why don't you call the San Diego planning and zoning commissioner? There had to be all kinds of permits needed to build right along the coast like that. At least you could get a make on Roscoe—maybe even the others if they really are partners—which I don't believe for a second. While you do that, I've got a little project of my own in mind."

"I trust whatever it is can be implemented from that bed."

"You will recall Roscoe has a boat, a forty-seven-foot Pacemaker. That's plenty big enough to have the range and capacity for the Baja run. It's a good bet that's how they're bringing the stuff in. I've got a buddy I met in the Power Squadron who's coast guard. It would be interesting to see how many trips that boat's taken south of the border lately. I may even want to have a close look at her myself. If it is the vehicle they're using, there has to be some concealed space aboard where they feel secure stashing it—maybe a double hull with a phony bilge. The boat would be checked by the customs people every time it comes back from foreign waters."

"Commendable! Bed rest appears to stimulate your mental processes."

"Sure, that's to be expected. I only have so much blood; most of the time it's in my legs because you keep me charging around out in the field."

"I see," Win nodded, looking better than when he arrived. "According to that theory, I should be able to anticipate a steady flow of brilliant deductive reasoning from you over the next few days."

"Certainly! That was just one tiny sample. Now I'm going to follow my own clever advice and call my friend at the coast guard station." I threw aside my covers and began the complicated maneuver of getting out of bed.

Win shot me a look of grave concern as he arose, but he was wise enough not to waste his breath arguing or trying to help. Telling me he was on his way to the office to carry out his part, he left.

As is all too often the case with my brainstorms, this one was a complete washout. By late afternoon I'd gotten word back: The *Wahoo*, Roscoe's ship, hadn't so much as made a run to Ensenada since he'd owned her. And Win's results weren't any better. Roscoe Blaise was clean. He held a California real-estate broker's license as well as a developer's license and a list of permits a mile long. No record, naturally, or he wouldn't have held the licenses and permits. He was listed on the county books as sole proprietor of Blaise Development Corporation, so if he had any partners they were "silent" ones. Apparently the condos at Sea View marked his first attempt to make it as a builder. Up

until a couple of years ago he'd been slugging it out in the
trenches as a residential real-estate broker in Bay Park.

I spent most of Thursday and Friday on the phone, picking
the brains of everyone I could think of in any position to know
anything about local drug trafficking. I quickly became appalled
to discover how common such people were, and the matter-of-fact
way in which they viewed the enterprise. Simple case of "find a
need and fill it." Oldest and truest adage in the world of business.
During those two days I called in a lot of debts, managing to work
my way backwards from users to vendors to suppliers and, ultimately, to an importer or wholesaler. Those who accepted my
bona fides and talked to me had absolutely no reason to lie. If
they could have used me to harpoon a competitor they would have
done it. Not one had ever run across the name Blaise. So for sixty
hours—all the way up to Saturday morning—we might as well
have been baying at the moon.

CHAPTER 8

Saturday morning I walked into the dining room, grabbed a cup of coffee, and waited impatiently for my heart to start.

"You give at least the illusion of being fully ambulatory," Win remarked dubiously. "Are you?"

"Yeah, except my left leg wants to take shorter steps than my right, so I find myself going in circles a lot."

"At least you enjoy the advantage of a valid excuse; I find myself in a similar position, intellectually speaking."

"Don't look at me," I warned him. "Considering the return on all my bright ideas, I've retired from the genius business. From now on I'm strictly a legman again."

Win seemed preoccupied and didn't answer. I proceeded to make a sizable dent in the egg rations, much to Louis's delight. Either he'd gotten lucky that morning, or my standards had lowered during my stretch upstairs in solitary. "What's the latest word on Dirk?" I asked Win.

"Mr. Price reports he seems to be coping moderately well.

He apparently exercises excessively to achieve physical exhaustion in order to distract himself from his environment. Even so, he is becoming increasingly agitated, paces incessantly during their interviews. The grand jury meets next week—Tuesday—to consider the preponderance of evidence against him."

"Can they make it stick without a corpus delicti?"

Win looked morose. "There doesn't seem the slightest doubt probable cause will be found, in spite of that absence. He'll undoubtedly be bound over for trial. Mr. Price will seek an early court date, but with little expectation of success. The court will be sympathetic to the district attorney's request for time to continue searching for the body. Damn—this is onerous!" he suddenly shouted angrily. Frowning at my empty plate, he asked, "Are you quite finished?"

"Sure; I'm all set for at least an hour." I think it was the first time I'd ever heard him use even that mild expletive. It was a clear sign of his extreme agitation.

"Then come along. I'm determined to unravel this absonant mare's nest at once." He got up and walked toward the office, his cane never even getting close to the floor.

"Now there's an idea," I muttered to nobody in particular, and got up and followed at a more sedate pace. When he began cussing and using esoteric words, that was a sure sign the fur was about to fly.

We were busily engaged in a fine debate—more like an argument—over what would be our next move, when Louis stuck his head in the door twenty minutes later. "What is it?" Win snapped. Normally he never snaps at Louis. The rest of us are fair game, but never Louis. It's too much like kicking a sick puppy.

"A man to see Matt, Mr. Winfield," Louis mumbled.

"Has he got a name?" I asked.

"A Mr. Roscoe Blaise, Matt; I made him wait outside."

Win and I engaged in a contest to see who could get the most altitude out of his eyebrows. As far as I could tell, it looked like a draw, with a new world record established jointly. Win recovered first. "Would you consider introducing me to your friend?" he inquired facetiously.

I grinned right back at him. "Okay, I'll share the wealth. But just remember—he came to see me. It must have been something I did that dazzled him into coming here to confess everything."

"If only the gods were so indulgent," he replied thoughtfully. "Still, I've no doubt we'll profit from this meeting in some small way."

Roscoe came waddling in, looking for all the world like a chastened schoolboy. When he spotted Win his eyes popped. "I didn't expect to see you, Mr. Secretary," he told Win almost reverently. "I mean, it's certainly an honor to meet you, sir, but I hope I'm not disturbing you."

Win leaned back and let him have a broadside: "As a result of your knavery, Mr. Blaise, I am indeed disturbed. Beyond endurance. If it really wasn't your intention to disturb me, you might have avoided endangering the lives of everyone in this house, for a start. Now then, so much for false amenities—why have you come?"

Roscoe looked confused. He appealed to me. "What's he talking about, Mr. Doyle?" His Humpty-Dumpty physique gave him a comic air, his ruddy balloon face was the picture of wounded innocence.

"Just answer the man's question," I told him flatly. "What did bring you around? Come to take a body count? Sorry to disappoint. We're all hale and hardy." I studied him intently, searching for signs of shock or dismay at finding me more or less intact.

"I can't imagine what you must think of me, both of you," he said hesitantly. He kept looking back and forth from Win to me, as if hoping for a sign of sympathy from one of us. "I just found out myself what happened out at my place four nights ago. I've never been so embarrassed in my life. Right away I fired the three men involved, then I came here to try and apologize. I'm really sorry, Mr. Doyle. And I came to see if there's any way I can make it up to you."

"So that's the tack you've elected?" Win mused. "We're to believe you innocent of all peccancy? Nothing more than the guiltless victim of your own misguided trust?"

Roscoe pleaded with Win, wringing his big hands like a truant schoolboy. "I don't blame you a bit for feeling like that but I can only tell you the truth and hope for the best. Everything I've got in the world—or ever will—is riding on those condos. I swear to you, I had no idea those jerks were using me as a cover for their dealing."

He switched his plea to me. "Well, Mr. Doyle; was I there in the middle of the night when you caught them with the stuff? Was I?"

"I didn't have a chance to call the roll," I told him. "Somebody might have stayed behind to mind the store—I figure that would have been you."

He lifted his hands toward heaven in silent supplication, gave a sigh of defeat, and collapsed into a chair. "I felt I had to try. So I tried. Now I got nothing more to say."

"That much at least is untrue," Win told him. "There's a good deal more you have yet to say. You might begin by explaining why—after allegedly discovering your employees were engaged in a felony—you allowed them to go free. I am no attorney, thank God, but unless I'm sadly mistaken, you've just confessed to charges of accessory after the fact concerning the crimes of smuggling, illicit drug trafficking, and attempted murder."

"I guess it's true; my fate is in your hands, gentlemen. I did it last night in a fit of rage. Looking back, I guess I should have turned them in but all I could think about last night was getting them the hell away from Sea View." He sat up a little straighter in the chair and took a deep breath. "And I'll be perfectly honest about this. Maybe subconsciously I wanted to save my own skin. Turning them in might have held up construction somehow—they could have easily gotten even by implicating me. By the time I hired an attorney and proved my innocence I'd be bankrupt. The publicity alone would have been fatal. My licenses? My bonds? The truth is it wouldn't take much to put me under, so maybe I was looking out for number one—okay?" He hadn't made eye contact with either of us since he sat in the chair; he seemed fascinated by the sight of his big belly spilling over onto his thighs.

"Just how would you have us believe you discovered their culpability?" Win inquired.

Roscoe ignored the dripping sarcasm. "The cops came down on the place like a ton of bricks Thursday. But you know that; I assume you sent them. Anyway, you could tell they thought they had inside information; the only thing they were interested in was the storage shed. One of those three jerks—it was Joe—acted like he was having kittens the whole time they were there. I stewed about it for the next twenty-four hours. Something didn't smell right. None of them was drawing a paycheck—I told Mr. Doyle that—but they all had money to burn. And they really didn't give a good goddamn about the project. In fact, the more I stewed about it, the more I realized they seemed content to have it go on forever. Whenever the cookie jar was empty, they'd come up with another fifty thousand or so to keep things rolling, but never enough so any real progress could be made. Now I understand why.

"Anyway, yesterday I confronted all three guys together. At first they tried to laugh it off, but I was pretty worked up by then. Finally, they admitted they'd been running coke in from Mexico and simply defied me to do a thing about it. And that's when they told me about Matt's being there Wednesday morning and getting shot. They made it clear they'd implicate me in that as well if I told anyone. That's when I ordered them off the property. I also made it clear I would turn them in if I ever so much as caught sight of any one of them again."

Win cocked his head and looked a question at me.

The best I was willing to do was lift my shoulders an inch and lower them. If Roscoe was lying, he had a gift for it. But then, most successful crooks do.

"Mr. Blaise," Win said, "either you're an ingenuous dupe or a clever malfeasant with unmitigated gall. Time will tell me which appellation is the correct one. For now, you may go a long way toward convincing us of your tenability by telling us where we might find your former associates."

Roscoe obliged by rattling off an address in Carlsbad, saying they'd all shared a house. "Why should you care, though?" he asked Win. "Why not just let the bums go? I think I can guarantee they won't hang around this part of the country."

"But we care a great deal," Win assured him grimly. "You seem to have forgotten why we're involved in the first place. Our sole mission right now is to solve the murder of Marlee Reynaud. If we are to credit your account, it follows that those men killed her. Presumably for the same reason they attempted to kill Mr. Doyle. She was a bright, inquisitive woman who often spent her evenings working in your interests. It's not difficult to suppose she inadvertently unearthed knowledge of these clandestine activities, and your men's feral response to Mr. Doyle's presence makes it quite clear they were capable of violence. Now do you begin to grasp the gravity of your error in letting them leave freely?"

Roscoe's head shook rapidly. "No! No, you're dead wrong on that score. Danny, Joe, and Tommy were all three with me aboard the *Wahoo*—that's my boat—when Marlee was killed. I'm positive because the next day, when we heard, we all talked about how sad that she hadn't accepted my invitation to come along. She'd have still been alive."

"You must forgive my lack of enthusiasm for that alibi, Mr. Blaise. It always fails to impress me when one of my suspects volunteers to vouch for the other defendants."

Roscoe shoved himself to his feet, and I could see more color coming into his face. "Now I guess I came here to take some crap, so I've shut up and taken some, but not that particular load. It just so happens on that day—Sunday, a week ago tomorrow—we took one of my favorite runs. We left the slip on Harbor Island at noon and ran due west for just over four hours to the south end of San Clemente Island. There's a tiny cove there—barely room for half a dozen boats. We caught some lobster, brought up some nice abalone, and didn't start back until midnight. I always make the run back late because I love to see the night creatures in the sea—I mean the luminous ones—and they don't even begin to rise until then. The times—the exact course—everything's in my ship's log." He stated it as if that made it sacrosanct.

"So you say. I repeat, I'm not impressed," Win told him.

Roscoe stuck out his jaw, what little he had. "Would you be impressed if I told you the log is also signed, including the time and date, by half a dozen naval officers? There's a small base right there on the island and we invited some guys aboard to share the catch. They were sitting there on the beach with nothing to do so I offered them a beer and it went from there. Now according to what I read in the paper about the estimated time of Marlee's death, they were still aboard making a big dent in my booze locker when she was killed."

Win's face clearly reflected dismay. I suppose mine did too. "May I assume these names will be made available to Mr. Doyle?" He didn't sound dismayed, he sounded angry.

"Look, guys," Roscoe pleaded, "anything, anytime—that's my motto. Here!" He scribbled something on one of his cards and handed it to me. "Just show this card if anyone gives you a hard time. The name of the marina, slip number, and combination to the main hatch—it's all there. You'll find the log at the lower bridge, in the top drawer. Be my guest.

"Now what about this matter of you getting shot? You'll never know how relieved I was to find you on your feet. It happened right in my office, so naturally I feel kind of responsible. I mean—let's face it—I feel terrible. Just tell me what I can do to make it up to you. At least see that I get the medical bill—okay?"

It was a masterful performance—or it wasn't. "No, but thanks," I told him. "The box of candy was more than enough."

It will never cease to frustrate me when someone lies to me so convincingly I buy whatever it is they're selling. It just doesn't seem reasonable or fair. As a trained detective I should be able to tell—right? Wrong! The totally blank look on Roscoe's face was genuine. It was incredible, but for the first time since he'd entered the room, I was seriously considering the idea he was innocent. Considering it, hell; I was all but convinced of it. There was no way he knew one single damn thing about those poisoned chocolates.

"Candy? What candy? You want candy, I'll send a truckload. First him," he nodded at Win, "making with a lot of words I never heard of. And now you with candy. Between the two of you, I might as well be in a foreign country."

He backed toward the door, hands spread palms up, as if in supplication. "I guess I've said what I came to say; I leave the rest up to you. If it would make you feel like big shots to ruin an honest man, I guess you can. So be my guest. If not, and you ever need anything, or have some more questions, you know where to find me." Roscoe had enough sense to realize that an offer of handshakes all around would not be appropriate, so he settled for a fractional bow and left, closing the heavy door quietly behind him.

He left Win and me staring at each other. Neither wanted to be the first to say it. I lost, as usual. "Maybe you could use your influence to get Dirk put in one of those country club prisons—you know, like the Watergate crew."

His look evolved into a glare. "I fail to see the humor in this, Mr. Doyle," he told me bitterly.

"Don't Mr. Doyle me, pal; I feel just as lousy as you. It's called gallows humor. I've even been known to whistle while walking through graveyards at night. It's the same principle."

"Is that how you perceive the situation? All we've been doing for one whole solid week is whistling in the dark? Am I to understand that you are prepared to ratify that man's account as unimpeachable?"

I tilted my chair back and considered. "It's complicated: To believe his construction site was some sort of halfway house for smuggling cocaine without his knowledge or participation would be ridiculous. But as for the rest of it, we might have to swallow it. Our Mr. Blaise is no fool, in spite of the 'good old boy' act. I mean, I doubt he bought off half the navy. Sure, I'll check it out six ways from Sunday, but right now I'd be willing to risk my next month's salary against a dirty dime his story will hold. And I'll even throw this in for free: If Roscoe knew one damn thing about any candy, then he and I are both in the wrong business. It sailed right by him."

Win traded his glare for a frown of frustration. "Then you're contending we're precisely where we were Monday morning when that cossack marched Dirk from this house in chains? That there is no connection between anyone at Blaise Construction and Marlee Reynaud's murder? You've been shot; we've all been nearly poisoned—all this in aid of nothing? We do not possess one single solitary hint of an idea—is that your contention?" Along the way his voice had risen; he began as a baritone and nearly made soprano by the time he'd finished.

"You put it about right. Before you turn into an Irish tenor, I'm leaving."

"Leaving for where?"

"First Carlsbad, in case I get the chance to thank the proper people for the candy. Next stop is Roscoe's boat. And don't think I'm not going to do more than check his logs. I'll stay over on my boat tonight; tomorrow I'll borrow a Sea Ray from a friend, make the run out to San Clemente, and have a chat with the navy officers named in the log. I wish I had photographs of those three. It won't prove much if they counted Roscoe and three others on the boat unless we know they're the right three."

"A reasonable itinerary. What the devil is a Sea Ray?"

"Twenty-six feet of dynamite. It'll make the run in less than two hours each way if the seas are calm. My kidneys may not like it, but that's their problem." I picked up Roscoe's business card and started to leave.

"Do you think it prudent, exposing yourself to that kind of physical hardship so soon? It only requires a relapse on your part to complete the perfect fiasco."

"It'll be good for me. Nothing more therapeutic than a fast

run aboard a good boat. The salt spray will rinse away my blues. You should come along."

He snorted derisively at the notion. "Hardly! While you play intrepid, I'll find a useful way to occupy myself. By the time you return tomorrow evening, I expect to have a cogent battle plan devised. I suppose I must proceed on the hypothesis that Mr. Blaise's statements will be validated. Indeed, I consider it axiomatic, as you do."

I stopped short in the open door. "Just get me a good seat on the flight to Baton Rouge." As I ducked out I caught sight of an angry grimace. I'd let him know how impressed I was he'd have to slave over a plan for two whole days. It took me two whole seconds to figure out there was nothing left but for me to go to Louisiana for what promised to be a long trip. It was beginning to look as if Marlee had attracted her killer from back home. It was a mean thing to do to him, but I was feeling pretty mean. The only thing worse than getting shot is getting shot for nothing. On my way to the car I looked around for a dog to kick.

The address in Carlsbad turned out to be a sizable ranch-style house on a quiet side street. There was a van parked in the drive and the front door stood open. A sign planted in the front lawn broadcast FOR RENT in big block letters, with the name and phone number of a local realty company.

I stayed in my car just long enough to check my revolver. There was still plenty of pain in my left side to remind me of the kind of people I was dealing with. Importing coke isn't for the small-change artists; those who get involved are in for keeps, and they play rough.

As I approached the open door I could hear the whine of a vacuum cleaner. It was being sluggishly operated by a young man with a scraggly beard. He was oblivious to my shouts, so I walked inside and pulled the plug.

He spun around, demanding, "You from the rental office?"

"Nope! Just a friend of the guys who lived here. Didn't know they'd moved. When did they leave?"

"I wouldn't know nothin' about it. All I know is, I got a call to hump it over here and clean it quick, so it can get shown. Ain't nobody living here now, I can tell you that." He padded over and replaced the plug in the outlet.

"Mind if I have a quick look around as long as I'm here? I think I might know someone who's interested."

"No skin off my nose, but make it fast. Soon's I finish this I got to shampoo the carpet. Don't want nobody prowling around then." He grasped the handle and the machine roared back to life.

It was the usual three bedroom layout with large kitchen, small dining room, and plenty of front room. The closets were empty, but the kitchen cabinets still contained an assortment of cheap plastic dishes and an odd lot of cookware. The patio in back was piled high with furniture, apparently removed from the carpeted areas of the house. Nothing caught my eye, so I strolled back into the living room. The only attractive feature was the large fieldstone fireplace. The raised stone hearth was piled with small tables and lamps to avoid having to lug them outside.

I waved at the kid on my way out the door. He ignored me. The office listed on the sign was located on the main street downtown. I drove there and found a parking space nearby. Inside, a harried-looking man of indeterminate middle age jumped to his feet at the sight of me, greedily rushing up to pump my hand. "My name is Pete Benchly," he gushed. "How may I help you today?"

"Matt Doyle, Pete; I'm here about that three bedroom rental house over on Lavender Lane."

The theatrical smile lost some of its luster. "Oh, interested in a rental?" Apparently renters didn't rate the same high-voltage smile as buyers.

"Not really, Pete; actually I'm a friend of the former tenants."

Even the second-rate smile disappeared. "If it's about that chair—okay, but if it's about the deposit—forget it! You should see the condition they left the place. Right now I've got an army of people over there trying to shape things up. They even spilled liquor on the mantel—took some of the varnish right up. My own fault I suppose for renting to single men."

"Keep the deposit, Pete; all I want to know is where they went."

Pete shrugged his narrow shoulders. "All I know, I got a call two days ago telling me they were leaving town right away. Didn't even have the courtesy to drop off the keys, so now, on top of everything else, I'll have to have the locks changed."

I asked him if they were current on the rent.

He couldn't entirely suppress his greedy little grin. "They'd paid through the end of the month, so that part of it's okay."

"How much was the rental deposit?"

"Same as the rent—seven hundred and fifty dollars."

"And no forwarding address? Which one called you?"

"I don't believe he said, and I certainly couldn't tell their voices apart. They barely opened their mouths, any of them."

"Yeah, that's what I liked about them." I returned to my car and headed for the on ramp to Highway 5. Poor soul; here it was the first week in April and he'd been paid through the end of the month. Plus another month's deposit, which was pure gravy. The talk about changing the lock was nothing but smoke. He'd use the office copy to stamp out a couple of new keys. Total expense under two dollars. The "army" he had over there was one lone kid who got minimum and who might draw as much as thirty-five bucks—tops. All the rest was cash in hand—windfall profit. It was the very best kind, because he'd probably have it rerented by the middle of the month. I wondered what the chances were the IRS would get their cut from the period of triple rent.

Win had once explained to me that in any of the desirable cities in Southern California, when you list a property for sale you're giving the broker first crack at it. If it's a bargain—and he'll do his best to make it one when he lists it—he buys it and to hell with his clients. You may not know he's buying it, but he is. He will often buy it through a designate—note the "or assigns" on the contract. He may flog it off to a pet investment group he owns points in. Ultimately, the house, apartment, or whatever, will be offered to the poor slob off the street, but only after all the "squeeze" is out of the price. A recent study done in Los Angeles estimates housing values there have been inflated at least 25 percent as a result of such tactics. What the world really needs, he told me, is a few more good books on how to get rich quickly through speculating in real estate. What those wonderful tomes all have in common is they never tell you where all that money comes from. Try and buy a home, sucker—you'll soon figure it out.

Some forty minutes later, I parked in front of the phony-looking Old Spanish motif of Harbor Island Marina. It was full tide, so the floating ramp leading to the docks was nearly level. Roscoe's Pacemaker was the aft cabin model with a flush deck, and looked to be in Bristol condition. Mounting the dockside steps, I boarded the pale teak decks, stepped over the coaming onto the cockpit deck, and spun the dial on the Zenith padlock. The port door opened, admitting me to the fully enclosed lower helm station. Starboard of the handsome ship's wheel was a tier of shallow drawers built into the mahogany console. As promised, the ship's log was in the top drawer.

Roscoe was a credit to his power squadron. Every trip going back two years was outlined in the prescribed manner: Names of everyone aboard, departure times, weather conditions, course, estimated and actual running time, it was textbook perfect. Scattered throughout were the little observations yachtsmen are given to: "13:31 hours, sighted school of dolphins; frolicked about the ship like playful schoolchildren." Guaranteed to make a skipper feel for all the world like Captain Cook. There probably wasn't a log in the marina that didn't include the same notation.

I relaxed in one of the sailcloth cockpit chairs and made a thorough job of the entire book. Nothing inspired me. Just another admiral of the fleet the moment his topsiders touched the deck. There wasn't a single line about drug smuggling or murder.

Before leaving, I got stubborn and spent three full hours

exploring every nook and cranny—with particular attention paid to the bilges. There are a surprising number of nooks on a forty-seven-foot yacht, and before I was through I discovered everything I'd expected—nothing! Unless you count a small area of dry rot on the port cockpit coaming.

I circled Harbor Drive around the perimeter of the bay toward Shelter Island where my own particular fantasy was moored. *Hobbit* is a thirty-seven-foot Crocker ketch. Over twelve foot in the beam, she's tubby, and the newer plastic toys leave her behind. But I love her. Built of cedar in 1940, she's my idea of a real ship. And fortunately they didn't cut her all up inside as is the custom so it could be claimed she slept eight. Headroom is a stately seven feet, and the below decks is mostly open.

My invariable custom the moment I step aboard is to shed my land clothes and don my boat clothes. These consist of rotting tennies, threadbare jeans—no label—and a misshapen T-shirt featuring samples of every can of paint and varnish I'd ever opened. I've never been able to verbalize it just right but aboard my boat—in these clothes—nothing can get to me. It's as if the bad vibrations are stymied by the border of water surrounding the boat. Even during my deepest funks the principle has held true. The awful-awfuls always end at the dock. Maybe I've rediscovered a very old natural law. Could be it's the real reason they went to all that trouble to build moats around castles.

For a refreshing hour I tinkered happily, running the diesel, checking the bilges, adding half a cup of water to the batteries—happy work! About four I wandered up the ramp—slanting at an ever-increasing angle as the tide dropped—and entered the brokerage office.

Dana glanced up, placed her hand over the mouthpiece of the phone, and said, "Hi, sailor—you got shore leave?" Then, holding up two fingers for time, she went back to describing the attributes of a Tollycraft.

Dana Marsh looked like a young Jackie Kennedy with either more flesh or less bone. Her white slacks were smudged at the knees from crawling around bilges and engine rooms, and her blue and white striped sweater even sported a mark or two.

She hung up after arranging to show the boat the following day. "Sounds like a hot prospect, Matt. There goes my Sunday again. Hope you weren't planning to shanghai me into helping you take out that old bucket of yours for a sail." She sat there smiling up at me—head tilted—thoughtfully tapping her teeth with the eraser end of a pencil. On a scale of ten she was only a nine point five; you had to deduct half a point for independence and sauciness.

"You never once referred to her as an old bucket when you were palming her off on me," I told her sternly. "As I recall, you used a lot of terms like 'classic beauty.'"

"Poetic license. *Caveat emptor*," she replied impishly. "Count your blessings; you were so green I could have sold you one of those junkers moored out at the free anchorage. Why do you look so pale?"

"Everybody looks pale compared to you. I'll get plenty of sun tomorrow. Can you reach Skip Fergesen on the phone? I need his Sea Ray tomorrow for a quick run out to San Clemente Island. Business. Tell him I'll top off the tanks when I get back."

She nodded, began fingering through a small file box of index cards on her desk. Extracting one, she frowned up at me. "So what's on San Clemente?"

"I have to talk to some navy types stationed there; it's not the sort of thing that can be done over the phone."

"Just wanted to check and make sure you knew there aren't any girls out there. You know, you could take two weeks off and go in your own boat." Chuckling nastily at her neat jab, she dialed a number, chatted away gaily for a couple of minutes, then hung up. "You're in luck—he had no plans to use it. Of course, he wasn't crazy about the idea; says not to run the mills at anything over thirty-eight hundred or your life is forfeit. And the port engine reads low, so you should trust the synchronizer."

"Thanks! I promise to be gentle with his baby. And about girls—you know damn well you've spoiled me for life. Not only did you palm off an old turkey boat on me that's visibly rotting right before my very eyes, you did also vamp me cruelly."

She slinked over and locked her arms around my waist.

"Vamped, did you say? Good lord, Matt; not even my old maiden aunt Tillie says vamped." Suddenly she noticed my pasty grimace. "Matt, what the hell's wrong with you?" she demanded anxiously.

"I don't know how to break this to you, but if you don't stop hugging me there's an excellent chance I'll faint."

She released her hold immediately and stood regarding me with a grave look on her face. "Seriously? Tell me what happened this time. I assume it's something to do with what I've been reading in the papers. Stand still, let me have a look."

"Never mind—it's just a scratch. You just happened to grope the wrong spot. Any place else is fine—take your pick."

Folding her arms primly, she leaned forward, stood on her toes, and kissed me chastely. It was a thoroughly pleasant sensation. No greasy feel of lipstick, no sticky residue or aftertaste, just the wonderful tactile delight of real, unadulterated girl.

"I'm staying over," I said. "Care to share a steak with me? You pick and I'll pay."

She eyed me suspiciously. "As if you don't know perfectly well how I feel about going out to eat around here. What they do to a piece of meat is almost as much of a crime as the prices they charge. And I can tell a hint when I hear one. That was my cue to invite you over to my boat for dinner, which, as you are well aware, would be delectable. All right, wipe that wounded doe look off your face; be there before six so we can toast the sunset."

I grinned at her and shook my head. "Dana, we always end up eating on your boat. And it's always delectable, but just to be fair, why not my boat tonight? I'll play galley slave and all you have to do is lounge around looking decorative."

"Swell," she made a grim face and gave me a mock shudder. "You want to cook me a steak over that rusty butane dinosaur you laughingly call a stove? Not to mention your whole boat smells like the inside of a tennis shoe. Thanks for the offer but no thanks."

"Okay, your boat then. But I want you to know I can spot a hint myself. That crack was nothing but a sly attempt to shame me into trading up into a bigger boat. You probably have some huge, ugly monster like yours in mind."

"I can't help it," she laughed. "I'm a born salesperson. It's instinctive. Besides—the way I figure it—even with the commission I collected for selling you that wreck, I'm running in the red on the deal. You come down here all the time, drink my wine, eat my steaks, make me all starry-eyed and girlish until I start letting suckers—I mean buyers—get away. The fact is, you're ruining me."

I kissed her this time, then headed for the door. "Who's ruining who? If you bump the slip rent on me one more time, I'll be eating all my meals at your place."

She chased me out of her office waving an arm and yelling. "If you don't do something about cleaning up that tub you call a boat, I'm going to have the harbor police haul it out of here as a derelict. Then you won't have to worry about slip rent. Get down there and work up an appetite, you big lazy bum, you."

"Okay, Boss, I'm going." We exchanged foolish grins, and I strutted off whistling happily, the pain in my side temporarily forgotten. Win often encouraged me to come down here and work on my boat whenever we began getting on each others' nerves. Claimed it did wonders for my disposition. And he was partly right—I enjoyed working on my boat, too.

The morning cloud cover was like a dirty woolen blanket overhead as I made my way along the dew-wet dock to Skip's boat. I stripped away the cockpit canvas, folded it, and placed it in the dock box. Retrieving the ignition keys from their secret hook under the gunnel, I switched both battery banks to "on" and turned on the blower.

It was a strain, but I made myself give it the full five minutes by remembering what was left of a boat at the next marina when the owner hadn't bothered. I tried to remember the ratio: one leaked cup of gasoline in the bilge equaled how many sticks of dynamite? Three? Six? Too damn many.

Both engines—350 Mercs—thundered to life at the first

touch of the button. Checking for good water flow from the exhausts, I cast off the mooring lines and backed her out into the fairway.

The name on the transom was *Scat Cat*. I gurgled my way past the harbor police dock at the required five knots, then drew a bead on the harbor entrance. I nursed the throttles forward in small increments until the tachs showed 3,000 RPMs. The speedometer read twenty-nine knots. The pulsating light of the synchronizer was diffused and fuzzy, so I nudged the port handle forward by fractions until it settled down into the small, sharply defined dot that proclaimed the engines to be perfectly matched.

I held her on a line well beyond the pair of lighthouses on Point Loma, then out beyond the kelp beds, then finally swung her nose a few degrees north of west and switched on the "iron mike." I watched for awhile, found the auto pilot was hunting too far south, disengaged, brought her a couple more points northerly, then kicked the pilot back in gear. Perfect! I briefly considered nursing her up to 3,500, but decided to leave well enough alone. At my current speed I'd arrive in just over two hours, and it was only 8:45. And the motion was tolerable. Each extra knot would exact a high price in both fuel consumption and physical abuse.

Occasionally the engines gave an animal scream of protest when the trough of a wave momentarily left the props high and dry, but otherwise their throaty roar was a happy duet. Spray off the starboard bow drove me to take refuge behind the forward port corner of the bridge.

I turned and looked back at the city. The outlines of the downtown buildings were fuzzy, muted by a dirty brown layer of smog. You didn't notice it much when you were a part of it; the sky would appear blue and the horizon would seem clear. It wasn't until you flew over the city or viewed it from offshore that you realized just how bad the pollution had really become.

The sea was calm except for the endless rollers marching from the far-off eastern Pacific to assault the California coast. There would be a chop built up by the time I returned but I'd have it on my port quarter. Running before it would be fine on the way home. Except for scanning the horizon up ahead once every couple of minutes, I was able to settle in and give some serious consideration to Dirk's predicament. Confinement was unthinkable for him—a hundred times worse than for most. It wouldn't likely cheer him much to know the sum total of our progress to date. Win had promised we'd get him out soon. What would be the effect on Win if we were unable to keep that promise? I damn well knew what the effect on Dirk would be. Not a very happy prospect, any of it.

The Sea Ray thrummed as a thing alive, slashing her way across the gentle gray face of the morning sea. Astern, I watched the widening scar she was leaving behind. It healed quickly. Fifty yards behind, there was no sign I'd ever been there.

CHAPTER 9

*M*onday morning arrived ahead of schedule, or so it seemed. I discovered an amazing variety of sore, stiff muscles competing for attention as I went through my morning drill. Five hours aboard a hard-charging small boat exacts quite a toll. Dozens of little-used muscles flex and work in response to the constant movement, attempting to adjust, even when you think you're just sitting and relaxing.

Randy waved a honey-soaked slice of toast in greeting as I entered the dining room. Win scowled darkly. "I had anticipated your return and your report sometime last evening," he complained.

"Fine, thank you; and good morning to you, too. I didn't get away from the marina until late. Sunday—in case you've forgotten—is supposed to be my day off. I settled for an evening, which is all too common as you well know." It was obvious he was feeling the pressure. When he got into a real funk, Randy and I referred to it as: "Win's got the black ass." It didn't figure to be a very pleasant day.

"An evening in the pleasant company of Miss Dana Marsh, no doubt. Apparently you feel such affairs are more important than reporting to me. Dirk's predicament shouldn't take precedence over your social life, of course."

I've never had much tolerance for sarcasm and he knew it. It has the same effect on me as fingernails on a blackboard. But his reference to Dana threw me. The subject had never been discussed. "What's this? Having me tailed so you're sure you're getting your money's worth? And if this is a monastery, I don't remember taking the vows. Must have been a slipup. And as for my report, you're welcome to it, but if I charged you a bent dime it'd be robbery." My own defiant glare was more than a match for his.

"It's good of you to find the time to mention it," he told me facetiously. "I'll be in the office, should it occur to you to stop in at your convenience." He arose grandly and made a great show of hobbling away from the table.

I glared at his rigid back, resisting the powerful urge to bounce my coffee cup off the back of his head. Eating my breakfast as slowly as possible, I chatted amiably with Randy, just to prove there was nothing wrong with my ability to relate to my fellow man. Then I hung around another five minutes, after Randy retreated to his basement laboratory, to chin with Louis about how things were going in the galley.

By the time I took my seat in the office I was cooled off and determined to stay that way, at least until Dirk was sprung. "Want to swap some more insults, or should I make my report?"

"I, too, have managed to bridle my vexation," he replied tolerantly. "Please report."

"Okay, but first about Dana. I don't recall ever mentioning her to you."

"Fortunately you don't constitute my sole contact with the world beyond these walls, though you may think so." His eyes twinkled. If there was anything in the world he loved more than being mysterious, it could only be attempting to appear omniscient. "It is quite true; you never have mentioned her. It gives one pause to wonder why not. Has it never occurred to you that I might possibly appreciate meeting the lady?"

"We're not to the stage yet where I bring her home to meet the family. Besides, I'm afraid to. There's always the chance you'd steal her away from me. I've seen the way you drive women nuts."

I spent the next hour recapping my trip to Carlsbad, my search of Roscoe's boat, and my interviews on San Clemente Island. When I was finished he just sat there with a vacant look in his eyes for a full minute before commenting. "Your account appears to be suggestive but far from conclusive," he finally told me distractedly. "Witnesses definitely place Mr. Blaise and his associates on the island at the time of the murder, but with the rather glaring exemption of one of the three."

"Right! That much is tight. I saw four of the six guys who'd signed Roscoe's log. No one was nervous and each one verified there were four men on the boat. Except nobody actually saw the fourth man. But they all bought the story that he was sacked out down below, suffering from sea sickness. Apparently it was mentioned often and the cause of a lot of chuckles. Roscoe was easy, of course, but even though I got pretty fair descriptions of the other two, I still can't say who the missing hood was. If he was missing. As I told you, the boat is a coho model with two cabins aft; it's perfectly possible that a fourth man was bedded down in one of those cabins. I made a point of talking to these guys separately—everything fits. Roscoe and at least two of his cohorts were definitely there the night Marlee died."

"When cursed with *mal de mer,* one usually opts to remain on deck in the fresh air," Win noted.

"That's true when the boat is underway, but once you're at anchor it would be normal to hunt up the softest bunk in the darkest cabin and crash," I told him.

Win beat out a vicious drumming with his fingers on the desk—for him it was a rare tantrum. "Doesn't it bother you at all that Mr. Blaise just happened to invite several strangers aboard, who in turn just happened to sign his ship's log?" he mumbled. He always mumbled when he was mad.

"Not a bit, unfortunately. I guess I skipped something pertinent—the book is full of similar entries. Roscoe does it all the time. Lots of yachtsmen do."

"Very well!" he conceded reluctantly, obviously resenting having to relinquish a perfectly good clue. "You were there; I wasn't. You saw the layout of the boat. Your conclusions?"

"It could easily be true. The layout of the boat makes it easy for someone to disappear below. And that model boat is noted for being top-heavy. The course from San Diego Harbor to San Clemente Island puts you broadside to the seas, so anyone prone to motion sickness would be a basket case by the time they hit the island.

"On the other hand, it's too damn pat. Somebody killed Marlee, and we know those three are killers. The only motive that makes any sense, at least so far, is that she found out about their sideline just like I did. It's a tough call, but make it sixty-forty in favor of one of the boys staying behind and doing her in."

"There's a problem with your computations," he growled.

"Yeah, the problem is we can't prove it either way."

"Wrong on both counts, I believe. The problem is, Dirk was set up to appear guilty, and none of these potential malfeasants would have any motive for doing that, since all possessed alibis. And wrong again in that we can't prove it. Even given the late hour of the *Wahoo*'s return, I hope and expect you'll be able to find someone who witnessed her docking. A boat entering a marina at such a late hour is something of a novelty—people check for security reasons—anyone who's up and about would normally make himself available to receive a mooring line and aid in docking the ship. Find that person and ascertain the number of men aboard."

Of course he was right; a noisy forty-seven-foot power boat entering a marina in the middle of the night would attract plenty of attention. Naturally it galled me that he thought of it first. "It's not something I can do by phone. I'll get down there right away.

Be back as soon as I can." I beat it for my car, telling myself there was no reason for embarrassment. After all, I was supposed to be the legman and he was supposed to be the brains of the outfit. So why did it bug me so when it worked out that way?

I was back in time for lunch. I dallied over coffee until even Randy had left the table. The tidings I bore were such that there was no hurry.

Win gave me a discerning look as I walked in the door of the office. As usual he was able to read me like a book and he frowned. "Your demeanor is quite eloquent," he sighed. "I assume you were able to verify that four men—Roscoe and his three look-alike henchmen—disembarked together."

"Yeah, it was easy and it was stupid of me not to think of it when I was down there checking over the *Wahoo* before. Old Harry Langstrom, the night guard, helped them moor the boat; they were all four aboard and they were the right four, too, since he's seen them coming and going quite a few times. But you know this doesn't close the book on it. Who's to say they didn't pick up one of the trio somewhere in the harbor before docking? There are dozens of places—bars, restaurants, fuel docks—where it could be done easily. In fact, if they went to all the trouble of setting up an alibi for the fourth man in the first place, they'd have been nuts not to do it."

"You're absolutely right, Matt. But I fail to see what we can do about it. If indeed that's what was done, presumably they selected someplace sufficiently suitable so that that fact is not available to us. Unless you have a suggestion?"

I think he loved to ask me that whenever he knew there wasn't a chance in hell I'd have one. "Short of hitting every conceivable place where a boat that size could tie up and asking everybody in sight, no."

"Hardly! It would take weeks, and in the end would prove nothing. What if he used a dingy? Or merely swam, or even waded out to the ship? Admit it—we've taken this line of investigation as far as possible." He leaned back in his chair, made a tent with his fingers, and gazed fixedly at them. It meant he was concentrating hard, or getting ready to. "Let us go back to your interview with the rental agent in Carlsbad. Please repeat the conversation *in toto*—verbatim, if possible."

I did—not knowing why—listening intently myself this time to find out what it was he'd picked up on. If it was there, I missed it—again. After finishing, I found Win sitting there with an oddly pleased look. It irritated me, so I decided it was time for me to take a trick. "So when do I take off for Baton Rouge?" I asked him.

His striking eyes switched their focus over to me. "You don't."

I admit it amazed me. "But that's our only chance now; what do you mean, I don't?"

"Simply that—you don't. A Mr. Stanley Morgan has that phase of the investigation well in hand. Mr. Morgan is a private operative native to that city, reputed to be an able man. I fully expect him to accomplish in three days what might take you weeks of floundering about. Forgive me for ruining any travel plans you may have had, but his efforts began last Saturday; I have every expectation of hearing from him by tomorrow the latest."

"Swell, now I'm a flounderer. Fine with me; I'm not all that fond of mosquitos anyway." Damned if I'd give him the satisfaction of letting him know I'd packed before coming down to lunch. He'd done it on purpose of course—to get even for the crack I'd made Saturday about knowing I'd be going to Louisiana.

"I intended no denigration. Mr. Morgan knows the city and its denizens. That's of enormous importance in such an insular section of the country. He will know where to look and whom to ask his decidedly delicate questions. More to the point, I expect nothing from that phase of the investigation, and you are sorely needed here."

"To do what?"

"Dirk's preliminary hearing is being held tomorrow. It's unconscionable to schedule it so soon—and I'm afraid but a mere formality—yet I'd like very much for you to be there. It may prove possible to offer him a word of succor, your hand perhaps. At the very least, make certain he sees you there. I know it will comfort him. I won't be there so you must go in my stead."

"What's on the schedule for this afternoon?" I asked, secretly pleased at being able to sneak upstairs and unpack. I'd never been to Louisiana, but from what I'd heard it sounded like a pretty good spot not to be going.

Win appeared ill at ease, which was decidedly a first. Without quite looking me in the eye, he asked hesitantly, "Would you mind terribly mowing the lawn, Matt? We all have to pitch in and cover for Dirk until he's released. If your recent wound permits, of course," he quickly added, in response to the dark look on my face.

I clamped my jaw and got up to leave. "Mow the lawn, huh? Now there's a great idea. Very productive, that is. I can't wait to tell Dirk tomorrow when he asks me what we've been doing to spring him. 'I mowed the lawn for you, pal,' I'll tell him. Don't think that won't make his spirits soar."

I stomped out the door. Even as I slammed it behind me I caught sight of Win grabbing for the phone book with an eager look in his eyes. He was certainly on to something, or at least he thought he was. But share it with me—forget it! If he had his way I'd read about it in the papers like everybody else.

The farcical excuse for a preliminary hearing was held in room 302 of the federal courthouse at 10 A.M. Tuesday. To schedule it only a few days after Dirk's arraignment was frightening evidence of just how far the authorities were willing to go to close the books. I'd arrived early enough to snag a seat down front. Between classes of school kids with their teachers, wistful out-of-work attorneys, and bored-looking old folks, it was pretty much a full house.

Dirk wasn't about to spot me when he made his entrance, closely flanked by a deputy. His head was lowered, as if he really didn't give a damn and wasn't about to contribute anything to the show. But as he was seated beside Hoffman, the lawyer touched

him and pointed over his shoulder toward me. Dirk glanced back
reluctantly, then favored me with a kind of shy, pitiful grin.
They'd allowed him to wear his favorite sport coat, and a tie I
recognized as one of mine. The sight of Dirk in a tie was somehow
oddly distressing. He considered them ludicrous looking—and
worse—potentially lethal.

"Hi, Tiger," I whispered. "Hope you're getting plenty of
sack time in. I'm going to run your tail off when you get back
home."

He nodded once, gravely, then turned and stood stiffly as the
judge strode in. Dirk looked as if he'd aged a year for every one
of the eight days they'd been holding him.

The hearing didn't last much more than half an hour. An
assistant D.A. called on one of Dixon's lieutenants to establish
motive, means, and opportunity. Next, a lab man backed it up
with a litany of physical evidence. Then they went back to the
time when, as a boy, Dirk had been forced to square off against
his own father, managing to make it sound as if the only reason
he'd failed to kill his stepmother too at the time was that she
escaped. Of course, it wasn't true! She'd run away to get help to
keep her drunken murderer of a husband from accomplishing his
goal of beating his thirteen-year-old son to death, just as he had
the boy's mother. Unfortunately, she wasn't present to straighten
them out on that point. The only other witness to the events of
that long-ago night was Dirk. They hadn't bought his story when
he'd been convicted of manslaughter for the death of his father,
and naturally subsequent events hadn't inclined them to begin
buying it now.

The lab guy testified the blood on the rug and knife was
Marlee's. And the prints on the handle of the knife were Dirk's.
Madge Burman showed up to tell them everything she'd thought,
heard, or dreamed. Hoffman jumped up and down a lot, but telling someone to disregard something they've already heard is like
telling a kid not to think about elephants. When Madge finally
described Dirk's departure that night—his pausing at the door to
say good night and not getting a response—she managed to create

a vivid image of a ruthless killer bidding so long to a corpse. The icing on the cake was when she told the judge how frightened Marlee'd told her she was of her stepson—the murderer. Hoffman inquired sarcastically, if that were so why would Marlee invite him to dinner and an evening alone with her? Madge made him sorry he asked by responding that no doubt her heart had been far greater than her judgment.

There were several times I felt like kicking the back of Hoffman's chair to see whether I couldn't get him going, but he wasn't really asleep. He raised a fuss every time someone referred to Dirk as a convicted killer, but you could see he was shoveling sand against the tide. He got his chance at last and I guess he made the most of it. He pointed out that not only wasn't there a scrap of conclusive evidence pointing to his client's guilt, the authorities were unable to prove the crime of murder had even been committed.

He closed with a strong pitch for establishing reasonable bail—at the very least—based on lack of evidence and the established fact that Dirk's continued availability would be guaranteed by no less a personage than retired Secretary of State Carter Winfield.

If the bored-looking guy in the black dress looking down on everyone from his raised place of eminence needed any time to arrive at a decision he must have taken it before he heard the case. Without an interruption he ordered Dirk bound over for trial on a charge of capital murder and held without bail. No court date was set, at the request of the district attorney. And apparently no one was much impressed with Hoffman's pledges. I guess they figured Dirk had already run from the scene of one homicide and no one—not even Win—could stop him from doing it again. Of course, because he'd already been convicted of killing his own biological father, the book closed on any chance he might have ever had.

Dirk sat throughout the proceedings, staring at a spot on the marble floor halfway between the judge and himself. He even looked guilty to me. Anyone who didn't know him—and that en-

compassed everyone on earth with the exception of four people—
would have gotten the distinct impression he was ashamed to look
them in the eye. And his shy air of solemnity could easily be
mistaken for a look of cruelty.

As Hoffman and he stood to go, I leaned forward over the
railing and patted Dirk on the back, for lack of a better idea. He
managed a fleeting look of gratitude as deputies led him away
through a side door.

Win was waiting expectantly when I returned to the office.

"Judging by the stricken look on your face," he observed
bitterly, "no miracles took place in court today."

"Nope! We'd better manage one ourselves quick, or Dirk's
going to turn into a vegetable—a very old vegetable. He looks
rough; we really have to get him the hell out of there, Win."

"Too well do I know. Credit it or not, progress is being
made."

Still standing beside my chair, I froze. "You've heard from
Baton Rouge? From what's-his-name? Stanley?" We were long
overdue for some good news; my heart rate was kicking into overdrive.

"Indeed, some half an hour ago. Mr. Morgan proved as thorough and efficient as I'd hoped—a refreshing rarity these days.
Take your seat and listen to a report from me for a change."

I dropped into my chair. "I'd listen standing on my head if it
would help. Come on—give!" I urged him.

"The trail begins in 1972 with twenty-nine-year-old Marlee
Bode—she'd resumed her maiden name after the death of her
first husband—enrolling in business college in Baton Rouge. She
was an above average student, securing a position with a construction company even before graduation. Four years later she
married a steelworker employed by the same company, one Marcel Reynaud. She immediately resigned her position in order to
undertake the duties of full-time wife. Five years later her idyll
ended when her husband suffered a fatal accident on the job. The
widow is subsequently forced to return to work in her former position.

"Six more years pass. She enjoys several promotions and is apparently held in high regard by her peers. But suddenly last year she seemed to become restless, constantly complaining to co-workers of her rising dissatisfaction. She soon announced her intention to move to one of the smaller beach communities of Southern California. Since she was known as a determined woman who never failed to follow the thought with the deed, no one was surprised when she did precisely that last fall. She left behind her only the regret of her employers—no debts, either financial or emotional." Win sat there looking fatuously pleased, as if he'd pulled something off.

"Terrific! So now tell me the significant part. You know— the part you're holding back."

He gave me an injured look. "I have omitted absolutely nothing of substance. Apparently you fail to understand. Negative evidence was exactly what I was hoping for. The very last thing I fancied was the necessity of combing the swamps back there for months in search of a phantom killer from her past. Don't you see what a blessing this is, Matt?"

"Yeah, we're twice blessed, we are," I snorted. "First we had to accept the fact that our most likely suspects were off the hook, and now nobody back there is worth a glance. I guess that settles it—nobody did it. Why don't we call Dixon and give him the good news?"

"I fear the call would be both premature and inaccurate, but surely we're light years ahead for the knowledge our investigation needn't span the country."

"Maybe, but I don't trust a guy that paints somebody all white. We're supposed to believe she was universally loved by all? I don't buy it. What about her in-laws? Did this Stanley think to check them out? Maybe they're looney tunes and hated her for moving; or maybe they even blamed her for their son's death somehow. After living there all that time, it looks to me as if her leaving was some sort of flight. Maybe she enjoyed some kind of protection back there that didn't hold up out here. Look, I admit it's thin as hell, but it's possible. Who knows what this Stanley guy missed?"

"I believe I mentioned he was thorough," Win reminded me testily. "Marcel Reynaud was the product of an orphanage. Mrs. Reynaud's associates did not revere her by any means. I said she was held in high regard; she was also considered intolerant of errors and omissions as well as something of an introvert. Mr. Morgan's written report will feature a number of interviews containing such derogatory remarks, but it's patently obvious she did not bring her killer with her when she moved west. She emerges as a quietly determined woman; not the sort who inspires the range of deep emotion necessary to generate murder. She would merely seem to be one of the vast majority who become victims only through inadvertence, by finding themselves in the wrong place at the wrong time."

I was on my feet, striding up and down the roomy office, threading my way through the bottleneck formed by the juncture of the two opposing desks. "I swear to God I don't see a glimmer. What are you suggesting? Do we just throw in the towel and trust the system? We know Dirk is innocent, so why worry? Is that what all this is leading up to? Jesus, Win—if you could have seen the poor guy today."

Win sighed heavily. "I only wish we had that option to fall back on. Don't misunderstand me—the system works well enough up to a point. I'll allow an innocent person is likely to be found so under ordinary circumstances. But other factors can assume control at certain levels in our system of jurisprudence, especially in certain types of crime. Crimes which shock or offend the public conscience—which is more difficult than you may imagine—for instance. That is one time our advocacy system tends to break down. In such cases outside considerations often take control. The press make it a *cause célèbre* because it involves famous personages. Because reading about it titillates people, too much is written about it. This turns it into more of a political contest than a legal one. In an extraordinary effort to appear as Caesar's wife, the authorities often base their judgments on appeasement rather than blind justice. The entire case may become more like the Super Bowl than an exercise in judicature. Opposing factions square off amid the fanfare of publicity, political pressures, and the natural human desire to look good in the big one.

"Our advocacy system, Matt, is soundly based on noble principles, but in actuality it takes all onus for justice from the shoulders of the courts—where it rightfully belongs—and places it squarely upon the defense attorney. If he should be incompetent—and the majority are, as are their peers in all other professions—tough! Far too much injustice is rationalized away because of our unbounded and unreasonable faith in this system.

"The truth is, I'm undoubtedly Dirk's major liability now because, as my agent, he's the baseball in what is tantamount to a World Series court case. Instead of investigating this crime intelligently, the police are under constraint to consider everything from the narrowest possible view. 'Can you ram this through the grand jury?' The district attorney replies, 'Yes,' and so it's bulldozed through. Never mind the facts—appearance is everything. This allays the stinging headlines which would have prevailed if there were no one in custody. Charges of undue influence emanating from this house would be used as brickbats to beat the police, district attorney, and mayor. And add to this already supercharged atmosphere Inspector Dixon's antipathy toward this household and everyone in it, and you have the existing equation for injustice. No evidence is being sought or considered, except as it serves to further indict Dirk."

I'd long since stopped pacing, stung by his dissertation. "Christ! You make it sound as if we ought to be tunneling under the jail."

"Keep your shovel at the ready, Matt. But I still have reason to believe it won't come to that. If I am Dirk's gravest liability because of the focus of media attention upon me and thus my staff, I'm also his best hope of deliverance. Strike that—*we* are his best hope of deliverance."

"You have any specific ideas about how *we're* going to accomplish this deliverance?" I inquired hopefully.

"As I told you, progress is being made. Haven't I just elimi-
nated the awesome prospect of searching the uliginous bayous of
Louisiana for our killer?"

I hated hearing him get that verbose; it usually meant he was
fresh out of ideas. "Hey, that's right! You've narrowed it down to
a mere three million or so in San Diego County. That's if we can
rule out Orange, Los Angeles, and Riverside counties. If not,
what the hell—it still only makes it a mere eleven or twelve million."

Win rose quickly to his feet, snagged his cane from the arm of
his chair, and thundered, "You will desist baiting me. Curb your
churlish tongue and try expending your energy along more useful
lines. Begin by visiting the deceased's apartment immediately following lunch. After that I want you to interview anyone, and I mean
everyone, who had so much as seen Marlee Reynaud in passing—
Again!" he added, noting my dismay. "Those who seem to have
something to contribute—no matter how trivial—are to be brought
here to me." Giving me a long-suffering grimace, he breezed out
the door. The prospect of him questioning a witness personally was
eloquent testimony to just how bad things were.

Later when I joined him at the table, he was deep in discussion
with Randy concerning the likelihood of a wider-scale Mideastern
war. I got my jaw unclamped enough to admit some lunch, and
listened mutely to the chatter. I had the class not to mention that the
assignment I'd just been given was the exact same one he'd said was
a waste of time when I'd suggested it a week earlier.

The burly little reader of crime magazines was on duty in
another aloha shirt when I arrived at the ugly monolith Marlee
had called home for a few brief months. "How you doing?" I
greeted him warmly through the slot in the door. "You remember
me don't you?"

"Sure, I never forget a face." He swung the door wide.
"You're the cop with the job I'd want; you hang around waiting to
plug the guilty ones."

"You'd make a hell of a good cop. I'm headed up to number 28.
You got a passkey, or do I have to check in with the manager?"

He gave me a funny look. "Don't need no key—it's wide open. But it ain't much use going up there unless you're looking to rent an apartment."

Without waiting for further explanations, I hurried up the stairs one flight, and turned left to the end of the hall. He'd been absolutely correct; the door was indeed wide open. The reason it was open was because two guys wearing knee pads were installing new wall-to-wall carpeting. The entire apartment had been redecorated. I rushed from room to room, ignoring the protests of the rug men. Every inch of floor, ceiling, and wall had been redone. Nothing remained to show that it had ever been inhabited.

Disgusted, I left and began the tedious task of knocking on doors and asking the same questions over and over again *ad nauseum*. It was one of the jobs I hated most. The initial hostility— even anger—you run into much of the time is depressing. It made me wonder how door-to-door salesmen could bear getting out of bed in the morning. But then I doubt there are many of those intrepid souls left in this age of suspicion and fear.

There were six floors in the building, eight units to a floor except for the top which had only six. I concentrated on the first and second floors at first, figuring the tenants there would have had the greatest chance of seeing or hearing something. After that I began working my way up. By six o'clock I was on the fifth, had found only two dozen apartments occupied, and of those only seven people admitted to ever having so much as nodded at the murdered woman.

On my way out, I grilled the night man who'd come on duty in the lobby. He was older, almost emaciated, and decidedly unfriendly. He had nothing to add to the fact that Dirk had departed about ten-thirty on the night of the murder.

As he shoved the door open, it occurred to me to ask him, "When was the last time this lock was changed?" I pointed at the heavy glass door. "What happens lots of times, people make up duplicates for all their friends, so there ends up being a ton of keys floating around loose."

He gave me a smug look. "Not around here there isn't. Couple of months back we went to this whole new system. We don't use keys, we use these." He pulled a plastic credit card from a pocket. "Can't be duplicated by anybody except the manufacturer. We demand a fifty-dollar security deposit on every one so the tenants are damn careful not to lose them and they are only allotted one for each adult member of the family."

He was quite mistaken about not being able to duplicate them, but it did require an expert, and a fair amount of experimentation. Card keys incorporate several factors including size, thickness, and raised or recessed figures. But the big trick is the magnetic code unique to each system. Suddenly it became a whole lot tougher picturing someone unknown just waltzing in sometime after 11 P.M. and killing Marlee.

"How about this?" I challenged him. "One way people get around these is to wait until somebody comes along—going either in or out—and they just pop right through with them. If challenged, they could claim they forgot their own card; this place is big enough and with enough turnover so everybody must not know everybody else."

"Happened just like you said a few weeks ago. Some guy tried it anyway. The couple he followed in asked to see some ID and he told them to shove it. Well, he went on up to number 42—turned out he was a boyfriend of the girl lives there. The couple called the cops and the next thing you know they're here and leading him off with the cuffs on. See, the pair he snuck in with kept an eye on where he headed. We got a firm rule here: Everybody looks out for the other guy. Anyone lets somebody else in—they're responsible. The owners sent around a flyer telling all the tenants it would get them booted out in a minute if they were seen letting anyone in they didn't know. Anyway, what's with all the questions? Everybody knows how this stepson of hers got back in. He just helped himself to her card before he left the first time. I spotted him for a mean customer when I let him out. And she was already dead by then—right?"

I admitted it surely looked that way and glumly went back to knocking on more doors—the ones that hadn't responded earlier. The flow of returning inhabitants to the oversized rabbit warren encouraged me to forego supper and keep pitching. I was also getting damn tired of hearing how obvious it was Dirk was guilty. And so far all I'd done was turn up evidence to further indict him. I made a note to find out whether Marlee's key card had been found in her apartment.

I hung tough until nine. Marlee certainly hadn't made any bosom buddies I could find. I did come across several who'd been in her apartment, or at least as far as the doorway. They tended to verify Madge Burman's account about how Marlee would hang onto them in the hall chatting nonstop—seemingly reluctant to let them go. It struck them as decidedly odd, because the next time they'd see her in the building she'd barely give them a nod.

God help me, it was time to tackle Madge. She remained the only one in the building who'd seen or heard anything remotely pertinent, and I was determined not to go home empty-handed. Win's offer to interview witnesses was so unique I wasn't about to let it pass.

She responded to my knock with a look of annoyance etched in her dumpling face. "Oh, it's you! Officer Doyle, isn't it?"

"Not exactly, Madge. I'm a detective, but not associated with the police department."

She eyed me suspiciously through a two-inch crack in the doorway. "But you told me—"

"I can certainly see how you might have gotten that impression," I interrupted before she could get too wound up. "With all the officers you must have talked to last week, and then me coming along and probably asking all the same questions. Right now it's vital you come along with me and talk to my boss."

"It may be vital to you, but I'm right in the middle of a good movie on television."

At least she was honest, bless her chubby heart. Most people would have lied and said they were right in the middle of a good book, or busy trying to achieve world peace. Funny thing: Nobody likes to admit they watch a lot of television. Except Madge—I liked her better for it. "Wouldn't you rather meet Secretary of State Carter Winfield than sit through all those awful commercials? He turns down kings and presidents like they were bums, but he wants to meet you. It's only a few minutes away—in La Jolla."

"Carter Winfield?" Her little reddened eyes gleamed. "That fellow—her stepson who killed her—he worked for him, didn't he?"

"That's right! So you can imagine how distressed he is about all of this. It would be such a help if you would just see him for a few minutes. He seldom ever sees anyone—as I'm sure you know—so it would be quite a thing to tell your friends. But I must be honest with you, Madge; the reporters will be quite a nuisance, but there isn't a thing we can do about them."

"Reporters? What about reporters?"

"You know how it is. A couple of weeks ago he refused to see the French premier. The news hawks love to hang around just to see who we boot off the stoop. The last person he did see ended up on the Carson show." Her churlish attitude was now gone, displaced by a dreamy look. I'd selected the right approach; she'd have walked there.

"I guess it's my duty," she said, releasing the chain and admitting me into the hothouse apartment. "Just give me a minute to change."

"What you're wearing is fine, Madge."

"You men are so silly, Mr. Doyle. I'm afraid you don't know much about women's fashions. I'm wearing a housecoat. I'm most certainly not going to meet the press—I mean Mr. Secretary Winfield—in my housecoat." She scurried off, patting her hair frantically with both hands.

I grabbed the phone off the wall in the kitchen and dialed the private number of the office. The listed number would have been answered by Louis with me not there, but on the rare occasions when this phone rang, Win would answer himself. He'd know it was me now. On other nights, when I was there, he'd still answer, but he'd pretty well know it was the sitting president on the line, wanting to present him with some sticky wicket. How's that for an unlisted number?

"Yes, Matt?" He always sounded brusque. It was nothing personal—he simply hates phones.

"I'll be home shortly. With Madge Burman in tow. It's not much, but it's all there is. You remember who she is?"

"My memory is as good as yours," he snapped. "Have you any suggestions to offer concerning approach, or specific areas of cross-examination, which may prove fruitful?"

"Nope. Just pick her up and shake her and let's see what falls out. One thing which would help: Send Randy up to my room for the Nikon. Tell him never mind the film, just station him out front, and have him waste a couple of flash bulbs on her when we arrive."

There was a brief silence on the other end of the wire. "I see. And you've come up with nothing else of merit?"

"Nothing you're going to like." I hung up. Knowing it would take her a while to primp for her debut, I settled down in front of the TV and tried to make sense out of what was happening on the screen.

Madge emerged twenty minutes later, stuffed into a beige suit, wearing precarious-looking four-inch heels, and breathing as if she'd just run the forty in 4.5. I told her she looked great, turned off the set, and off we went.

Sure enough, Randy was on duty when we pulled up in front of the house. He fired more or less in her general direction half a dozen times between the car and the door, meanwhile asking questions like: "What government do you represent?" and "What do you think of the country's current trade deficit?"

He was having a great time. The only thing was, he neglected to ask her name. She corrected that little oversight quickly enough.

As I hustled her inside she complained, "Shouldn't there be more of them? At least a reporter? That man didn't write down one single thing I said."

"Don't worry; they don't write anymore. I think he had one of those combination cameras and tape recorders. You did just fine, Madge. He didn't get a single word out of you that will come back to haunt you after it hits the headlines. I only hope the boys at State pick up on that statement you made on foreign policy—it was beautiful."

I opened the massive carved door to the office and waved her in. She stopped just inside, obviously awed at the sight of Win, standing waiting for her behind his big desk. Leaning heavily on his cane—which made me suppress a grin—he inclined his still-handsome head graciously. "Welcome, dear lady. You cannot know what a rare delight it is to find myself in the company of such a lovely young woman in this, the December of my life."

I maintained a bland look—not without effort—hoping he wasn't about to break into a chorus of "September Song." Anyone who thinks chivalry is dead hasn't seen my boss when he's around a woman.

Flustered, Madge attempted the unfamiliar mechanics of a curtsy. She looked about as graceful as a camel starting to bed down for the night.

When I walked around to the front of his desk and held out a chair for her, Win corrected me. "No, no, Mr. Doyle; not that one. Bring forward the chair the Queen sat in." He indicated an identical chair over near the window. I lugged it over, still struggling to keep a straight face. I was having a tough time of it because it was true—a queen had once sat in it. Except that "queen" had been a fat hostile-aggressive businessman whose penchant for young boys had gotten him into hot water. He'd sworn he'd been set up for the charges against him by a competitor, and there was reason to believe it may have been true, but it was a case we'd happily passed on. Ever since, Win had relegated that particular chair to the farthest reaches of the room, to be used only in a pinch. It was nice to know he hadn't lost his sense of humor.

Madge settled into it with all the regal grace she could muster.

"In what manner do you prefer to be addressed, madam?" Win inquired solicitously. "Miss Burman? Ms. Burman, perhaps?"

"Oh, call me Madge, please."

"I could never presume such a liberty, though I appreciate the compliment. Shall we settle on Miss Burman then?"

"Yes, sir—fine," she agreed hastily.

Having ascertained that it wouldn't get him picketed by
NOW, he proceeded to lead her over the jumps. I watched, fascinated as he began by listening to her narrative and then went
back and dissected every word of it. Sometimes he let her ramble
off on a tangent, maybe to keep her loose or perhaps in hopes
she'd wander in some useful direction. Then he'd gently nudge
her back on the track, but always from an entirely different angle.

It was all very interesting to watch but I still couldn't see
that it was getting us anywhere. The whole sorry litany was still
coming out the same every time. I snuck a look at my watch. It
was after midnight. Win was beginning to show signs of strain to
my practiced eye, though he still maintained the appearance of
total enchantment with every word Madge uttered.

He was going over it for the tenth time, at least. "And this
custom—an annoying one naturally from your standpoint as her
nearest neighbor—never varied? She would stand at her door and
engage in a ten- or fifteen-minute dialogue with everyone who
chanced within, or anywhere near, her apartment. Always speaking in what was for her an unusually loud voice, sufficient to
override the dialogue coming from your television set?"

"Yes, she did it constantly. It nearly drove me crazy sometimes. And she'd just jabber about anything; half the time it made
no sense at all. Not that I listened, but the way that place is built
I didn't have much choice."

"Yet Mrs. Reynaud otherwise spoke in subdued tones?"

"That's for sure," Madge told him. "She was such a little
mouse of a thing. Half the time I couldn't hear what she was
trying to say and had to ask her to repeat herself."

Win's eyes flashed, and I suddenly snapped to attention.
"You present me with a conundrum, Miss Burman; how do you
explain it?"

"Con . . ." She stared at him blankly. He'd done a good job
of sticking to words she could digest, but now she choked on that
one.

"Conundrum," he repeated testily. "An inexplicable puzzle.
Barring emotional outbursts, people tend to speak at a consistent

level socially. It offends all logic when you tell me Mrs. Reynaud
was all but inaudible in her normal conversational tones, yet in
the next breath to state her voice was so loud when standing in
her doorway she obliterated the audio portion of your television
some fifteen yards away and through an intervening wall."

"Call it a con—what you said, if you like; I think she just
got nervous when someone cornered her in her apartment and as a
result she talked loudly."

Win smiled; it was his first genuine grin of the evening.
Standing, he told her, "Please believe me when I tell you I am
exceedingly grateful for the pleasure of your company this evening, Miss Burman. But I fear I've taken advantage of your splendid nature. Here it is, nearly one in the morning. Mr. Doyle will
return you home at once."

Madge tugged nervously at her skirt as we neared the front
door. When I opened it she exited grandly, then stopped, stared
in all directions, and turned to face me. "Where are all the reporters?" she wailed.

"You made the mistake of giving that guy your name and
address on the way in—remember? Don't blame me if there's a
mob waiting when we get back to your place."

Eight minutes later, I dropped her off before her ugly building. There wasn't a soul in sight. She barely heard me thanking
her for her time and bidding her good night. I left her standing on
the sidewalk, glancing furiously in all directions.

"Those press guys can be really shifty, Madge," I yelled out
the window. "Better check under the bed. I don't say the *San
Diego Union* would stoop to that, but there's always those rags
you see at the supermarket check stands."

The return trip gave me my first chance to ponder Win's
excuse for a hard night's work. I admitted it was—to use his
word—suggestive. But suggestive of what? Madge's theory was as
good as any I could conjure up. In fact it was better. So what was
so damn great about it that Win had been smirking like a cat with
a corner on the cream market when I'd left?

CHAPTER 10

Wednesday morning was Dirk's tenth day of captivity. No doubt everyone in that grand old house by the sea was aware of it, but to me it was like a field pack of lead strapped to my back. I fought it by forcing myself back into what had been our invariable routine—a prebreakfast run along the beach. It was hardly the same without Dirk there to drive me on. My left side was quiescent most of the time now, but it let me know it wasn't too crazy about the idea either. I hung in there for maybe a mile and a half. The iodine scent of the freshly beached kelp—together with the harsh astringency of the early morning sea air—performed its old magic. Later the sun would breast the high sandstone cliffs standing sentinel duty over the beach, but for now it was the cool, shadowy primeval place I loved more than any other.

By the time I showered and rushed downstairs Win had left the table. I bolted my breakfast and rushed into the office to find Win glaring down at the *Union* spread all over his desk. "Greetings, Matt—are you prepared to report your findings from yesterday?"

"Morning. Sure, I can sum it up in a single word—zilch! Now that's covered, how about you telling me what it was you pried out of Madge last night that tickled you so much."

"Nothing specific," he answered vaguely. "At most, a mere inkling. Right now, a somewhat more complete summary of your interviews would be appreciated. We mustn't delay; studies have shown we forget at least half of all we hear within the first twenty-four hours, and 80 percent inside of a week. Appalling but true."

"Not me—not when I'm working." I knew a diversion when I heard one but there was nothing to be done. Crossing to my desk, I sat and began my dreary recital. Win sat erect, apparently listening intently, though not with his eyes closed as he did when he was really on to something. He didn't interrupt once—which was also a bad sign—but when I'd finished he did ask me to clarify a point or two, mostly concerning the mechanics of the new security system at the apartment building.

Finally satisfied there was no more blood contained in this particular stone, he stared into space for five seconds, then told me evenly, "Get Inspector Dixon on the phone, Matt."

I picked up the receiver and punched the familiar number. After working my way through a couple of minor obstacles cluttering up the city payroll, I heard his usual nasty "Yeah?" on the line. Resisting the urge to zing him first, I merely nodded at Win.

He picked up his phone as if it had scales and squirmed. I settled back to listen with all the anticipation of a baseball nut about to hear a World Series game. "This is Carter Winfield, Inspector; I wish to ask you a simple question concerning the death of Mrs. Marlee Reynaud."

"Forget it! Not after that crummy act you pulled down at the federal detention center. You'd love to toss one of your famous monkey wrenches into the case against your pet goon, wouldn't you? The only surprising part is, you're expecting me to help you do it. You must really be desperate."

Win grimaced under the Herculean effort of keeping from blowing. Considering how much he hated phones and the way he felt about Dixon, it ranked as one of the world's great struggles.

"Your attitude is insupportable, Inspector. I merely arranged to visit Dirk, which was surely my right as his patron. As for my challenging your case against him, either your charges are sound—and thus unassailable—or they are fallacious and rightfully doomed anyway. My request is certainly a modest one. Was Mrs. Reynaud's key card found in her purse?" He even managed to make his voice sound modest, which was quite a trick under the circumstances.

The only sound from the phone was a faint crackle and ethereal hum. I could picture Dixon's big, red face contorting in concentration, looking for the hook. He is far from stupid, but Win has a bad effect on him.

"Just what in hell are you up to?" he finally demanded, out of sheer frustration.

"I serve justice, as do you," Win replied placidly.

"Sure you do. Like hell you do. But you can have that for free—what it's worth. At least it'll save having that wise-ass Doyle down here pumping everybody from the mayor on down until he gets it anyway. There was no purse found in the apartment. Your boy figures to have taken it along with the body, hoping we'd figure it for a robbery."

"It's entirely possible there's an alternate explanation," Win purred into the phone. "In any event, I thank you for answering my question with what was—at least for you—a minimum of vituperation. Good day." He replaced the phone gingerly, his face a study in peaceful abstraction.

I was understandably reluctant to disturb him. There was always the remote possibility he was actually accomplishing something. I leaned back, relaxed, and prepared to wait him out.

It was three long minutes before he deigned to recognize my existence. "I've an errand for you, Matt. Would it be possible to fetch that gentleman from the trailer park opposite Sea View? The one who offered his advice constraining you from the purchase of one of Mr. Blaise's condominiums?"

I'll admit I blinked in total surprise. I'd amused myself by projecting the likely train of his thoughts. A futile hobby admittedly, but usually I'm somewhere within the same galaxy. Not this time. "Easiest thing in the world. But please don't tell me we're back to square one with Roscoe for a suspect?"

"I'll be better able to answer that after I commune with this fellow. I warn you, it is essential you remain unseen by Mr. Blaise. We must not risk that under any conditions. Can that be managed?"

"Sure! I'll park way over at the east end of the trailer park. But I still don't get it. What could you possibly want with him? And what harm could it do if Roscoe spotted me there?"

"A simple case of overprecaution; it's remotely possible we might be putting the man in danger if you and he were observed together. As to why—it would seem this fellow has conducted what amounts to surveillance of that building site from its very inception. Don't you think it might prove instructive to find out what he's seen?"

"Only if we wanted to learn how not to build condos." I stood up, stretched, and left with the distinct impression he was just trying to get me out of the office so he could pull something. It would be so like him to hold back, then whip it out of his hat together with trumpets and flourishes. Usually I had a pretty good idea of what was coming, but not this time. I couldn't have been any more in the dark if you'd taped my eyes and dropped me down a coal mine.

When I rounded the blue and white aluminum coach, the same old geezer was sitting in the same old lawn chair, as if they were both national monuments. He reminded me of Percy Kilbride in the reruns I'd seen of the old Ma and Pa Kettle movies from the forties. His scrawny neck seen in profile made him look a little like a turkey.

He turned at the sound of my feet crunching on the white gravel surrounding his trailer. "Hi," I waved; "remember me? You told me last week they didn't know what they were doing over there." I nodded in the general direction of the construction site across the road.

He eyed me warily. "I sorta remember. What do you want?" His voice betrayed the fearful dread of the elderly living on a fixed income. The slightest financial shock could spell utter disaster and they know it only too well; still they remain the single most vulnerable prey for every kind of slick and dirty operation under the sun.

"My name's Matt Doyle," I told him, positioning myself so my back was to Roscoe's office, in case he took a notion to glance across the road.

The old man tentatively offered me a bony claw. "Barney Clyde."

"Nice to meet you, Barney. I'm here to tell you that the former secretary of state—Carter Winfield—wants very much to confer with you. He lives less than ten minutes from here and he sent me to get you."

Barney's watery eyes grew larger, and he was silent for a few seconds. "What's he want to talk to me for?"

"I'm not really sure, Barney. It would be confidential—most of his conferences are. All I know is he's terribly interested in seeing this section of the coast preserved from senseless exploitation. I told him about you—that you seemed to be a knowledgeable man when it came to building. My guess is he wants to pick your brain about what's been going on across the road there."

A golf-sized Adam's apple bounced up and down his scrawny neck a few times as he swallowed. "I guess maybe I could give him an earful at that. Why, I always did say he was the best damn secretary of state there ever was. Be obliged for the chance to tell him so." Barney levered himself up from his ratty chair. Mounting the few wooden steps to his trailer, he told me: "Be right back. Got to get my wallet and leave a note for the missus. Hate to miss seein' the look on her face when she reads it."

Fifteen minutes later, I was making introductions back in the office. The two men shook hands warmly. Barney—after a shaky start—stuck to his word and told Win his eight years in office had been the best thing that ever happened to this country during his lifetime. Win merely responded with a smile and a slight nod. It could have been a gesture of gratitude or an agreement; in any case he didn't seem inclined to argue the point.

"Now then, Mr. Clyde, let's settle down to a discussion of more contemporary affairs. You informed my associate those builders across the road from you didn't know what they were doing. I'd like you to elaborate on that statement, if you would."

Barney perched his lean frame well forward in his chair. "Shoot, I could give you a baker's dozen different ways that fool Blaise is screwin' up. That project's been goin' on now for over eight months, and there ain't nowhere near half them units done. He's for sure losin' his shirt over there. See, what he's doin', he's subcontractin' all the work out and he don't know one thing about coordinatin' it right. For instance, instead of doin' each job all at once, he'll pour foundations for maybe a third of it, call in the rough carpenters, then the roofers, plumbers, electricians, and all like that. Sometimes there'll be weeks go by with nothing bein' done at all. That's because, what happens, say the roofers you got lined up weeks back, they got a bigger job in the meantime, so when you're ready for them they ain't about to show. So what does Blaise do? Why, he sits on his fat behind and he waits for them. And the sad part is he'll have to go through all the same hassles lots more times, because that's the way he's doin' the whole deal—one little piece at a time."

"Perhaps the determining factor is fiscal necessity," suggested Win. "Possibly he must complete and sell a small number of units in order to fund the construction of others."

"That ain't the way you do it—never! Not on a small project like that. You end up spendin' two, maybe even three times what it would cost to do it right. Hell, that whole place should be done by now, and like I say, they ain't even halfway. And what chance does he have of sellin' any, with the place lookin' like a junkyard?

"Look, I was a contractor myself, back in Kansas City. Started with a borrowed hammer and ended up runnin' a gang of twenty-five, thirty men. Just for laughs, I been keepin' a log on that place across the road. You know: how many guys working how many hours, that sort of thing. I got the hourly rates by callin' the union halls. I can estimate the materials easy. The numbers I come up with are already well over a million bucks and that don't include one thin dime for the land. And he's probably workin' on borrowed money, so you can throw in one hell of a bunch of interest, too. There's twenty-four condos priced from one hundred and twenty-five thousand up to one hundred and seventy-five. Call it a hundred and fifty average. That's three million six *if* he gets his price and *if* he sells every one. And these projects always have to end up hirin' brokers to sell the units, so don't forget there's commissions to be paid.

"See what I'm gettin' at? That idiot's going to end up spendin' way more than the total value of the project any way you cut it. Three million maybe on improvements—there's got to be a terrific amount of landscapin' done, and that's gonna come high—plus land cost, interest, and cost of sales."

Win sat mute, frowning. "You are a veritable cornucopia of knowledge and information, Mr. Clyde," he muttered distractedly. "Given the current soft market for real estate in general—and condominiums in particular—it would seem inevitable Mr. Blaise is indeed doomed to fiscal calamity."

Barney's head dipped in rapid assent. "You damn betcha! I just hope Mr. Kline got his cash up front for the land—it must have sold for a bundle. Don't know why I should give a hoot in hell—after him going back on his word like he did—but he always seemed like such a fine man before."

"And who might this Mr. Kline be?" Win inquired gently. "In what way has he reneged on his promise to you?"

"Reuben Kline. He owns the trailer park I live at. Real well-to-do type, but a nicer man you'd never meet. Used to visit the clubhouse every year a few days before Christmas, put out a spread you couldn't hardly believe for all of us that lived there. One year after the meal he even called bingo and handed out fifty-dollar bills to every winner. My wife Edna won one of 'em, too. Another time he brought along a movie and showed it. Brand new, it was—not even in the theaters yet.

"But this last Christmas—nothing! Never a peep out of him. My guess is he's ashamed to show his face on account of the way he went and let that fool Blaise build on his land. See, he promised us nothin' would ever go in there as long as he lived—said it was what made the trailer park so special. Edna and me—lots of us from the park—we used to walk over there for picnics all the time. There was some tables Mr. Kline had built there and everything. Just to watch the sunset sometimes, you know. Now, instead of an ocean view, all we got is them ugly apartments staring at us. Might as well be in some second-rate park in southeast San Diego."

"A pity, to be sure," murmured Win, the animation on his face belying his blasé tone. "One is led to assume Mr. Kline was forced into his decision by pressing exigencies. Where might Mr. Reuben Kline be found?"

"Lives up in Newport Beach somewhere; the park manager would know."

"Excellent! Now, Mr. Clyde, why don't you just sit back in your chair, relax, and tell me everything you've observed from your point of vantage."

"About what?" Barney asked, suddenly wary.

"Anything you wish. Whatever strikes you as unusual or even remotely interesting concerning Mr. Blaise or his apparently ill-considered project."

Mollified, Barney took Win at his word and embarked on a rambling dissertation, beginning eight months ago when the first bulldozer had rumbled onto the lot. He made it clearer with every sentence, the only thing that could have saved Roscoe from impending financial ruin would have been if he—Barney Clyde—had been tapped to run the show.

My eyes glazed over after a while, but Win still seemed fascinated with every word, even when Barney went into great detail about how the prevailing winds blew all the dust caused by the construction right into his mobile home.

The sallow old man had obviously been waiting for an audience for a very long time. You could plainly see he'd be good for hours. But after another fifteen minutes—during which he largely repeated himself—Win put a halt to the torrent of words. "I'm afraid I've imposed upon your kindness entirely too long, Mr. Clyde. You could do me one final benefaction if—when Mr. Doyle returns you to your home—you would procure the address of Mr. Kline for me."

"I guess I could," Barney allowed reluctantly. "But I wouldn't want to cause him no grief, even if he did back down on his word."

"Don't concern yourself," Win assured him. I admired his self-control; the compulsion to correct anyone uttering a double negative in his presence was all but overwhelming.

"Okay, but leave my name out of it if you talk to him." Barney jumped to his feet to accept Win's outstretched hand. "I'd sure hate to get kicked out of there, what with seein' all them famous TV stars comin' and goin' all the time."

The script had called for him to let go and follow me to the door, but Win held his hand. "You've obviously omitted something of interest from your narrative, Mr. Clyde. I too am fascinated by the luminaries of the theater." (A damn lie; the nicest thing I'd ever heard him say about actors was they were one-dimensional psuedo-people suffering from severe cases of arrested development.) "Tell me about the ones you've seen." There was a hard edge of excitement in that voice I knew so well.

"Well, I seen quite a few the last five or six months, you know. Mostly I don't know the names—they're the younger ones whose movies I don't see—but I recognize 'em from the Carson show, and like that on TV. There's that guy who does the cop show on Channel 3—he's been there lots of times. And there's that girl—the real skinny blonde, you know—from "Single Parents." She's there plenty, too. I'd say more than a dozen all told, most more than once."

Win had released Barney's hand and was standing there regarding him thoughtfully. "Is the purpose of these illustrious visitors apparent to you? Do they appear to be considering the purchase of a condominium, for instance?"

"Naw, they don't pay no attention to them. They only come for the pretty tiles."

"Pretty tiles, Mr. Clyde?"

"Tiles, you know. Mexican tiles. The kind they use to make you think the roofs are tiled, which they're not. But these tiles are real nice—I'll give 'em that. Blaise, he gets them straight from Mexico. This ratty old truck with Baja plates and Mex writing on the doors is always dropping off bundles of the damn things. Must have delivered enough to tile half of North County."

"And personages, some of whom you recognize as theatrical performers, depart bearing a quantum of those tiles," mused Win.

"Them and plenty of others. There's hardly a day goes by when somebody doesn't stop by for a batch. Looks to me like them pretty tiles caught on real big somewheres."

"I dare say you're right. Thank you again, Mr. Clyde. I'm enormously indebted to you. Your powers of observation far outstrip your talent as a grammarian, thank heaven." He spoke slowly—his mind otherwise occupied—sitting staring out the window. He no longer knew or cared we were there, so we left.

He hadn't moved a muscle as far as I could tell when I returned forty minutes later. I dropped into my chair and began rummaging through the deep bottom left drawer of my desk. Finding the Thomas Brothers map of Orange County, I flipped it open and began looking for the address on the slip of paper in my hand.

"I see you've secured the location of Mr. Kline's habitat."

He was watching me when I glanced up. His young-looking gray eyes were animated, the glassy, contemplative look gone. "106 Via Oporto—it's on Lido Isle in Newport. Very much in the high rent district."

Win looked over his shoulder at the wall clock. It was a few minutes shy of noon. "I'd like you to pay the Klines a visit, Matt—this afternoon."

"I'm way ahead of you for once. I'll wear my new gray trop-
ical worsted, since it's Lido Isle. It would be a long drive to find
no one home. I'd better call first."

"No! Surprise is our best ally."

"Okay, I could use one. What's my pitch?"

"Since I know practically nothing of the man I can make no
cogent suggestions. Utilize your own facile artifices. You will
know the appropriate tack to use when you meet your man. In the
meantime, can you think of any means by which we might deter-
mine Mr. Blaise's financial situation?"

"Easiest thing in the world. I'll have our bank manager run a
TRW tape on him. You'll have it this afternoon."

"Excellent! Call him at once, then we'll adjourn for lunch."

I wasted five minutes at the dining table trying to get a peek
at what was going on in his head. All I did get was a load of crap
about how it would be better if I went ahead without the burden of
preconceived notions which might prove entirely erroneous. No
danger of that. It was a little like sending a guy out hunting, but
not letting him in on what the game was going to be. Would it be
rabbit or bear? Like that proverbial hunter, I left for Newport not
knowing whether I was likely to end up feeling silly or dead.

CHAPTER 11

*I*t was a leisurely hour drive north on Highway 5. There were a few spots along the way where you couldn't see sprawling housing developments or shopping centers. Damn few. Where rolling green pastures and fat cattle had been only a few years ago, now there were endless projects with names like Rancho Nuevo and Villa Capri. The rare virgin spots all sprouted billboards announcing future housing developments or business complexes. In spite of the lyrical names and the six-figure prices, the houses all looked dismally sterile and cheap. But it would be a cat burglar's dream; they were built so close together it would be no great feat to jump from roof to roof. The vast megapolis south from Los Angeles to the Mexican border the pundits used to predict was virtually a reality.

I swung off onto Route 101 through Laguna Beach, with all its artsy-craftsy tourist lairs and a red light every block to make certain you got ample opportunity to succumb to the carefully contrived charm. There was a glorious stretch of green between Laguna and Newport. It was a riding stable overlooking the sea.

Almost enough to overcome a lifetime antipathy for horses—almost.

In Newport Beach, I turned left and rolled down the hill toward the harbor. A narrow, steeply arched little bridge led past a yacht club onto Lido Isle. Everything was only three-quarter scale except the cars and the people. The inadequate streets were jammed with cars that could barely pass without touching. Mobs of people wandered in an apparently aimless fashion in various stages of undress. Progress was measured in inches. I shuddered to think what the place would be like during the summer.

Fortunately the main street was only a few blocks long. I passed through a residential area of tiny frame houses on postage-stamp lots. In an urban inner city it would have qualified as a slum, except every house and lot was in immaculate condition, and I knew any given cottage would command a price the equivalent of one of the finest homes on the mainland.

As I neared the water on the north shore, the houses increased in size. Via Oporto paralleled the water and I soon found 106. It was a low, rambling ranch-style of white brick with brown shutters. It rambled quite a bit—especially for Lido Isle—say, over four thousand square feet. An American flag fluttered from a thirty-foot steel pole in the front yard. A gunmetal gray Mercedes sport coupe sat quietly ticking over in the circular drive.

Before my fingers could reach the bell the door flew open and I was face-to-face with a disconcertingly beautiful girl. Black curly hair elegantly styled over sharp features, each of which taken individually was perfection. The total effect was something on the order of Liz Taylor thirty years ago, if she'd have been more athletic and taller. The girl before me was pushing thirty but not there yet, dressed in designer jeans and a simple checkered shirt—the kind you can steal on Rodeo Drive for a mere three hundred dollars.

She looked me up and down as if I were an exhibit being offered at discount. "I suppose it's too much to expect you can memorize lines and not bump into the furniture," she stated pessimistically.

"I never yet heard a line worth memorizing so who knows?" I responded archly. "But I definitely don't bump into furniture; I merely use it to lean on. You might not know it to look at me, but I'm exceedingly frail. In fact, I'm the aesthetic type."

"I can see that—about as frail as a Missouri mule. No, make that a jungle cat. You move marvelously. Please tell me you're a gifted actor and make my day."

Her voice, while brusque, was also a musical instrument of great range and clarity. I had to stifle a very strong urge to take two steps forward, throw her over my shoulder, and race for the nearest cave. "I'd love nothing more than to make your day— maybe even your night—but I don't think we ought to begin our relationship with a lie."

"On the contrary, lies are the very best basis for a relationship. Nothing good could possibly survive honesty." She stepped down from the doorway and pulled the door closed behind her. This put us less than an arm's length apart. She barely made it to my ears, so she had to tilt her head back to peer up at me. The sun caught her fair in the eyes, so she put on a pair of expensive-looking silver sunglasses.

The shades dampened the effect enough to enable me to remember why I was there. "My name's Matt Doyle. Is Reuben Kline around?"

I could barely make out her eyes now, but she tilted her head to one side as if in sympathy. "My father is home—he's always home, poor dear—but I'm afraid it wouldn't do you a bit of good to see him. He's extremely ill. Perhaps I can help though. If it's business, I handle all of his affairs now. My name is Tina Kline."

"I hope you can, Tina. My boss is Carter Winfield—know who he is?" Famous as he was, I'd learned not to assume anything with the under-thirty crowd. Most of them didn't know who the current cabinet members were, or who the allies were during the Second World War. They've soft-pedaled history and geography in the schools lately. Great idea! Now we can repeat all our same mistakes over again.

I got a fleeting impression of the faintly seen eyes behind the glasses dilating momentarily. "Certainly! He's practically a national monument, for Christ's sake."

"Almost. Then you may also know of one of our employees—Dirk Bomande—who's been arrested for the murder of Marlee Reynaud. She was an employee of a development company in Solana Beach called Sea View—twenty-four condos now under construction? Your father is financially involved. Though I suppose it's entirely possible he never knew the victim, my questions concern his partner, Roscoe Blaise. I have information for your father as well, and I'll guarantee it's worth his time to hear me out."

Tina stood rooted, with her fists planted on her slender hips, regarding me critically. "God—you're so utterly perfect!"

"I doubt it—perfect for what?" If it was a stall, it had real promise.

"Sorry! You'll have to forgive me. I've got an entirely one-track mind just now. I'm in the midst of shooting an important film and there's a part—not a lead, mind you, but pivotal—calling for a very physical and yet charismatic type. Kind of like an Errol Flynn who can come across like Bogart when he speaks. I've been casting for weeks without getting within a mile of what I want. And here I open the door and there he stands. You're him! It's no wonder I'm not tracking very well." She shook her head at the sheer wonder of it, then seized my hand and tugged hard. "I'm going to be very, very late. Come on—we can talk all you want in the car."

For a guy who'd just been told by an expert he was a cross between Flynn and Bogart, I thought I maintained my composure pretty well. "Huh?"

"Please just come—I'll explain all in the car. I'm the one you want to talk to anyway. My father's suffered a severe stroke. To put it another way, he's a rutabaga." She made the outrageous remark with somewhat less emotion than the guy who gives the stock market report on the six o'clock news. My orders were to go with the flow, so I slid into the passenger seat of the sweet little bomb.

Nobody has ever accused me of driving like a little old lady from La Jolla, but Tina maneuvered the coupe as if saddled with a death wish. Fortunately she kept up a nonstop monologue; I probably couldn't have separated my teeth long enough to ask any leading questions.

It seems Tina'd become a virtual orphan within the crushingly brief period of one week about nine months ago. First her mother had OD'd on vodka and Valium, and then her father had suffered a massive cardiovascular arrest not two days after the funeral. He was, as Tina so quaintly put it, a rutabaga, and there she was alone in the world and left holding the bag. The bag he'd left her with was a fine big bag, but her father's assets needed constant attention, like so many plates that had to be kept spinning atop their frail limber sticks. In Tina's desperate scramble to keep the momentum, she'd agreed to enter into a limited partnership with Roscoe Blaise. The little coastal plot had been nonincome-producing, and the annual taxes were enough to buy a family home in a ghetto neighborhood. She was more than a little disappointed at the slow progress of the project but hadn't given it a whole lot of thought because she was up to her ears and far beyond in quite a project of her own.

It was a very hairy half hour later when we pulled up outside a sound stage in Burbank. She spun out of the car and all but dragged me inside. Her "project" consisted of a huge set that might have been Charles Addams's ultimate Halloween. Even with the studio lights burning, it was a gray on black world of grotesque Rackham-like trees, ruins, and what I took to be stylized tombstones. Several dozen people—all appearing to be under thirty—stood grouped in tiny living islands lost within the cavernous building.

Tina's brisk entrance galvanized them into frantic animation, with the notable exception of one seated young man who gave all the indications of being comatose. "All right, children," Tina shouted, her voice retaining its charming musical qualities even at full volume, "the clock is running. Sorry I'm late, but how's this for an excuse? His name is Matt; isn't he a lovely addition to

our merry little band? He materialized right out of thin air at my
front door—further proof we are favored by the gods."

I was suddenly surrounded by as bizarre a bunch of looney
tunes as I'd ever come across. Except for eight or ten who were
obviously technicians, the rest were in costumes ranging from a
Roman toga to a four-star general. Among the girls I spied a
witch, an angel, and one who could have been Lady Godiva except her hair was too short. Apparently whoever it was was dis-
guised as a girl. It was a first-class job of camouflage. They all
seemed to suffer from a consuming need to touch me. Standing
there in my Hart, Shaffner, and Marx, Countess Mara tie—with
my revolver clipped to my belt—I felt like a rabbi at a Bund
rally.

Tina made quick rounds of the camera and lighting crews,
giving them brief, crisp instructions, then she waved the "children" quiet. It was an impressive display of complete control over
what I would have thought a wholly undisciplined mob; the instant her hand went over her head, silence reigned supreme.
"Magic time is in five minutes. Now don't you dare start thinking
of clever little lines of dialogue. Just remember what I've told
you: Keep your minds blank until I point to you, then speak whatever pops into your head. Say as little or as much as you like, and
God help you if you assume a role, or even attempt to act in any
way."

After carving that particular dictum deep in stone, she took
my arm, pinned it against an impressive breast, and led me to a
nearly full rack of costumes set back against a far wall. "I think I
rather like the idea of tights, a leather jerkin, and perhaps a
cocked hat, Matt, but it's whatever turns you on, dear."

I was pretty well along toward being turned on by then and it
had nothing whatever to do with a cocked hat. I folded my arms
and shook my head, thereby proving once and for all the theories
concerning body language. "You're not actually serious? I flunked
high school drama. Look, you've got more than a dollar or two in
overhead at stake here; I don't want to screw it all up for you."

"Perfect! I couldn't be more pleased to hear you flunked.

Now hurry, please. All you have to do is pace around up there against that marvelous setting. What we're attempting to do is an entirely new form of theater, unheard of in film. It's truly a quantum leap from the Antonioni school . . . never mind—I'll explain more later. I'm not even going to tell you the context of the scene; it could spoil what may just be a uniquely spontaneous segment. Don't give me that churlish glare—didn't you and I vow to help one another? So untie those arms and slip into something bizarre and comfortable."

It was the only way to justify my existence in the group, and I was willing to bet the farm there were answers floating around the room worth sweating for. Blaise, Sea View, Mexican tiles, and murder all pointed toward a Hollywood connection and—though most people don't know it—Hollywood is in Burbank now. At least, the Hollywood we associate with those big, silver screens is. And I found I was drawn toward Kline; she was the conduit connecting the two disparate locations. Battered by personal tragedy and deeply immersed in the demanding role of producer/director of a film, she'd be ripe for exploitation.

So I changed, but passed on the Robin Hood outfit Tina'd favored; instead I opted for a monk's robe, complete with cowl. It served a couple of purposes admirably: With the hood up no one would ever recognize me, in the unlikely event anyone I knew ever saw this film, and it gave me the essential space needed to hide my revolver. I certainly wasn't about to leave it lying around loose in that cuckoo's nest.

As I shuffled reluctantly toward the vast stage, Tina glanced over and ordered me back again to swap my oxfords for a pair of sandals—no socks. This caused a general wave of giggles among my fellow thespians. Finally all the actors were assembled. I counted fifteen of us. No additional directions were offered; we weren't even told how or where to move during the upcoming scene. The dreaded call for "action" was given by Tina and the cameras presumably rolled.

We all began schlepping back and forth across the dimly lighted set. An overhead mike tracked one or another of us; a blue-tinted spot framed whichever individual Tina indicated with her outstretched arm. She'd hold her point for varying lengths of time, drop her arm, then raise it emphatically at another one of us. Whoever it was found him- or herself quite literally "on the spot."

Judging from her facial expressions it seemed impossible to disappoint Tina. She appeared equally satisfied with the guy who looked like one of the three Musketeers and recited a clever monologue in verse, and the barbarian in skins and leather who was so spaced out he got all tongue-tied and settled in the end for an emphatic, "Aw, fuck it!"

The Lady Godiva sans hair informed us she was a "Living phantasmagoria—the source of all that was in the world—be it good or ill." She was good for a couple of minutes, longer than most.

Inevitably, my turn came. I stopped, as I'd seen the others do, when the spot hit me. I peered out from the dark recesses of my cowl and said in a monotone, "Forever and forever and forever. Why must I expiate the sins of men I never knew, forever and forever and forever?"

It seemed to fit the outfit, not that the rest had shown much concern on that score. After the third time through my little query, Tina got the idea that was about as far as I intended to pursue my existentialistic quickie, and the light moved on. I definitely thought mine was one of the better performances. Suddenly I felt like a complete ass, realizing I was really getting into the whole insane farce. It was to laugh.

The entire sequence took thirty-five minutes to film. Tina's welcome cry of "cut" sent me scampering for my clothes. The remainder of the cast was apparently content to stay in—or out—of uniform. They clustered around Tina, jabbering happily like so many insecure puppies eager for a kind word or gesture. No one objected when I elbowed my way over to her side.

"You were marvelous," she shouted at me over the gabble. "And your instincts were sound when you selected the monk's robe. There's something self-righteous about your aura—I can see that clearly now."

"Sounds more like an insult than a compliment, but thanks anyway. When can we talk some more?"

"Not now! Full shooting schedule for the rest of today. You can either hang around and watch, or be back here around seven—that's party time."

"Guess I'll run a couple of errands then."

"But you will be back," she insisted.

"Wouldn't miss it, Tina. Besides, my car is still parked in front of your house in Newport. I've been kidnapped."

Tina nodded with obvious satisfaction. Then, jolting me with the full wattage of her awesomely lovely smile, she turned her back and began talking to the troops again.

I fought free of the crush and left the huge building. After the gloom inside, the bright blaze of the sun made my eyes water. While I waited for adjustments to be made, I considered my options. There was really only one primary. Detectives are policemen, after all. They may believe you heart and soul, but you'd better know they'll always check. Win had sent me to see Reuben Kline, and when I got home I'd damn well better have seen him—even if it was lying in a coma. I had to get inside Tina's house on Lido Isle. There was plenty of time. I trotted toward the main gate in search of a cab, but then I came up with a better idea. Tina's Mercedes was sitting right outside the sound stage in a reserved slot, and I'd watched her nonchalantly toss the keys into the ashtray. Why not? Considering the way my plans might shape up for the afternoon, Grand Theft, Auto, would be the least of my worries.

The car handled like a dream compared to my four-year-old Chevy. I took the time to stop and chat with the guard at the gate. "I'm running some errands for Tina Kline—you probably recognize her car. Won't have any difficulty getting back in here later, will I?"

The competent-looking middle-aged guard eyed me silently for several seconds. "You came in with her less than an hour ago, didn't you?" he asked rhetorically. He damn well knew I had, or he'd have figured me for a car thief and pulled his sidearm by now. There are too many rent-a-cops living for the day they can do just that, and he struck me as one of them.

"Sure did. Figure to be back about seven. You still be on?"

"Hell, no; but don't worry. I'll log you out with a note you're due back then. Be no problem, as long as you don't bring along any company."

"No company—just some party supplies. Thanks, Perry." He wore a chrome name tag on his left breast. The sound of his own name pleased him. It's the sweetest sound any of us ever hear.

I muddled around Burbank a while, too stubborn to stop for directions, but eventually picked up the Newport Freeway. The middle of the afternoon was a lousy time for what I had in mind, but so it goes. I'd built up a minor head of steam and knew better than to allow it to dissipate.

Via Oporto was easy. Coming in from the north this time, I crossed a short, narrow bridge over a canal and curved left. My car was still where I'd left it. While driving, I'd devised several clever schemes, all of which had one thing in common: They were too risky in the daylight and based upon too little data.

So instead I pulled in the curving drive and parked right in front of the double doors of the house. My ring was answered promptly enough, but first I caught a glimpse of movement among the still-drawn drapes. I was fairly certain if it hadn't been for Tina's car sitting in plain sight, I'd have gotten no response whatever.

When the door opened, I found myself facing what central casting would send if someone requested a female marine top kick. Fat and forty were both understatements, but there was no mistaking the essential core of inner toughness. She was big— five ten or better—and her hostile eyes probed mine with blazing intensity. "What is it?" she demanded, as if I were standing thirty feet away.

"Sorry to bother you. Perhaps you know, Miss Kline and I went to the studio together shortly after lunch. That's my car out there in front—just in case you've been wondering. Anyway, she asked me to dash back here to pick up some notes she needs for this afternoon's filming." I was doing my slightly nervous fawning bit, guaranteed to make almost anyone feel superior. At my size it's quite a trick, but since most of us no longer carry clubs, other criteria prevail and it is possible.

The door opened the rest of the way and she stepped aside with a residue of reluctance. "Where are these papers?" It was abundantly clear I was not about to be given the run of the house.

This forced me to make a guess, and I could only hope it sounded halfway plausible. "Her desk, she thinks. If you'll be kind enough to show me where it is, I know exactly what to look for."

She sniffed derisively, which I took as another tribute to my thespian talents. Without further comment, she spun and marched across ten yards of ankle-deep gold carpet, turned right, and opened a heavy carved oak door, leading me into a library-cum-office. The unbroken wall on the right was solid books, mostly on real estate and investments. On the left, double sliding glass doors opened onto an attractive flagstone patio. Straight ahead was another identical door to the one we'd just entered.

The big nurse—that's what I took her to be, though she wore no uniform or insignia—crossed the room and stood with her back to the other door, arms folded defensively. She couldn't have told me what I'd wanted to know any more blatantly if she'd agreed to sign an affidavit.

I made a great show of rifling through the papers on the desk, examining each one quickly but carefully. My mind was racing. Suddenly I remembered the antihistamine tablets I carried in my trouser pocket—defense against the profusion of eucalyptus trees that abound in many areas of Southern California. We were not compatible. Clutching my chest, I started gasping and wheezing and fumbling for a tablet. "Don't be alarmed," I hissed, doing my level best to alarm her. "I need . . . a little . . . water. Be . . . okay . . . *ahhh!*"

At first, I was afraid she'd call my bluff. Or worse, demand a close look at the little yellow pill. Any nurse and half the general population would immediately recognize it as a common over-the-counter modality. But my routine hadn't left her a whole lot of slack. In spite of a guarded glare of suspicion, she rushed out of the room.

It figured to be a quick trip; I could hear water running within ten seconds, but by then I'd already released the inside lock securing the glass patio doors. I even risked opening one, closing it again quickly. If there had been an alarm activated, better to find it out then. It would have been a simple matter to claim an overpowering need for some fresh air. Breaking out was one thing; coming the other way later would be a different matter.

To allay her suspicion, I let her find me sitting slumped over the desk. Accepting the half-filled glass of water with trembling hands, I popped the tablet in my mouth and choked down a sip. Slowly, I allowed my vital signs to normalize, making quite a show of struggling for ever-deeper breaths.

"Heart?" she asked without caring. The first thing she'd done upon reentering the room had been to glance repeatedly at the far door.

"No, thank God! Bronchial tubes. Sometimes when I get nervous or overly excited they constrict on me. It's as if I'm being strangled. Hope I didn't frighten you."

"Hardly," she replied condescendingly. "I assume what you took was a Brondecon, or something similar with epinephrine. They now have much better products available—aerosols—which work much more quickly. Perhaps you should consider another doctor; one who's somewhat more current with the literature." Like most medical personnel, she was an elitist at heart and couldn't resist putting a layman in his place.

"You might be right. Mine's about eighty, I think. Thanks."

"Have you found whatever it is you were sent for? I really do have other things—"

"Right here—found it just where Tina said." I waved a lined yellow legal pad I'd come across with several pages of nonsense that may or may not have had something to do with the film. At least it was something which would pass muster if that big stump of a nurse demanded a look.

She trusted me about as far as she could heave a piano, so I beat her to it by handing her the pad. She briefly scanned the first page, flipped through it, including the blank pages, then handed it back. I got the impression she'd have liked to frisk me as well.

My effusive thanks as we retraversed the sea of shag garnered nothing more than some additional contemptuous sniffs. Then the big stump stood in the doorway and watched me pull away in Tina's car.

It wasn't much after four; dusk wasn't due until after five-thirty. I couldn't wait. There would be too many people around by then anyway. Fortunately, the rear yard bordering the canal had appeared to feature a lot of lush plantings, so I elected to run the risk. Parking the distinctive-looking car several blocks distant, I backtracked along the sidewalk to the house next door to Tina's. Along the way I noticed a metal sign planted on a lawn advertising the fact that there was a neighborhood watch program in effect. It did little to lighten my somber thoughts, but now I was committed.

Strolling jauntily, attempting to look as if I belonged, I veered directly for the high wooden gate on the far side of the neighboring house, lifted the latch, and passed quickly but not furtively through. Once behind the house, I swiftly crossed over to the Kline property and paused in the lee of a squat palmlike shrub to have a look around. The only activity appeared to be the traffic over the bridge about a block away. Currently there were no boats moving up or down the canal that marked the back property line. I could hear the sounds of children yelping not too far off, but no kids were within sight.

I shrugged and walked silently to the concrete and stone patio. The library drapes were still open and the room was empty. Better yet, the door leading to the living area was once again closed. I tugged tentatively at the handle of the heavy glass plate door. It slid open like a dream. I stopped it at two feet and slipped inside. Then I voted to close it again, just in case Big Stump happened to poke her nose in. The big question from the very beginning had been whether she'd be on station in the next room where I was confident I'd find the patient. And after all the mental gyrations were finished there was only one way to find out, and there wasn't a single damn thing I could do to improve my odds. So I walked over, turned the knob slowly, and nudged the door open with my shoulder.

The good-sized room was richly furnished, dwarfing the pale figure of a man lying in the middle of a sterile-looking hospital bed. Man and bed were oddly out of place amid the expensive antique chests of drawers, bedside tables, and massive dresser. The guardrails were both raised, and an IV drip slowly made its ominous way from the suspended bottle, down the transparent plastic tube, into the vein of the prone man's left arm. The room was in semidarkness, with only a low-wattage lamp to offset the effect of the heavy drapes over all the windows.

I stood beside the bed-cum-cage and studied Reuben Kline. For a man who'd supposedly suffered a massive CVA and been totally immobilized on both sides, he seemed remarkably hale. I knew the facial muscles should have been entirely lax, flaccid to the point of drooping. But they weren't. The quickest and surest test that a layman—that's doctorese for dummy—can conduct is known as plantar stimulation. My long-ago training as an army field medic assured me it could do no harm; yet I still experienced a strong sense of reluctance as I peeled away the bed covers to expose his bare feet. It was a struggle to overcome the natural hesitancy to tamper with sick people without a professional's blessing. I steeled myself by remembering what a joke "professionals' blessings" had turned out to be in the army.

Using the tip of my index finger, I rubbed the center of Kline's right arch. The foot soon bowed satisfactorily, the toes clenching like the vestigial fist they were. I repeated the simple test on the left foot. Results were identical. Satisfied, I tucked the covers back in exactly the way I'd found them.

"Maaash."

My nerves of steel turned out to be jello. I hunched in defense against attack, but my feet got tangled in my frantic haste to spin and face the door. The reaction was autonomic, entirely beyond my control. On a conscious level I was fully aware that the sound had emanated from Kline's own lips.

Willing my heart rate back below two hundred, I leaned over the nearest rail and looked into his barely open eyes. There was a vestige of keen intelligence piercing the veil of heavy stupor. And there was fear—overwhelming, palpable fear. "Maaash," he breathed again. The effort obviously cost him more than he could afford to pay; the pale lids slammed shut with frightening finality. The second time I thought I'd picked up the faintest trace of an *R* sound. If so, it was an amazing display of grit. An *R* is one of the trickiest consonant sounds to make. Why was the word *marsh* so important it expressed the first and only thought in the poor man's muddled mind?

Suddenly, the most important thing in my muddled mind was to get out of there. I made myself take a good look at the IV bottle but the label had been removed. Unheard of. Then I beat it fast. The one hole in my scheme would be the unlocked patio door. The best I could hope for was that Big Stump would chalk it up to an oversight on her part, in which case it would no doubt never be mentioned to Tina. It was a swell theory—except Big Stump didn't strike me as the patio type. Her complexion had all the color and texture of unbaked bread.

As I drove north I was faced with what Win would refer to as a conundrum: Was it possible Tina could live in the same house with her father and Big Stump and be innocent of collusion? Why should she be expected to know the real reason he'd been laid low? Her own career didn't leave much time for such considerations, and her remark about her father being a rutabaga had hinted at a lack of filial concern. There was nothing unusual about a son or daughter experiencing resentment toward a parent who dies suddenly or becomes incapacitated. And Tina had experienced both within a very short time—her father dropped into an apparent coma and her mother committed suicide. Quite a double whammy for anybody. More data was required.

It was pushing five by the time I parked Tina's wonderful set of wheels in the auto park tower next to Continental Bank on Wilshire Boulevard. One of the myriad little facts I'd gleaned from my fast shuffle through the Klines' papers that afternoon was the name and branch of their bank. It had so far been a hell of a day for hunches, so I'd decided to push my luck.

Waltzing in cold would have been dumb, so I'd prepared my script well. I'd phoned twenty minutes earlier, sweet-talking my way through receptionist, secretary, and an assistant vice-president and ended up scheduled to chat with the president of Continental—one Ronald Coburn. I couldn't possibly have gotten what I wanted from any of the others in a million years, but Coburn—maybe. He could afford to relax the rules when he felt like it and trust his instincts. All the others would be tightly clad in their hair shirts, practicing paranoids, lucky if they made it to the bathroom successfully during business hours.

From the considerable variety of business cards available in my wallet, I selected the one I deemed most suitable. It bore my correct name—as indeed most of them did—in raised gilt script. There was nothing else on the card—no address, no phone numbers—except for a title, Executive Vice-President N.A., and the name of my company, Lloyd's of London. The card was designed to create the unmistakable impression that it was extremely unlikely I would ever need or desire any further communion with whomever it might be given to. Therefore should I deign to append an address or phone number, it would practically qualify as a collector's item. People invariably found the card to be reassuring in the extreme. The paper stock was as thick as a credit card and heavily textured. It was far and away my favorite.

Entering the huge baroque cavern was a lot like finding yourself on the set of a big-budget fantasy film. The three-story lobby featured a cascading falls surrounded by a circular pool. Handy for laundering money, I presumed.

I stayed in character, ignoring all the sweet young things somehow always to be found in the front lines, and walked confidently past a number of increasingly larger desks. I handed my card mutely to a gimlet-eyed man whose desk plate proclaimed him to be assistant manager. It was the best I could manage without actually opening doors. "I'm slightly late for an appointment with your Mr. Coburn," I told him brusquely, creating the impression it was somehow his fault. The "your Mr. Coburn" was a nice touch, too, I thought—making it perfectly clear he wasn't *my* Mr. Coburn.

He thought he was going to stall me, and even reached for a phone. But the card, my manner of introduction, and a frigid stare combined to jolt him to his feet and invite me to please follow him.

At the dead end of a long walnut-paneled corridor he opened a door with Coburn's name on it and stood aside to allow me to enter. He then closed it with each of us on opposite sides. During our safari he'd handed me back the card, which I appreciated because they're damn costly and I was running low.

It was immediately obvious why my guide hadn't felt it necessary to enter. Coburn's outer office was fully staffed by an exceedingly fit-looking man not much over thirty and of an impressive size. I was willing to give attractive odds there was some sort of handgun either upon his person, or at least within easy reach.

This one barely glanced at the card, said my name quietly into the intercom, then stood and led me through the final door behind him.

Ronald Coburn was properly distinguished looking, complete with silvery white hair where any remained, regular features still sharply chiseled, and an upright, almost military, bearing, though he was seated. Even his smile was carefully calculated—friendly but not effusive. There was a questioning look in his hunter's eyes. "You're not the regular Lloyd's representative we're used to seeing around here, Mr. Doyle." There were questions implicit in his rich baritone voice.

It was my cue to give the name of his regular rep and make with the explanations. It didn't necessarily mean he was suspicious; it was designed to put me on the defensive. Coburn would be a master at putting people on the defensive. But it was a game for two. "It's getting a bit late in the day for the usual pregame activities, Mr. Coburn. I'm certain we're both busy men with little time to waste on idle chatter, so let's dispense with it.

You may well decide what I'm about to ask of you is irregular. It isn't, but admittedly it's open to interpretation. I won't offend you by invoking confidentiality; I'll ask that you afford me the same consideration.

"Your bank currently handles the business accounts of the Kline family. Specifically, the father, Reuben, and daughter, Tina. My firm holds a very substantial policy on the daughter's film production company, Kaleidoscope Productions. Miss Kline is operating as both producer and director on her current film. What's even more irregular, all funding is entirely her own—she has no other financial backers. Or perhaps it would be more correct to say, the funding is her father's. Now then, it has come to our attention her father has recently become totally incapacitated due to stroke.

"To put it frankly, Mr. Coburn, we're more than a little concerned. It's estimated her current production will cost a minimum of another four million dollars to complete, edit, and distribute. Without meaning to impugn anyone, let me just say, when things begin going bad for a private production company such as this one, we oftentimes find ourselves faced with a very considerable claim. It's fairly incredible how much more common fires are on the set of bad movies than good ones, if you see what I mean.

"Earlier this afternoon, I spent several hours on Miss Kline's set out in Burbank. Quite honestly, I must tell you I was appalled. Admittedly I know nothing whatever about the film industry but if what she's doing out there ever makes it into a theater anywhere I'll be positively amazed. What I've seen has made me edgy—I smell trouble. According to her financial statement submitted at the time the policy was written she was on firm ground. But the production is way over budget now. She's also bogged down in some disastrous condominium project in San Diego County. And with her father's illness, well. . . . I leave it to you. Call it professional courtesy. I've come to you to ascertain the amount of ready cash your institution holds in the names of Reuben Kline, Tina Kline, and Kaleidoscope Productions, Inc."

Coburn had visibly relaxed during my lengthy discourse.

"This could have all been handled over the phone, Mr. Doyle. As their underwriter, you have every right to verify the financial statement you were given."

"And so we did, sir; but that was many months ago. Now the question arises of whether or not Miss Kline has access to her father's funds. We're able to roughly estimate the balance remaining in her corporate account, but it would seem she lives . . . ah, let us say life in the fast lane. So we wonder about that, too."

"Nothing more satisfying than putting to rest the fears of a worried man," he told me expansively. Reaching for a gold phone, he began requesting facts and making swift and precise notes on a memo pad. After two or three minutes, he covered the mouthpiece and asked: "I presume you have no interest in the account of Marsha Kline?"

It caught me completely off guard. "Marsha?" I heard myself mumbling stupidly.

"Reuben's older daughter." Taking my confused silence for a negative response, he returned his full attention to the phone.

Marsha! Not marsh—Marsha! Reuben Kline had through an incredible effort of will spoken the name of his elder daughter—twice! I wondered why.

"This should set your mind at ease," Coburn interrupted my thoughts. "Reuben Kline's accounts total one hundred and twelve thousand dollars—rather less than I would have thought—but then no doubt Tina drew against them heavily at one time, and there wouldn't be much point in replacing funds in his accounts now. I'm certain he had at least half a dozen of our jumbo CD's—a minimum of a hundred thousand each—at one time last year. I can find all that out if you like but I doubt you'll care. Ancient history. By the way, Tina does have every legal right to comingle her father's funds. We have a certified power of attorney on file granting her that right without reservation.

"Now here's the good news. Tina's accounts total four hundred and seventy-eight thousand and change. And Kaleidoscope currently shows seven million, eight hundred thousand, plus."

"Far better than we had reason to believe," I managed, struggling to climb back into character. My mind wanted to be left alone in a quiet place to explore the ramifications of another daughter named Marsha, if indeed there were any. "But it's still going to be a near thing if she continues to suffer production delays and that construction deal in San Diego goes sour."

"I told you I'd put your mind at ease," Coburn reminded me cockily. "Ms. Kline is currently averaging weekly deposits of well in excess of one hundred and fifty thousand dollars in the Kaleidoscope account. It's up from four million only four months ago, in fact, so that's obviously a very conservative figure. Best of all, that's net increase—allowing for all the expenses of current production costs. Smile, Mr. Doyle; Lloyd's is safe as houses on this one."

"But I don't understand," I said honestly. "Where could all that money be coming from? Do your records show that?"

"Indeed they do, and I anticipated your request for that information as well," he smiled smugly. "Apparently the deposits are from another production company—Star Child, Inc.—which I believe was the corporate structure Marsha Kline formed to produce an earlier film. I seem to recall it won some award or other. Don't ask me the title, but it must be quite a hit. It's the custom among independent film producers to form a separate subchapter S corporation to house each project they become involved in. In that way, one loser can't pull down another, more profitable venture. So Star Child, Inc. is pouring venture capital into Kaleidoscope at quite a prodigious rate; obviously to take full advantage of the reinvestment credit and avoid paying taxes on the profits of the first film. A legitimate and very businesslike way of conducting one's affairs in this town," he added happily. I could understand his proprietary attitude; what banker wouldn't be tickled to have a client like Tina?

I unfolded myself, clasping Coburn's hand warmly. "You're as good as your word—my mind is indeed at ease," I lied through my teeth. He joined me in a stroll all the way down the hall, attempting to make small talk, but I just couldn't muster. My mind was spinning with possibilities. I'd even neglected to retrieve my phony Lloyd's card from his desk when he wasn't looking. I always made a point of that. It's not that I'm cheap; it's just that when you're leaving the scene of a felony it's considered bad form to leave physical evidence lying around.

CHAPTER 12

*I*t was still a few minutes shy of seven when I pulled to a stop beside the guard kiosk at the entrance to the studio. Perry had kept his word. The new man quickly checked his clipboard and waved me through. I reluctantly parked the Mercedes exactly where I'd found it, in the full knowledge my own car would feel about as responsive as a Sherman tank for a long time to come.

My mind had not stopped spinning from the time I left Rueben Kline's bedside, trying to put the pieces together. And after my visit to the bank, it was all I could do to remember to stop and start the car at intersections. In fact, I was so at sea I had to stroll slowly around the lot another twenty minutes before going inside. My immediate problem was figuring out how to play it with Tina and her space cadets. A call to Win would have been a blessing, and one was long overdue, but there didn't appear to be any pay phones along the deserted alleys surrounding Soundstage 4, the site of my acting debut. My circumnavigation of the entire area complete, I shrugged off my misgivings, sighed, and entered never-never land.

The quiet cushion of night stopped at the door; I entered a strident world of too much light and sound. The number of people had increased, and the original group seemed intact, but it was tough to be certain. I had pegged them mainly by their costumes, which they no longer wore. Too bad—I was going to miss Lady Godiva.

There was a long trestle table loaded with deli items more or less in the center of the room. Having a strong sense of priorities, I headed directly for it. I've always found that breaking and entering and fraud give one an incredible appetite, for some reason.

Tina was not in sight. Earlier I would have found that disappointing, but now it was a relief. Every fact so far spelled Tina up to her neck in one of the slickest scams I'd ever heard of; but every instinct in my body screamed otherwise. Either she was an innocent pawn, or I should burn my license and apply for the night manager's job at McDonald's.

I piled a plate with an interesting selection of munchies, found an empty folding chair, and proceeded to stoke my empty hold while observing the beautiful people at play. Everyone seemed to be talking and no one listening. Waves of music erupted from speakers near the ceiling all around the room like barrages of assault artillery. Even accounting for the high decibel count, everyone seemed far too loud, too animated. They all had a brittle, frenzied air about them. It was like being a nondrinker at a drunken party. At first I chalked it up to the well-stocked bar that formed the top of the T at one end of the deli table. My presence certainly wasn't attracting any interest, in sharp contrast to my reception earlier in the day. Maybe they'd seen the day's rushes and I stunk. Everyone seemed so damned intense, so frightfully earnest; when you got close enough, you fully expected to find them debating the meaning of life. On the contrary, I heard nothing more significant under discussion than automobiles, hair stylists, and tax shelters.

There is a popular concept, bred by TV mysteries, that all you have to do is circulate in a party crowd and information will gravitate your way like iron filings to a magnet. It is, alas, far from true. I could have spent the next three hours making nice with everyone and my chances of hearing one single item of the slightest interest would have been all but nil. You have to ask questions—very specific questions. And the trouble with questions is they inevitably tell the listener more than you would like them to know, but there's no help for it.

Strictly as protective coloration, I crossed over to the bar, filled a tumbler with ice, and poured tonic over it with a few liberal squeezes of lime juice to make the color right. If asked, I was drinking vodka tonics, but insisted on making my own. Sign of the serious drinker. Successful mingling requires a full glass in hand. The nondrinker is taken as an indictment and resented mightily.

And so I became a social animal, holding my glass as if it were a badge of honor, grinning gaily. I pulled up short in front of the Lady Godiva girl—you see, I had noticed her face—and effectively cut her out of the herd. "Hi, again; my name's Matt—remember? I thought you were great this afternoon."

She nodded in what I took to be complete agreement. "I'm B.B. You were good, too. I mean you had, like, this heavy presence, you know?"

Up close, I noted the rapidly shifting eyes and almost breathless animation. Her speech was clear, but too fast, a little like a 33 record being played at 45 speed. It wasn't typical of the booze reaction—in fact, it was only then I realized she didn't even have a glass in her hand. "Truth to tell, B.B., I was scared stiff. And something bothers me. Today was just a lark, a favor to Tina; I won't be in any other scenes. Won't that cause problems in continuity? I mean—here this character in a monk's robe pops up in the middle of the film, then disappears forever."

B.B. shook her head. "That's an example of the rigid films of the past. We're avoiding all those old compulsions like story line, continuity, all that shit. It's long since time films moved beyond that. Up until now, movies have been like portrait painters; some great ones, sure, like Rembrandt, but along came the Impressionists and blew them right out of the water. Now they fight for a street corner at Disneyland—paint your portrait for ten bucks! We're going to do the same to films."

She'd recited it like a kid in catechism class. "All over my head, B.B., but the Kline sisters must be doing something right. I hear Tina's sister's last film is grossing a bundle."

B.B. gave me a funny, vacant look. "Who the hell told you that? I heard it was enough to send a diabetic right into a coma. I've never seen it, but neither has anybody else—it was never released. Tina says her sister arranged to have it shown right here at UCLA; the students all walked out laughing. It was supposedly sort of a combination "Leave It to Beaver" and "Ozzie and Harriet." That ought to be enough to gag any goat. Can you—"

Suddenly, there was a large obstruction between us. The mad-looking pair of eyes barely a foot from mine belonged to the barbarian who'd flubbed his lines that afternoon. Or did he emerge as the star of the scene? Who knows?

"Come here, B.B.," he demanded, never taking those insane eyes from mine. "Let's go—Now!" He spun away angrily, placed a meaty hand on her back, and propelled her toward the door in the corner where I'd noted a fair amount of traffic coming and going.

Jealous lover, I concluded, scanning for my next target. During the next half hour I piled up mostly negatives—including the fact that no one I talked with had ever met Tina's sister, Marsha. I did find they were an incredibly close-knit little repertory group—including the technicians—and were intensely loyal to Tina. Yet surprisingly, they didn't evidence all that much enthusiasm for the film. Many were openly disinterested. I added another question to my form, and in talking to eight, failed to find one with any meaningful credits in any phase of the theater arts.

"Here, Matt; let me buy you a drink."

I about-faced to find Tina holding out a drink. It was a vodka tonic, with a thin slice of lime split over the rim. She still made every other woman in the room an ugly duckling by comparison but the eyes were different. I couldn't put my finger on it; she blinked and it was gone.

"Better take it; it's the only salary you'll get for your performance today. I can't give you a dime unless you join the Screen Actor's Guild."

My own glass of tonic was long gone. I hadn't bothered replacing it because fewer than half the guests were drinking. There was no way I could gracefully refuse. "Thanks! I figure, on the basis of the laborer being worthy of his hire, I'm being overpaid. Free supper, plus drinks." I took the glass and pretended to survey the crowd as I clinked the ice against my teeth. I was very careful not to accept any of the drink into my mouth. "You run a happy ship," I told her as I turned back around. "I was hoping Marsha'd be here tonight—I'd love to meet her."

It was completely off the cuff. Tina stiffened as if I'd struck her a blow. "No, you wouldn't. My sister's a spoiled brat. With both Mom and Dad gone, there was no one left to hold her hand and so she split. Last I heard of her, she was wandering around Europe somewhere, ruining the scenery over there for a change."

It was the first thing I'd ever heard her say with real emotion. It certainly wasn't love; if it was sibling rivalry it was the most acute case on the books. When I was a kid we had a cat who used to watch me the same way Tina was looking at me now. We had to get rid of the cat because the neighbors complained it killed off every songbird within a quarter mile. We didn't miss it.

"How long does the party last? Don't let me rush you but if it's going to be late I should start thinking about a cab. My car's still at your house, and I have to get back to La Jolla tonight."

"Of course," she assured me, once again the amiable Venus. "Just drink up and have some fun. I can wrap things up here in about half an hour. This is anything but a formal party—just our usual way of unwinding after a long day at the office. What I'm trying to achieve demands a special ambience, and I think it's coming through in the film."

She spun around and disappeared through the door in the corner, where it seemed to me nearly everyone in the room had gone at one time or another during the course of the evening. I was suddenly fascinated with that door, but not with the barbarian

who stood guard beside it. I sauntered over to the bar and
promptly ditched Tina's drink into the half-melted ice bucket,
substituting one of my own formula. I looked up to find the barbarian positively glaring at me from clear across the room. It was
obvious he'd watched me dispose of the drink, and apparently the
act displeased him a great deal. I wondered why. Was he hoping
I'd get a little looped, so the odds would be more favorable when
he called me out? It didn't make much sense, but there's supposed to be one in every crowd, and maybe he was it. He certainly looked the part.

Forty-five minutes later I was still no wiser, when Tina reap-
peared, saying her good-byes all around. Just as we hit the outside door she snapped her fingers, explaining she had some vital
instructions to give the camera crew and to please go out and wait
for her in the car. When I said I'd prefer to wait right where I was
she pleaded for me to go out and start the car for her. She explained she always liked to warm the engine at least five minutes
after it had been sitting all day.

I went through the charade of asking for the keys; she told
me I'd find them in the ashtray. If she was aware I'd driven her
car all afternoon she was a better actress than anyone in the
room—not that it was much of a compliment. I stepped outside
and gulped my first breath of fresh air in hours, thoroughly relieved to be free of the din inside.

I used the time to plan the coming half-hour drive. Tina was
a puzzlement. I savored the dark vacuum of the night to try and
marshal my thoughts.

Silence was indeed golden, right up until the time it was
broken by a sharp "snick" sound—the same sound was repeated
half a second later. My body reacted long before my brain finished processing and identifying the unique and unmistakable
sound of the hammers being pulled back on a double-barreled
shotgun.

"This is better than you deserve, you son-of-a-bitching
narc!"

For a microsecond, I'd considered the safety of the door behind me. It would have been a fatal error. Instead, I forced myself to stand facing the deadly sounds, faked a motion toward the door, then dove away from it, rolling as hard and fast as if my clothes were on fire. The monstrous blast of the gun filled the concrete valley between the buildings, echoing and reechoing. He was no more than thirty or forty feet away, giving the pellets—or whatever load he was using—something on the order of a two-foot pattern. He wouldn't have to be much of a marksman to make the second barrel count. I'd suckered him on the first one; the pellets had scoured the metal door nearly free of paint in the middle, and there were tracks in the concrete wall beyond. This much was clear, under the narrow cone of the light mounted directly over the door. But he was tracking me nicely now, and I was caught lying in the middle of an empty street.

He was a shadow figure in semidarkness midway between the totally inadequate mercury vapor lights at each intersection. It wasn't the time or place for anything fancy—it was survival time. My revolver had been drawn and at the ready before I'd hit the ground. No conscious thought had been required—it was pure reflex, a mindset well established years ago. I fired at the darkest section of the ghostly image. I didn't stop until I got results.

Concurrent with my second shot, the palpable *blam* of the other barrel sent a shock wave over me. The assault on my eardrums was brutal, but the impact of being at the wrong end of a discharging twelve-gauge was truly awesome. I actually heard the pellets passing overhead. It was impossible for me to tell whether my first bullet caused him to pull high or he was just incredibly inept. Either way, it had been a very close thing.

At least he was down. I scrambled to my feet and went to him fast, in case he was still in shape to reload. There was no hurry. One of the first two shots had knocked him down with a hit high on the right shoulder. It had to have been the third and final bullet, because of the angle, that caught him under the jaw and exited high on the back of the head. I wished to hell I'd settled for two shots, but wishing wasn't going to do either of us much good.

It was the barbarian, of course. Funny, I'd never even bothered to ask his name or a single thing about him. I hadn't considered him very important.

It seemed incredibly strange, standing there in the street after a gun battle—alone—with dozens of people less than forty yards away. Gay, happy people, dining, drinking, and laughing within rock-throwing distance of the most brutal activity of which man is capable. Though I knew soundstages were built to be soundproof, it still struck me as bizarre.

The feeling dissipated when I heard the whine of a golf cart coming down the street. It was a rent-a-cop. It took a bit of convincing to get him to leave a confessed armed killer at the scene while he went back to his post and called it in. I offered to swap jobs with him when he balked, but that didn't appeal either. A look at my private investigator's license helped but he couldn't quite shake the notion the world would be a better place if I were to hand my gun over to him until the proper authorities arrived.

Patiently, I pulled out my wallet again and showed him my permit to carry, then asked him whether he would care to stand there unarmed after what I'd just been through. He finally got the message and left.

I glared down at the husk of the barbarian, cursing softly. I was about to meet a whole new group of people, thanks to him— LAPD Homicide, and probably an assistant D.A. or two. It was certainly my day to be a social gadfly.

It could have been a lot worse. In the past it often has been. LAPD has the reputation of being the most efficient and elite department of any major city in the country. Based on my experiences that night it might even be true. Or maybe I just got lucky and drew the varsity squad.

The first black and white on the scene relieved me of my piece and jailed me in the back seat, but I didn't hold it against them for an instant. Standard operating procedure. At least the scenario was self-explanatory—though it would have been nice to have had a witness or two.

It wasn't too long after midnight when all the sound and fury finally died. The dear little computers admitted my existence, identity, licenses, no doubt in that precise order. Ever notice how relieved and even grateful we are when the machines recognize us? Do you worry that some day they won't? I was sitting opposite Chief Inspector Fogarty, deputy head of Homicide, nursing what had to be the world's worst cup of coffee. We were both winding down, as comfortable with each other as a public cop and a private cop can ever be. My statement was signed and the foremost concern on my mind was getting to Newport, retrieving my car, and finding my way to my bed.

"You must ask very good questions, Doyle," Fogarty stated out of the blue. He was a whip-thin man of about fifty who'd been dark all of his life, but was now developing a head of lush, light gray hair. His eyebrows hadn't gotten the word yet, and he could easily have dyed the crop and dropped ten years, but he wasn't the type. His quick, clever eyes were those of a man who could never be bothered with such trivial nonsense.

"How do you mean?"

"You figure it. You say all you set out to do was double check the connection between this Tina Kline and a builder named Roscoe Blaise, who employed the woman your buddy is accused of murdering. That takes maybe five minutes if you talk real slow—which you don't. But you spent more than half a day at it, and end up rattling somebody's cage to the point where they wanted you dead. How about telling me what some of those questions were?"

"You're trying to make too much of it, Inspector. The questions were innocuous; your own people must have found that out when they questioned the lot. My working premise was maybe Blaise had run into money troubles and was using the building site as a depot for a drug scam. If his partner—Tina Kline—was short of funds too, it would shore up the theory nicely. Of course she didn't necessarily have to be a party to it but it would fit better. Unfortunately it didn't hold up at either end. As you know, I had the San Diego police comb the condo site and they found it clean. And Tina Kline enjoys an embarrassment of riches, so it figures to be exactly what it smells like. Mr. . . . sorry, what was his name again?"

"Sidney Potter."

"Sidney is a doper. He sees me hanging around, pumping people, though I never said a word to him. Say he's not just a user—he's a distributor. He's swinging through his paranoid phase, so whatever I do or don't do feeds his conviction that I'm out to get him. He may well have seen my gun when I was getting in or out of my robe for the filming. And he's only the most recent in a long list of people who took me for a cop, which I guess I sort of am. Maybe it's just that simple."

"Could be," Fogarty replied, adding: "It's also possible the sun will rise in the west tomorrow," letting me know how impressed he was with my logic. Following another contemplative pull at his mug of coffee, he said: "There's that embarrassing little matter of Continental Bank."

I'd had an afternoon to account for. The only way to hold out on an expert is to tell most of the truth exactly, always including something mildly incriminating. I'd had no choice but to come clean about my call on Coburn at the bank. It had served to reinforce my story about only being concerned with Tina's finances. Without it, Fogarty wouldn't have bought the total package for a bent nickel. Of course, he wasn't anyway, but at least I had him regarding me as a victim of something neither of us understood. He was too clever by half—I liked him.

"There is that," I admitted. "All I can say is I was in a hurry and didn't ask for anything that isn't part of the public record, or at least available to everyone from the IRS to the credit card companies. Not much of a crime when you think about it, is it? Kind of thing people like skip tracers do every day."

"The Lloyd's people might think otherwise."

"Yeah, being English and all, they might at that. Could cause problems if someone were to mention it to them." I wasn't all that worried. Fogarty was nothing if not a pro. A Homicide pro. It was clear he couldn't care less about such a petty peccadillo, unless it somehow tied in with a murder investigation. He was only thinking of using it on me like a can opener, but he was having a tough time finding a starting point.

He stared at me unblinking for a full ten count, a very disconcerting habit of his. I imagined it had served him well over the years. "You absolutely certain you have nothing more to add to your statement? Say some small detail that just this second occurred to you?"

I gave the question the attention it deserved, shook my head, and told him, "I'm sure." It's essential to keep your answers brief while lying. The trouble was, Fogarty knew that as well as I did.

He shrugged his shoulders and sighed. "You're not dumb enough to buy it, Doyle."

"I don't like it any better than you do. I just don't have anything better—not yet."

He nodded. "Maybe! If it's so, I hope you get something better before it's too late. Go home. But you owe me, Mr. Lloyd's vice-president. If you don't keep in touch—I will. It would be simple to put Mr. Sid Potter away in the 'closed' files, but I've never had much success playing it that way. You were set up— we both know it. Part of the reason lies within my jurisdiction. Now I don't share the popular view around the department concerning private ops. A man's either worth a good goddamn or he isn't, regardless of where he draws his pay. I propose a fair exchange: Anything I find worth telling will get passed on to you, but heaven help you if you don't reciprocate."

I stood up and shook his hand. "You can count on it," I told him, meaning it. Of course, the pledge wasn't retroactive. "Where's the nearest place to snag a cab this time of night, Inspector? My car is still parked in front of Tina Kline's place way down on Lido Isle in Newport."

Fogarty had unbent his spare frame to its full height of about six three, but suddenly he froze. Those penetrating dark eyes stared at the wall for several seconds. "I think maybe you've got a ride," he muttered softly. Snatching his phone, he asked the switchboard to get him the Orange County Bomb Squad. While he was waiting to be put through, he asked me for the address, and a description of my car. I gave him both numbly. Someone came on the line and he told them to proceed, but to wait with their report until we arrived, regardless of the outcome.

Probably it would have occurred to me, too, during my trip south. I'd like to think it would have—in fact I have to think it would have. It's true Fogarty thought of it right off the bat, but no one had just attempted to turn him into mincemeat with a pair of blasts from a twelve-gauge shotgun either. Such an experience has a tendency to preoccupy the mind for a while.

The chief inspector rated a car and driver regardless of the hour, so we both sat in the back. Perhaps because he had thought of it first I resented the fact that he was taking it entirely for granted the bomb squad would find something.

"After all," I said, "these things aren't available at the local Safeway—not yet anyway. It takes time to devise those kinds of goodies."

"What devise? Two sticks of dynamite, a detonator cap, and a few inches of number twelve wire—*boom*—you're in business. Or, in your case, out of business. And let's not forget one of your prime suspects is a contractor with easy access to all sorts of explosives. Last time you visited there you were shot by one of his employees—right? For Christ's sake, Doyle; maybe you're not as quick as I first thought. Now I want you to tell me everyone who could have known where the car was parked for the last thirteen hours."

"Everybody and nobody. I'm not trying to be mysterious or philosophical. Anyone and everyone at Soundstage 4 knew I rode in with Tina. Some or all of them might know her home address. Tina's the only one who's for certain."

"You didn't ask anyone else about a lift? Ask someone if they were headed south? Or lived around Newport?"

"Definitely not; I'd expected to ride back with Tina all along. And I wanted more time with her."

"I don't blame you. What about someone else at her place? You see anybody there?"

Though I'd known it was coming, it rocked me. Fogarty was like a hound with a first-class nose, constantly worrying around until he picked up the scent his instincts told him was there. But I still considered Big Stump prior knowledge. Having successfully rationalized the verbal semantics in my mind, I lied with a reasonably clear conscience. "No one; I met her outside. She was leaving as I arrived. Doesn't mean no one saw me. Must be some sort of staff, since her father is supposed to be an invalid." I realized I was expounding too much. Common mistake of the liar. Great tendency to keep talking, embellishing the fib. Eventually you end up tripping over your own tongue.

That was about as far as we could go with that line of questioning. Fogarty seemed fascinated with the notion of my working for Carter Winfield, asking endless questions about Win and our work methods. Many of my answers made him laugh, and I was the first to admit when it came to procedures we were laughable. I even invited him to stop in next time he was in San Diego. I figured it would do Win a world of good to see that all homicide inspectors weren't apes.

As if on cue, Fogarty said: "We got quite an earful on you from one of my counterparts in San Diego—an Inspector Dixon. I got the impression he didn't like you."

"He has his reasons. My boss and he are like oil and water. Besides, Dixon doesn't share your live and let live attitude towards private ops."

"Is it true he used to be in criminal lab work? I heard he was damn good at it, too, but on the phone he sounds as if he's got a couple of loose bolts." Fogarty posed the question reluctantly, as if Dixon's shortcomings reflected on all of his peers. In a way, I guess they did.

"Only when my name—or Win's—is mentioned. We've gone around him a few too many times and handed people over to the D.A. or whoever would make Dixon look the worst. It all started when he tried to stop Win from getting his investigator's license—claimed he was too old. Since then, it's turned into a vendetta at times. But Dixon's as good as any, and better than most."

My response seemed to satisfy Fogarty. It was a small price to pay for his consideration. And there'd been times I'd even thought it might be true. But not lately.

As we passed over the short bridge to Lido Isle we could see the area around my car was daylight bright. We pulled up behind a generator van with its motor running quietly inside a sound shield box, supplying current for the half-dozen spotlights encircling my tired-looking old Chevy. Fogarty and I hit the street together from opposite sides.

A curly-haired young man in a light green jumpsuit and flack jacket stepped forward to meet us. "Sergeant Jensen, sir." He hesitated, unsure of which of us was official.

Fogarty took him off the hook by introducing himself, then indicating me. "This is Matt Doyle—the poor schmuck who couldn't wait to jump in and drive that car home," he told Jensen by way of identification.

"It's just as well he didn't, sir. It's a rudimentary device: three sticks of quite fresh dynamite—detonator caps on two, the second being a backup on the off chance the first failed. It wouldn't have. We checked; they were both good. Standard installation: spliced into the hot wire from the ignition switch." Jensen looked at me sympathetically. "Put it this way, Mr. Doyle. Ninety-five percent chance it would have killed you outright. The other five percent you don't even want to think about."

I knew the look. He was thinking he wasn't going to be there the next time, but I would. And we all knew there figured to be a next time. Twice in one day indicated a certain air of determination on someone's part. There were signs of a definite trend.

"You've swept the vehicle?" Fogarty asked. "You're sure the dynamite wasn't just the decoy for a more sophisticated device, well concealed somewhere else?"

"Of course!" Jensen's reply held the faintest trace of contempt and the word *sir* was conspicuous for its absence.

Fogarty grinned in acceptance of the rebuke. "Sorry—stupid of me. I'm grateful for your splendid cooperation and I'm certain Mr. Doyle is as well. I'll have a chat with your division chief in the morning. Thank you, Jensen."

I tossed in some sincere thanks of my own, pumping the kid's hand until I realized he was grimacing in pain. As the squad of three men from Orange County stowed their gear, and the street lamps resumed the task of bathing the street in soft light, Fogarty told me: "Doyle, you are going to put a tax hike on the upcoming ballot for sure. Do you realize you've got the police of three counties working on this case for you? San Diego, Los Angeles, and tomorrow there'll be Orange County cops walking this street, questioning everybody for any sign of activity anywhere near this car. Boy, you're a menace. Where are you going to strike next? Riverside?"

"No," I assured him sleepily, "home."

The likeable inspector gave me a strange look. "You do that, Doyle—you go home. Then give some real serious consideration to staying there. I don't know what's going on here, but there's nothing wrong with my instincts. They're top notch—saved my ass too many times to count. And right now I'm scared standing here next to you, scared damn near shitless I might get caught in the fallout."

There was nothing more to say. I clamped him on the shoulder, squeezed hard for thanks, and climbed into my now alien-feeling car. I was unable to keep from tightening my jaw when I turned the key in the ignition.

CHAPTER 13

I slept until noon, not nearly as self-indulgent as it sounds, since it was 5 A.M. when my ear finally touched a pillow. Lunch was a hit-and-run affair. Louis just lays out a spread and it's strictly do it yourself. Frequently, it's the only meal of the day that's edible. Even he can't screw up cottage cheese, fresh fruit, and sandwich supplies. By one o'clock, I was wide awake and sitting where I belonged.

Win was also seated where he belonged. After a distant greeting, he waited in what he perceives as a patient manner. I was trying to reorganize my muddled maze of thoughts; it promised to be one of my more challenging chores of reporting. "Whenever you're ready," he finally growled sarcastically.

"I'm ready! Let's see whether you are." I took a deep breath and plunged right in. I'd considered myself a pretty fair report man when I'd come to work for Win some years earlier, but I'd been nowhere near the standard he demanded. He'd turned me into a human tape recorder, only better, because I recorded expressions, body language, and a host of other nuances and observations no machine could touch. I'd learned to rate my performance by the number of times he interrupted—stopping me for clarification of a point or to request a repeat. I guess I was on my stride that day because there was a host of interruptions. The whole report—given chronologically—required nearly two full hours. When I finished we just stared at each other in utter silence. Both of us were seeing the same damn thing—a very unhappy man.

Win finally broke the silence. "First: I ask that you overlook—if not forgive—my truculence earlier. In my defense I can only quote, 'They also serve who only stand and wait.' Yesterday was a difficult one for me, spent anticipating your return or, at the very least, a phone call. Second: It would seem you have pledged our cooperation to this Chief Inspector Fogarty. Am I to take it you made this alliance in good faith? Under no coercion?"

"Right! As stated."

He got a slightly pained look. "Very well; then we are honor bound by it. Third: You failed to mention suffering any damage during your mortal exchange with Mr. Potter. Bearing in mind your sometimes excessive pride, I am compelled to ask whether you are indeed 100 percent fit."

"Yes, no damage, except one hell of a fine new suit is ready for Louis's ragbag. Actually, for a guy someone tried to kill twice in one day I'm pretty frisky."

"Three times," he corrected me softly.

"I only count two."

"You're mistaken; the actual count is three, I assure you. Had you not been utterly beguiled by this siren, you would have seen it too. I refer of course to the drink—the vodka tonic—offered you by Tina Kline. If you'd imbibed of it, there would have been no need for Mr. Potter to lay in ambush for you. Recall his inappropriate look of anger when he observed you disposing of the lethal drink untouched. Now you know the significance of that baleful expression. I have never been so deeply concerned, Matt. Between Dirk's incarceration and your normally acute powers of perception in abeyance, I fear the worst."

"What powers of perception in abeyance? If you're dissatisfied with my conduct yesterday, I'd sure like to know where you think I went wrong."

"On the contrary, you rode the winds of chance to their apogee; I commend you for the veritable wealth of data you've accumulated. Don't misunderstand! I am shaken by the fact—but for sheer happenstance concerning the drink, and the intervention of another concerning the bomb—you'd have been dead by now. Little wonder the implications strike me as extremely grim."

"Nuts! You know damn well I'd never drink anything given to me by a suspect, and during a case everybody is a suspect. Never have and never will. So much for 'sheer happenstance.' It was good procedure paying off, is what it was. As for the car bomb, believe me when I tell you I thought that one through very candidly all the way home from Newport this morning. I'm absolutely certain that by the time I'd ridden in a cab all the way from Fogarty's office in LA to my car, there is no way in hell I'd have just jumped in and turned the key. It's a fact! Nonnegotiable."

"How would you have proceeded?"

"Easy! I've done it before. I'd have gotten my flashlight from the glove compartment and given the car a very thorough check—believe me. And the first place I'd have looked was right where the bomb was stashed."

"Very well, I believe you. Knowing your capabilities as I do, I have no reason to doubt it. But what if a slightly different device were employed? One that ignited upon opening the driver's door? Or say the bomb was triggered when the glove box was opened? Or a pressure-activated mechanism set off by your weight upon the seat?"

"Then I'd be dead," I acknowledged simply. "We can play 'what if' until hell freezes; the point is I came through intact, and that includes whatever faculties I began with."

Win attempted a smile, but it was a poor effort. "Your point is well taken, Matt; unfortunately, so is mine. They underestimated you. They elected to act within a very brief time frame which didn't allow for more sophisticated methods. Two mistakes which they are unlikely to make again. Don't you grasp the depth of our dilemma? The police of three counties are involved but only in small, unrelated aspects of the case. They fear us—not the police. And rightfully so. They are totally committed to our destruction; we would be dolts not to accept the fact."

I'd never seen the old man in such a state. "So what do you suggest?"

He paused only a few moments before issuing new orders. "Have everyone meet here in the office in one half hour. I need that much time to digest the full implications of your astounding report."

He was staring into space when I left to spread the word. "Everyone" consisted of Louis from the kitchen and Randy from his lab in the basement. As a platoon, we were a little on the light side. Both men were brimming over with questions about the unprecedented gathering but I assured them I wasn't the one with the answers.

Left with twenty minutes to kill, I went outside and made a perimeter check around the house. If asked before I would have said the big, old Spanish-style barn of a house was pretty secure. Now I saw it in a different light. The two-foot-thick walls gave the illusion of invulnerability, but unfortunately no one was likely to try kicking in the walls. I began counting the ways it would be easy to gain access and gave it up in disgust when I reached a dozen. It was just another old house after all, far from the inviolate fort we'd liked to imagine. Before my circuit was even complete I had to resist an irrational urge to rush back inside. I had that funny, prickly feeling along my spine you're said to experience when someone's watching you intently. I shrugged and chalked it up to frayed nerves. But I still had it.

Win formally invited everyone to be seated. We all did, each after our own fashion. Randy sat well back, yet hunched forward—elbows on knees—peering owlishly at Win through those quarter-inch-thick glasses of his. Louis sat primly upright—decidedly ill at ease—occupying only the leading edge of his chair.

I slouched into mine, pulled out my middle desk drawer, and used it for a footrest. It occurred to me that any psychologist worth his salt, and there must be a few, could do a pretty fair workup on each of us with nothing more to go on.

Win didn't waste time on preliminaries. "This house and everyone in it is now under a state of siege. You are each entitled to know the circumstances, therefore I'll answer any questions you may have later, time permitting. As of now the following directives are in effect: No one is to leave this house for any reason. Understand me—I mean the *house*—not the grounds. No deliveries of any kind will be accepted—there will be no exceptions. I note your distress, Louis; I appreciate this stricture inconveniences you more than the rest of us. Nonetheless it is absolutely essential. I regret the need to distress you, but it's only fair to advise you no fewer than three serious attempts were made on Matt's life yesterday. This is all connected to Dirk's unfortunate predicament, as you've probably surmised. There is every reason to suppose additional acts of violence are even now being devised against all of us. Matt will see the two of you are armed. I realize neither of you has the slightest expertise with firearms, but carry them at all times anyway. You can't be forced to use them, but they may serve as a deterrent, or at the very least, an effective alarm.

"I must now proceed to serve a generous portion of crow—and I will be dining alone, gentlemen. I've never thought myself a fool, but surely I've been living in a fool's paradise. This house is all but defenseless. Considering the line of work we're engaged in, this cruel fact is utterly indefensible. Unlike our neighbors—suddenly so distressingly far away—we have no barred windows, no security system whatever. I'm humiliated. In my arrogance I have placed each of you in imminent danger. I do not beg your forgiveness—it is unforgivable—but I ask your forbearance until this siege is lifted."

He seemed to be finished eating crow, so I fished into my bottom right drawer and came up with weapons for the troops. Louis got the little Izuzu .25 calibre. It was a cheap imitation

Berretta made in Spain. It fired anywhere over about a twenty-degree arc but it was small and flat and Louis couldn't hurt himself too much with it. I checked to make certain the clip was full and the safety on. After showing Louis how to release the safety I offered it to him. He accepted it between thumb and forefinger, the way I'd seen him handle things that got left in the refrigerator too long. He gazed at it in utter incomprehension, then dropped it in a pants pocket. I couldn't help glancing over at Win; he was lifting his eyes to heaven in supplication. I suppose he was praying Louis didn't hurt either himself or any of the rest of us. I know I was.

Randy got the old Webbley Colt—a damn fine gun, except for its size. Again I checked. The next chamber in line was empty, the only real safety you've got on a revolver. I explained this to Randy, and showed him how to cock it. He just stared at the big pistol in horror. When I handed it to him, he took it with two pudgy hands and seemed at a complete loss where to go from there. He finally settled for holding it in his lap as if it were a bouquet of flowers. I almost asked Win whether I shouldn't issue extra rounds, but decided to lay off gigging him for the duration. He was already too miserable for words—it wouldn't have been any fun. He's often told me I have a perverse mind, and I guess maybe I have. The sight of those two armed and primed to repel invaders gave me the giggles. Win, on the other hand, looked as if he wanted to bawl.

"That will be all," Win told them briskly. "Return to whatever duties you were engaged in. Louis, you will have some calls to make, canceling whatever deliveries are due. Give some expedient excuse. Randy, I'd like you to give some thought to an alarm—rudimentary to be sure. It must be something which may be implemented by tonight. I realize we haven't time to accomplish much but concoct anything, if only some tin cans hung from a string."

"I think I can do better than that," Randy assured him. The troops got to their feet and headed for the door. Randy looked like an altar boy in his white lab jacket, holding the Webbley in front of his belly like a chalice. My giggles came back.

"Randy," Win called at his retreating back, "is my watch repaired yet?"

"Almost! If you need it I can finish it within a couple of hours. What have you decided about the timing?"

"Ten seconds will suffice, I should imagine," Win replied thoughtfully. "Does that present any particular problems?"

"Not really; I'll have it late this afternoon."

After the exit of the palace guard, I was left to my own devices for several minutes. My devices consisted of cleaning my nails and glancing at Win to keep up with the latest assortment of furrows developing on his normally unruffled face.

"Matt, is it necessary for me to explain why we must face this situation as best we can? Why we haven't the option of summoning aid?"

"Not to me it isn't. I thought one of the others might bring it up. I've been all through it just as I imagine you have. It's no use. Either we wouldn't get the help we need, and we'd be a laughingstock, or we would get it and we'd only blow the investigation. And we'd still be a laughingstock."

"Exactly!" Win growled with some of his old fire. "Now, attend me, please; we have a great many tasks to accomplish." I resented the way he made it sound as if I were the one holding up the works but it was a good sign. "Taken in order of urgency, the first is to call your young lady who sold you your boat, Miss Dana Marsh, and send her away somewhere—anywhere—immediately."

"Two things: Dana is not my young lady, or anybody's. And sending her somewhere she doesn't want to go when she doesn't want to go there is a chore roughly equivalent to solving the Mideast crisis."

"Be that as it may, the alternative may well be abduction and death. In such circumstances I've found it helpful to walk around in my adversary's head. None of the others here has anyone beyond these walls who might be used as a gun to our heads. You might—that's something only you can say. If you can look me in the eye and tell me her death would not be an unbearable burden, so much the better. If you're unable to do so—make that call *now*! Those people are desperate and have but two choices: to breach these walls or kidnap Dana Marsh. Which would you elect?"

I was soon punching out the numbers of her marina office. She answered on the third ring. "Brokerage office, Dana Marsh." I couldn't help giving a little gasp of relief at the sound of her voice.

"This's Matt—no time for explanations, trifle mine. Just toss some things in a bag and go away somewhere for a few days. Better yet—buy new things after you get there. I'd say three days max. Trust me on this, okay?"

"Matt, your sense of humor has taken a turn for the worse, which I wouldn't have thought possible."

"Don't I wish. No, this is the straight gen, kid; you've got to do it *now*! Makes no difference where but it should be at least five hundred miles away. Call me when you arrive. I'll let you know the second you can come back. No more than three days—I promise."

"Are you crazy? I've got a client due here in twenty minutes to look at a boat."

"The possibility of a commission isn't worth dying for, Dana."

"But it's the ninety-foot Feadship I listed, for Christ's sake, Matt! Do you have any idea what the commission would be on a . . . did you say dying? As in dead?"

"Yeah, I'm afraid I did. I never dreamed. . . . Oh, hell, I'll tell all when you get back. Will you go?"

"If you're positive this isn't an exaggeration, I guess I haven't got a whole lot of choice. Damn you, you've got me shaking in my deck shoes." She sounded rattled for the first time since I'd known her.

"It's no exaggeration, so go—Now!"

"I'll call. Bye." It was one of the things I liked best about her. When there was nothing more left to say, she said it.

"Mission accomplished," I reported redundantly. "What's next?"

"Excellent! One less chink in our armor. Darkness sets in at 5:45 P.M., I believe. About six I want you and Dr. Bruckner to slip outside and ascend to Dirk's apartment. I'll ask the two of you to stand watch-on-watch throughout the night. It's the sole location which bears on three whole sides of the property. As our best marksman—indeed our only one—you should man that position. It's also possible those concerned know something of the layout of the house. Entirely too many people do. If so, they may neglect to concern themselves with Dirk's quarters."

"I don't like the idea of leaving you and Louis alone."

"It's the best compromise. We'll be in communication via the in-house phones. Louis and I will stand alternate watches as well. Which reminds me: You neglected to issue me arms."

"You want a gun?"

"What would you have me do? Thrash my assailants with my bare hands? Or perhaps stand aside and rely on Louis to deal with them? Of course I wish to have a gun."

I could only shake my head in wonder. Maybe the guy was right who said if you live long enough you see everything. "I'm afraid all that's left is a Woodsman .22 target pistol. If you hit anyone with it the odds are about nine-to-one you'll just make them angrier."

"Academic, I assure you; give it to me. If nothing else I might provide some diversionary tactics and inspire our less-than-intrepid band to greater heights." I gave him the long-barreled weapon, together with the necessary instructions. He listened up like a good recruit and even handled it as if he knew which end to point. Hell, it wouldn't have surprised me to find out he was a crack shot. Slowly, accidentally, over the years I'd come to learn he'd been terribly good at a lot of things.

"Win, this all for one and one for all bit is a lark and I for one am having the time of my life, but aren't we forgetting something? I know we're not about to abandon the fort here and leave it undefended—that's not even open to discussion—but why not call Fogarty and have him direct the Orange County police to blitz the Kline house and get Reuben out from under? Any first-year medical student could see he hasn't suffered any damn stroke. It's obvious he's being restrained against his will with massive doses of some kind of sedative. He probably has all the answers about what's going on. Once we get him out of there and dried out he may be able to blow everything wide open."

"I've considered it, believe me. Chances are excellent all we'd accomplish is getting the poor man killed. If your visit with him yesterday has been discovered, I fear he's already a dead man. If not, there's no reason to forfeit his life now. There's a likelihood Miss Kline was contacted by Mr. Coburn and appraised of your visit to his bank. This would be standard practice, given the size and activity of her accounts. If so, she will have made the assumption your bogus visit to her home and your ersatz bronchial attack were an excuse to discover where she banked. This could be most fortuitous, and there is every reason to hope she remains blissfully unaware of your second call. This morning you stood before that very house with a number of policemen, yet your instincts kept you from confiding in them concerning Mr. Kline's precarious situation only a few yards away. Those instincts were sound; it must surely have served to reassure Miss Kline of our collective ignorance. If he lives, he will be safe enough for the time being. And we scarcely need him to 'blow everything wide open,' as you so euphemistically put it. Every major aspect of the case is now clear to me."

I gave him a full ten seconds to finish before I shouted: "You actually know who killed Marlee Reynaud and set Dirk up to take the fall?"

"I know them, yes. You'll note the use of the plural pronoun, for it was two different people, not one, who committed those despicable acts. Oddly enough, each was ignorant of the other's intentions. And both acts, odious as they certainly were, make up but a small portion of the pattern of bestiality and malefaction which runs wide and deep throughout this affair. Our mistake, Matt, in conducting this investigation was our grave underestimation of the stakes—we set out to bring a killer to bay. Now we're the ones at bay, faced with a veritable Hydra of evil."

His monologue was spoken in the most somber of Church-illian tones. The effect was just as chilling as he'd no doubt intended. It also told me absolutely nothing, which I knew damn well he also intended. "This is no time for your usual clam act, Win," I told him angrily. "When I see you sitting there with a gun in your hand, that tells me the situation is not normal. I insist you fill me in now. Perish the thought, but what if something happened to you? Dirk would stay right where he is, for openers. And arming Louis is not going to solve our problems."

"Dirk will be a free man tomorrow," Win stated with huge satisfaction. "And I've anticipated your demand, which is a cogent one. While you were gathering our meager forces I put in a call to your Chief Inspector Fogarty. I only pray he's as intelligent and objective as you paint him. Unfortunately he was attending a mayor's conference at the time, but I anticipate a return call within the hour. Rather than waste time repeating myself, I'll ask you only to wait until that call comes through, at which time I invite you to listen to the entire sordid tale."

He was better at waiting than I was. "Instead of sitting around, why not dump the works on Dixon? After all, he's the one we'll ultimately have to convince before we get clear title to Dirk."

Win's eyes sparked at the mention of that name, as they always did. "That Neanderthal? I wouldn't waste my breath. At best he'd do nothing but cavil—at worst he'd merely make some insulting remarks and hang up."

He was right and I knew it, but I knew he'd enjoy telling me. Louis rapped softly, opened the door far enough to inject his face, and solemnly announced dinner was being served early. We adjourned to the dining room, where Louis astounded me by sitting at table with us and digging right in. It was truly a day of the rare and unusual; he'd never done it before. I guessed it was a sign of his new job description. What may not have been proper for a chef was *de rigueur* for an armed combatant about to go on night patrol. I gave him a big grin to show my approval. I would have guessed by now that he'd have forgotten the gun was even in his pocket, but apparently I was wrong.

"Have you enjoyed success with your project?" Win inquired tersely of Randy.

"No problem. I decided on clear monofilament fishing line with twenty-four-pound test. I'll string a perimeter all around the house—fairly close in—using the natural plantings in the borders. Should be all but invisible as soon as the sun sets. Make it a foot and a half or more off the ground, so it won't snag the rabbits and squirrels that work the lawn at night. Anybody barges into it, a buzzer goes off. I can lead in through any opening you want—a window, a door—so let me know where to mount the buzzer."

"I'd hoped for something a bit more subtle," Win carped. "Your proposed alarm will alert them as effectively as us."

"Sorry!" Randy snapped. "I thought it a good deal better than the string of tin cans you said you'd settle for. Give me three days and a chance to order supplies and I'll give you photoelectric eyes in every palm tree. Subtle takes more than an hour." Another first: I'd never known Randy to bark at Win before; he usually addressed him like an acolyte to a bishop.

Win acknowledged the rebuke with a single nod which spoke volumes. "Forgive me, Dr. Bruckner—Randy. My mind is a seething caldron. It chafes to have discovered nearly every piece of this devilish puzzle, yet instead of celebrating our success, we sit besieged before our own hearth. But I promise you this: We need only survive this night, and the siege will be broken." He went back to moving the food around on his plate, a custom he had which made no sense to me at all. If he was at table, he put a tiny bit of food on his plate. Of course, he never ate a bite of it, but he always took some. The coming night would be easier on Win than the rest of us—he never slept more than a few hours a night anyway.

When the cheerless meal was over, I noticed Win pick up the phone in the dining room as he passed. He was checking to make sure the line was still operative. A seething caldron was right. Next, he directed Randy to mount the signal device just inside the front door. Though it was now nearly six, there was plenty of light left when we went outdoors and began stringing line. I kept jerking my head in all directions, on the lookout for any movement. I felt a little foolish, but that didn't stop me from doing it.

We made a fair job of it, tapping tiny eyelets into every tree or shrub where the line passed. Randy had strung a bunch of these onto the line before we began, with his usual meticulous attention to detail. The house was encircled. I was backing toward the front door, carefully maintaining what I hoped was the correct tension on the line.

Win's voice bellowed at me from the house. "In the office, Matt—quickly!"

"In a second; just let me secure this—"

"Drop it. It no longer serves, I'm afraid. Hurry!" The imperative in his voice hit me hard then. I rushed inside. He stood rigid as a post just inside the door, saying flatly, "The phone . . . it's for you."

I saw a ghastly look in his eyes and quickly looked away—I didn't want to think about what could be that bad. It may have taken me as many as six steps to cover the fifteen yards between the front door and the phone. "Matt Doyle," I managed to croak into the holes in the mouthpiece.

"Oh, Matt—I'm so sorry," Dana cried in an unfamiliar, anguished voice. She certainly sounded sorry. "The client for the Feadship showed up early, just as I was leaving for the airport—I really was. He offered to drive me, so we could at least discuss the price on the way. I thought it would be all right; there was a driver and we got in the back of this new . . ."

The gut-wrenching sound of a hard slap punctuated the end of the sentence, followed immediately by a sharp "Stop that!" from Dana. Several agonizing seconds later she resumed. "I guess I'm not supposed to make references to specifics, like the make of the car," she explained stiffly.

"Are you all right, Dana?" Though I was bursting with fury

and fear and pride for the way she was handling it, that poor platitude was all that came out.

"Slightly bowed, but unbroken. But you can bet next time you tell me to get out of town . . ."

The infinitely precious sound of her husky voice faded, to be replaced by a far less pleasant one familiar as it was discouraging. It was Danny, who'd cornered me in the trailer/office at Sea View and ended up unconscious on the floor for his trouble. It would be tough faking him out a second time, and he was the type who'd want to make amends. "You'll have lots of time to chat with her, Doyle," he growled. "Your broad is here at Sea View waiting for you. If you want her to stay alive, you got twenty minutes."

"Wait!" I screamed into the phone, glancing frantically at Win for I don't know what. He sat taking it all in on his extension; his face reflected my own as a mirror. He gave no gesture—no look—but no message could have been clearer. This particular decision was going to have to be made solo. "Don't do anything you'll regret—I'm on my way."

I just let the phone drop and tore open the bottom drawer of my desk. It took two precious seconds to come up with the dark carbon steel throwing knife Dirk had labored so hard to teach me to use. Pulling up my right trouser leg, I strapped the blade in its sheath to my calf. My mind was blank; I was only vaguely aware of Win curtly issuing orders to someone. I had my gun in my belt holster, for all the good I knew it would do me. Snatching my car keys from their usual nest in an ornamental ashtray on my desk, I bolted for the door.

I found Win blocking my way. He was looking down the hall but I realized he was talking to me. "I said remove the knife, Matt."

"Like hell I will. They'll have my gun before I even get out of the car, supposing I live that long. Odds are they'll have the knife a few seconds later, but there's a slim chance not. Slim chances are about all I've got right now so what's to lose?"

"Possibly a great deal. As you say, the gun is a foregone conclusion. But if they get the impression you're a walking arse-

nal in disguise they may decide to divest you of all your possessions—even including your watch."

I stared at him stupidly. "My watch?"

"Yes, and that would indeed be unfortunate. Hurry now; remove that ugly weapon from your leg, and your watch as well."

It didn't seem the ideal time for a debate, so I did as I was
told. The throwing knife went back in the drawer, and my Bulova
went in the ashtray on my desk.

Randy rushed in panting and handed Win something. Win
in turn held it out to me. It was a somewhat beat-up old Timex,
much larger than the current crop because of the oversized batteries required by the earlier models. I stared at Win with raised
eyebrows; he passed the look on to Randy.

"It's functional, Matt." Randy took the ugly timepiece from
Win and pulled the stem out—very gingerly, I noticed. "You can
even reset it if you should change time zones. If the case were to
be opened, it would pass only the most cursory of examinations.
Try not to use this stem though. I'm afraid the watch loses a
couple of minutes a day, but I suggest you just allow for that in
your mind and not bother correcting it."

"Congratulations! You've invented a watch that is big, ugly,
and keeps lousy time. I hope the Nobel Prize committee knows
about this. Now if you'll both excuse me I've got a date with
Dana."

"Pay strict attention, Matt," Win demanded quietly. "This is
that slim chance you were hoping for."

"This little beauty has hidden merits," Randy continued.
"The case is molded plastique explosive, fixed by a process I've
developed. Very stable, so don't be concerned. The stem is the
triggering mechanism. Remove the stem completely and in eight
to ten seconds she'll blow with the equivalent force of half a
dozen sticks of TNT—according to the conversion tables."

"You two actually expect me to wear that thing? Whose
bright idea was this?"

"I foresaw the possibility of such an impasse occurring one

day," Win replied. "Randy supplied the solution, of course; I merely posed the problem."

"It's perfectly safe, Matt, really," Randy told me. "The detonation can only be triggered by an electrical charge from the battery. No way can that take place unless the stem is completely removed, which requires considerable effort. Other than that, you can bang it around all you want. Heat won't affect it, certainly not at any level you're capable of enduring."

"If it's so fucking safe, why are you handling it like a hot potato?" I demanded, taking it from Randy roughly and slipping the cheap gold expansion band over my left hand. It felt awkward and heavy. I half expected it to blow with every one of the audible ticks of its primitive mechanism.

"Okay, now I'm a walking Roman candle—wonderful! Tell me the gods' truth, Randy. I heard Win ask if his watch was ready earlier this afternoon. You told him another couple of hours would do it—which means this little jewel is hot off the drawing board, doesn't it? My question is this: Would you be comfortable wearing this monstrosity around your wrist? Forget comfortable; would you even be willing to wear it for a single day?"

Randy stood there staring at his handiwork with a horrid frown. "I can't lie to you, Matt; it was a tremendous relief to get it out of my lab."

Damn! I wish to hell you'd learn to lie," I told him in disgust. Then I shrugged, mumbled, "As if any of it makes a particle of difference," grabbed them both by the shoulder, and sprinted for my car.

CHAPTER 14

*A*ll the lights were blazing in the trailer as I skidded to a stop amid a cloud of sandstone dust. There were no other signs of life. The feeble light of a new moon, rising low in the eastern sky, did nothing to penetrate the sinister gloom beyond the range of the office lights.

Waiving all preliminaries, I shoved the door open and stepped up inside. Danny sat on one corner of the secretary's desk grinning nastily up at me. "Where is she?" I shouted.

"Gone away, but not far," he responded amiably. "It was decided to play it close just in case you got another case of the cutes and arrived with a squad of cops. You got to watch it, Doyle; you're getting a terrible reputation for that sort of thing."

His idle chatter was designed to distract—make noise to mask the sound of the second man. Suddenly I flinched at the numbing pain of what I presumed was a gun jamming hard into my lumbar vertebra. "Either he followed orders and came alone, or they've got him on a very long leash." It was the same voice I'd heard while clinging to my perilous perch on the nearby cliffs. The one called Joe. "Did you shake him out yet?"

"Naw," Danny replied laconically, still grinning, his hard agate eyes bright with evil merriment. I could tell it was a scene he'd played in his head many times; he was visibly savoring every moment. "You remember the last time you and me and Tommy went up against this one? He's real tough, Joe. You reach out a hand to search a man like this, you're likely to pull back nothing but a bloody stump."

Danny wasn't a tiny bit worried—not when I still hadn't a clue where Dana was. He was merely amusing himself. Boys will be boys. I pulled away the left side of my jacket, exposing my revolver. "Look, all I want from you is—"

I never got to finish telling Danny what it was I wanted. My skull exploded over my right ear. I distinctly remember the pain and some impressive fireworks, but it only lasted an instant, and then all systems shut down.

My synapses began taking calls again in random sequence, a few at a time. One of the first things the main control center took note of was the leaden weight of arms and legs. I was cruelly bound with wire at wrists and ankles, leaving the limbs engorged with blood, while the extremities themselves were pallid and utterly dead. I was tracking well enough to realize if the trip were a very long one, severe circulatory damage would cripple me for life.

There was no doubt about my going on a trip. I was sitting up in the back seat of a black Chrysler Imperial. I suddenly thought to glance toward my dead hands. Until that moment, I'd actually forgotten the watch's existence. It was still there, hiked up enough on my swollen forearm to allow the wire to be wound tight at the smallest part of my wrist.

Its presence was warmly reassuring, but even as I considered my situation I came to a devastating realization: I recognized the tiny rococo seaside estates on my right. I knew exactly where we were: approximately twelve miles south of Tijuana, traveling on the old service road that parallels the fine new toll road running the entire length of Baja, all the way to Cabo San Lucas.

This knowledge led directly to an inescapable conclusion: If they didn't care whether or not I knew where I was and how I got there, then it was certain there wasn't going to be any return trip. The realization certainly didn't surprise me—it's just that certainty is harder to handle than theory. It's the difference between a young man knowing he's going to die some day, and some poor sod in a ward being told he's got a day or two, tops.

"How'd you get me through the border checkpoint?" I asked whoever felt like talking. I was no longer content to be left alone with my thoughts. Danny was seated beside me, turned slightly to keep an eye on me. Joe was up front driving.

Danny indicated a blanket on the floor. "Plan was to say we were delivering our dear sick friend to the cancer clinic down here. You were out—snoring peacefully. The lap robe hid your hands and feet. It was a beautiful act. A real shame the U.S. side was unmanned and the Mexihots waved us through without a glance." He almost sounded disappointed.

It was the usual drill. There isn't a whole hell of a lot you can smuggle into Mexico profitably, and with over ten million visitors annually entering through the San Ysidro checkpoint, there isn't much novelty left to keep up the Mexican customs guards' interest.

We passed a sign informing us that Ensenada was fifty-two kilometers south. Soon after, we turned east over an old stone bridge spanning the toll road. Looking south about a third of a mile, I could see the familiar lights of the beach hotel and restaurant/lounge where I'd often dined; it richly deserved its fame for the local lobster.

Spiraling down from the bridge, the big car bounced along a deeply rutted track. From here on it was strictly terra incognita for me. It looked as if the stony fields on either side would have made a smoother ride, from what could be seen in the expanding cone of the headlights. We bottomed out dozens of times, but Joe was working the shoulders well and avoiding the deepest of the pits. It was obvious he knew the road well. Twenty minutes and maybe seven miles from the toll road we arrived at our destination.

The shabby, sprawling, one-story adobe building featured a weathered sign proclaiming it to be the home of Tejar Superior Compañía. We continued around behind the factory, where the lousy excuse for a road disappeared completely. I counted eight smallish structures arranged in a horseshoe pattern around a central compound, the open end to the east. The structures ranged from the meanest shack to a metal Quonset hut the size of a modest house. Night-lights mounted on thirty-foot poles illuminated the area, and there were lights in most of the windows of the motley group of buildings.

Joe pulled up in front of what looked to be the poorest of the wooden shacks and killed the engine. The door flew open, and Roscoe Blaise waddled out, his ruddy moon of a face split wide in a facetious welcoming grin. He opened my door. Danny merely raised his feet and kicked me out into the red dust at his boss's feet. I managed to deny them the satisfaction of so much as a groan, though the pain throughout my limbs was beyond belief by then.

"Things appear to have worked out according to schedule," Roscoe commented to no one in particular.

"Does the schedule include me losing my hands and feet?" I demanded, furious. If it did, I figured I'd better attempt to pull the stem out of that damn watch while I could still manage it. There was a slight chance I could get it between my teeth, though my elbows didn't seem to remember how to bend. The thought of taking Roscoe and his two pals with me helped, but I couldn't see where it would do Dana much good.

"Don't be silly, Mr. Doyle. You and your lady friend are to be my honored guests for a short time—that's all. It's the only way I know to stop your never-ending prying into my private affairs. You must understand this clearly: No harm will come to either one of you unless you bring it on yourselves. Just think about it and I'm sure you'll see the logic of it. If anything were to happen to you two we'd lose our control over Carter Winfield.

You're here strictly as insurance—you wouldn't be worth a dime to us dead."

He was doing his best to sell it, but I wasn't buying. It was pure crap, designed to make me a little more manageable, and a lot less desperate. It was a damn shame they were no longer underestimating me. Though I never bought it for an instant, I decided then and there to help make the sale to Dana. She might hate me for it later, but right now it was the only gift I had to give. In case I didn't bail us out, there was no point in having her spend her last few hours in sheer terror.

Roscoe bent over me, close as his bloated belly permitted. "Dear me—I see what you mean. Do you suppose you could walk if we were to remove the wire from your ankles?"

"Maybe the day after tomorrow," I told him grimly, "if I'm lucky."

He directed Danny and Joe to bring me inside. They each grabbed me under an arm and began pulling, with no regard for the wear and tear on either my clothing or my hide. Those two were the direct types; they were doing little to reinforce Roscoe's sham concerning peaceful coexistence.

The homely structure was a bunkhouse—obviously never intended to house upper management. The twenty- by thirty-foot, one-room building featured an unfinished planked floor, matching walls with two small windows sealed off with heavy plywood, and a corrugated iron roof. It would make a great oven in the summer. Four mismatched, twin-sized beds were spaced at intervals on either side of the shabby room. It looked like a barracks for inductees into the world's poorest army.

I could see Dana stretched out on a bunk at the far left, and the sudden wave of relief obliterated the astounding ache in my limbs for a few blessed moments. Opposite Dana—on the far right bunk—another woman lay curled in the fetal position, facing the wall with her back to me.

I couldn't tell much about her except her personal hygiene left a lot to be desired. The place smelled like the inside of a lion cage during a zoo strike.

"Here, I think." Roscoe indicated the first bed on the left.

"Guy's made of lead," Joe complained. They were making heavy work of getting me up onto the bed. I relaxed those muscles I was still on speaking terms with, which didn't make it any easier. Small pleasures for small minds.

"Undo those wires," Roscoe ordered. I could have kissed the ugly bastard. He looked a little like a stubby Gert Frobe—the actor who played Goldfinger in the Bond film.

"I don't like it," Danny balked. "Listen to me—I know this guy."

"Just because he knocked you on your can? What are you afraid of? It'll be hours and hours before he'll be able to lift a finger or wiggle a toe. Get them off while I get the phone. We don't want to cause him permanent damage," Roscoe added as an afterthought, halfway out the door. He'd nearly forgotten his role as genial host there for a moment.

They obeyed. During the half hour since I'd regained consciousness, I was convinced getting rid of my bonds would be the most wonderful thing that ever happened to me. It wasn't—at least not for the first fifteen minutes or more. Though I wouldn't have thought it possible, the anguish increased geometrically as my dead extremities came screaming back to life. But I endured it happily, knowing it signaled a resurgence of life. The fact was, my outlook was improving as rapidly as my circulation. Roscoe was fetching a phone—that had possibilities. Sitting there on the bed with my hands limp and useless as broken flippers at my sides I looked and found Dana's eyes. "I told you one day I'd pirate you away to a remote romantic spot in the middle of nowhere."

She responded with the slightly lopsided smile I loved so. "My advice is change travel agents. I've heard of economy class, but this is ridiculous."

Now I could see she was tied hand and foot to the metal frame of her bed. The sight of the bonds and her obscene helpless position brought the gorge rising to my throat. I choked it down. My time would come. Adjustments would be made.

Roscoe returned bearing a wireless phone. He started to hand it to me, pulling it back almost as if embarrassed when I just sat there staring at it helplessly. "Sorry—thoughtless of me. Give me your office number; I'll dial and hold the phone for you. Here's the idea: explain to your boss as long as he sits tight, no one gets hurt. We have a certain . . . ah, project to complete. As soon as it's over we'll all be long gone—so neither side has anything to fear from the other. It's absolutely vital to convince him of that, because if he continues his investigation in any way, both your lives will be endangered. Then we would be forced to silence him by sending along various portions of your anatomy—that sort of thing." He explained it in a completely businesslike manner, pleasantly enough, as though he were describing the merits of a new car he was trying to sell me.

"How the hell can he continue any investigation? With me here and Dirk in jail? What are you afraid he'll do—send his houseboy after you? The old guy has all he can do to stand, and his attention span is getting shorter by the day." I took the opportunity to ease their troubled minds in every possible way.

"Maybe—maybe not. He looked in pretty good shape to me when I was there the other day," Roscoe remarked.

"Oh, sure; the guy's a real trouper. Puts up a good front for company. He was so exhausted after you left he had to go to bed the rest of the day. About this project of yours—what's the time frame? I don't fancy spending the next six months here at Casa de Crud."

Roscoe laughed appreciatively. "Nothing like that, I promise you. We're as anxious as you are to see this whole thing completed as quickly as possible. Call it two weeks at the outside—probably less."

And then Santa will drop by and take us home in a sleigh, I thought ruefully. I gave him the office number because there was no reason not to and there were a couple of reasons in favor. Win and the others would be hanging by their nails by now. At the very least, I'd be able to take them off the hook. Better yet, I had a thought or two that could lead to a much more informative chat with Win than Roscoe had in mind.

The volume setting was full on, and the ring at the other end was clearly audible to everyone in the room. Danny and Joe stood poised at the foot of the bed, glaring at me, as if warning me not to run off at the mouth. They didn't worry me much. Roscoe did—he held the phone. His face was barely two feet from mine as he stuck the mouthpiece in front of me. I focused at the point where his multiple chins ended and his slug-fat body began, and dreamed of the joys of driving my thumbs down into all that suet until they met up with his spine.

Win's voice, precise and cool, came on the line. "Carter Winfield." It was an improvement over his usual peremptory, "Yes?" He was obviously on his best behavior. Years ago, I'd tried to get him to tack on some minor pleasantry, like hello or good evening, but it was no go; he claimed there was an excess of verbiage in the world already, and he didn't personally feel like adding to it.

"It's me, Boss. Here's the situation: You promise to sit on your hands, and Roscoe and the boys will let me keep mine. You so much as ask yourself a question about their affairs, and you can start reassembling me right there in the office from the various parts which will be arriving in the mail. It may not be very original, but from my point of view it's still a real attention-getter."

"Are you intact?" He meant serviceable. "And is Miss Marsh with you and well?"

This was it! It was the one question I knew he'd have to ask—now I was counting on Roscoe's letting me answer it. "Affirmative on both counts. We're living high. Dining on eastern lobster and Seagram's Seven—my favorite fodder—as I'm sure you recall."

There was a brief but dangerous silence on the line. I risked a glance at Roscoe's face—he looked pleased. I shrugged, as if to explain there was no sense worrying the old man. "That's good to hear," Win finally responded. "But how long am I to suffer these restraints, and when may I anticipate your safe returns?"

"Couple of weeks or less, the man says."

"Very well. I make the assumption you can hear me, Mr. Blaise. I submit—albeit reluctantly—with the following proviso: Mr. Doyle and Miss Marsh are to be treated in a humane and civilized manner at all times. Failing that, you will find yourself the sole target of my total enmity. You would find no succor this side of the grave."

The icy, measured cadence of that final sentence wiped the smile from Roscoe's balloon face. He pulled the phone to his mouth and screamed: "What are you going to do about it, you old fart? Stop in here and check up on them? Just do as you're told and they'll be fine. And don't make me split a gut with your fucking stupid threats."

As Roscoe prepared to sever the connection, we all heard Win's reply clearly. "Some men—and a few nations as well— have seen fit to ignore warnings from me from time to time. I cannot think of a single instance in which any has failed to regret that serious error in judgment."

CHAPTER 15

*I*t was long after midnight. The three of us were silent inside the rough house. In spite of my pleas and protests, Danny had insisted on lashing me spread-eagled onto my bed. Strong, quarter-inch Dacron line led from my hands and feet to the four corners of the once fashionable bed. The rope was a vast improvement over the wire, but it would have been difficult to conceive of a more vulnerable and helpless position.

Dana and I had talked for a couple of hours—keeping it light—since we had to assume either the place was wired, or there was simply someone outside listening. I'd have loved to have been able to tell her the good news I hoped was true, but the risk would have been far too great.

At one point I'd asked her whether she thought the woman across from her was dead or alive. I'd yet to notice any movement, and I'd caught no sound of breathing either. Dana assured me she'd seen the woman's eyes flick open for a quick look at her when she'd first arrived.

Several times during those first couple of hours, either

Danny or Joe had flung open the door and switched on the over-head light. Not surprisingly, we were always right where they'd left us. Then they carefully checked my bonds, turned off the light, and left. Now it had been over an hour since the last spot check, and I could only hope the novelty had worn off.

I tested my systems. It took a direct order from Supreme Headquarters, but I found it possible to flex my fingers. I concentrated on that, having long since given up hope of reestablishing relations with my feet for the time being. My problem was the bane of every commander in the field—too long a supply line.

My mattress must have been stuffed with rocks, and there was a deep pocket where I lay in the center. It was more like lying in a hammock than on a bed. But the pocket was going to come in handy. When the boys had staked me out after the call to Win, I'd sunk deep into the trough of the mattress. I'd also re-tracted my shoulder joints as much as possible and flexed my buttocks, which served to draw my legs inward fractionally. Fi-nally, I'd splayed my fingers fanwise, thus slightly increasing the size of my wrists. Clenching your fist decreases your wrist size. (You accumulate such esoteric data in my line of work.) And I'd had to duplicate each of these actions every time I was checked. So far, so good; but I was afraid I'd never be able to maintain the illusion in the light of day. That fear—along with a hunch we weren't scheduled to see the light of another day—dictated action now.

The total benefit of all these minute deceptions was no more than a couple inches of slack, but I hoped it might just be enough. It had been enough to ease the restriction on my wrists and allow me to recover the partial use of my hands. Plan number one was to simply pull like hell until one of the posts broke off short but—after long study of the posts—I discarded the idea. Battered as the bunk was, the turned posts were solid maple, and a full three inches thick where the ropes were secured. All it would accomplish would be to tighten my bonds and possibly in-jure something in the bargain.

There was another way. Time would be a problem but there

was nothing I could do about that, so I forced it from my mind. If I bridged myself out of the slump in the mattress onto my heels and head, I'd create a few precious inches of additional slack. If I did it exactly right—lines taut at both feet and right hand—all the slack would become available at my left hand. I would have preferred to work it with my right hand because I'm not ambidextrous, and my control would be better. But it had to be the left. The posts gradually diminished in size, with the exception of two raised bands midway terminating in a wide oval cap. The cap was missing on my left-hand post.

I willed myself to go limp and lay there rehearsing the required steps. The catch was I had to do it right the first time. If exhaustion stopped me and I collapsed back into the trough it was all over. I'd try again, but each time I'd be weaker and increasingly unable to maintain the difficult bridge position for long.

Such moments aren't really worth savoring, so I arched my body up from the pocket of the bed and leaned against the pull of the three ropes to gain all the advantage possible for the fourth. I quickly lost all sense of time. Progress seemed agonizingly slow. Every joint in my body protested, and I was drenched in sweat in spite of the chill night air. Not only did I have to maintain the awkward body bridge while sawing my left arm back and forth, I had to constantly lift upward to work the loop toward its goal at the top. An instant's slack, and I'd have been right back to square one.

Each successive inch came twice as hard as the one before. The slack was disappearing as the left-hand rope assumed a more acute angle. I tried straining harder against the other three, desperate to find more rope. My limbs were screaming, but the thought of failure made all agony strictly academic.

My left shoulder popped as I writhed to work the coil over the last of the two decorative raised bands. The splintered top where the cap was broken off was still another three inches above the band, but I refused to allow myself to dwell on that appalling fact.

With a final supreme effort, I lunged at the post, working my trembling left arm back and forth furiously within the narrow scope of the available slack. The loop slid over the high spot in the wooden band and stopped. I glared at the remaining few inches in the full knowledge I had neither the stamina nor the required slack to go on. What was worse—the line was now snagged above the band, leaving me strung up like a Christmas goose. I was barely touching the bed. In a near panic, I did the only thing left to do—pit every ounce of my remaining reserves against the maple post, winner take all.

My effort was total. I hyperventilated a few times as Dirk had taught me, then yanked with everything I could muster, ignoring the specter of broken bones and torn ligaments. The results were almost too good; the eighteen-inch section of heavy post caromed off my skull with authority. A first-class light show followed.

All I really wanted was to just lay there peacefully and admire the strobe lights. But then it struck me as silly to go through all that just to calmly wait for one of the boys to pop in while I was still three-quarters trussed. I willed my half-dead fingers to function, sending them in search of the knots at my wrist. Laboring under considerable incentive, they somehow managed. I unbound my left wrist, then massaged my hands as long as I could bear it. After that I sat up and started on my ankles.

The post had broken at the level of the mattress, at the site of an unseen knot. Even so, I realized I could never have done it without the improved leverage I'd gained by working the line high above the bracing strength of the bed frame. The piece of hardwood reminded me of the fish billy I carried aboard my boat. It felt warmly reassuring in my slowly awakening hands.

I eased my feet over an edge of the bed. Even before putting any weight on them they felt immersed in molten lead. It was much like the sensation I remembered as a kid after a day of playing outside in subzero weather. All I could do was sit there rubbing and flexing, flexing and rubbing, praying the door wouldn't open for a little while yet. Later would be just fine.

Though I was somewhat hesitant to leave the bed for fear of creaking floorboards, I didn't remember hearing anything like that when Roscoe and his friends were moving around so I gave it a try. My feet felt as if I were strolling barefoot through a field of broken glass, but they arbitrarily followed orders most of the time.

Visibility was fair under the moonlight leaking through hundreds of voids in the walls and the bright arc lights over the compound in front. I hated to leave the area immediately around the door. If we did have a visitor, my only chance would come if I were within arm's reach. But I couldn't very well stand there and shout at Dana to wake up and untie herself, so I reluctantly hobbled to the far end of the shack and touched her lightly on the shoulder. Her eyes popped open instantly, wide with alarm. Their focus was all wrong. Knowing she couldn't see me, I whispered: "I think maybe you were right about my travel agent. Let's check out of here before they charge us for another day."

The panic drained away from the big brown eyes, and she managed a wan smile. "I always heard you couldn't keep a good man down." Her whisper was shaky.

I made short work of her bonds while explaining why I was in a hurry to restation myself near the door. She told me to go ahead; she'd join me there just as soon as her own feet reported for duty.

I lined up the dial of my half-pound watch in a streak of incoming light. I was amazed to see it was 4 A.M. already. It didn't make much sense to stand around worrying about a check that might not come before dawn. And I quickly discarded the notion of trying to draw someone inside by making some noise. They might come in all right—weapons drawn and in force. This would be the time of deepest slumber for most—somehow I had to bank on that and get us out of that stinking shack. And it couldn't be by the door; that was the one place someone was certainly monitoring. Thanks to the night-lights around the compound, it was bright enough to read a newspaper on the other side of that door.

There were no other exits and never had been. The pair of

tiny windows covered with sheets of new-looking plywood appeared to be the most substantial part of the structure. But the eaves offered a six-inch gap between where the wall ended and the metal roofing began. It was typical hido construction to allow for air circulation. Usually the space was sheathed in screening as defense against insects but they either hadn't bothered here or it had long since rusted away. It had to be my starting point—there was no other. The shed was old, and there was a good chance I'd find some areas of rot up there. I hissed softly, motioning for Dana to come. She'd been standing beside the other woman's bunk for some time. I'd even heard a hint of faint sibilant sounds from that corner.

She raised a hand to signify she'd heard me, but needed a moment more. The gesture jolted me—it was so like the sign she'd given me when I was in her office only a couple of days ago and she was on the phone. And now she was here—because of me. All I could do was grip the bedpost more tightly and wait.

When she joined me I clearly saw the anguished look on her face. "Oh, Matt; that poor soul has been here for months and months. She isn't even sure how long. She's not tracking very well, but physically I think she's reasonably fit. Yet, her mind is. . . . At first the Mexican workers from the factory forced her to. . . . Jesus, Matt! You wouldn't begin to believe the hell she's been through. Told me she finally resorted to smearing herself with her own waste to discourage the bastards. Several times—right in the midst of a rational sentence—she'll drift right off into nonsense babble. Once she began reciting a child's nursery rhyme."

I held my shuddering, devastated friend. There would be no more kidding her about the situation now. "Steady, mate—we'll all be out of here soon. Who is she?"

"I tried asking her, but all she said was her daddy called her his marshmallow."

"Bingo! Dana, two days ago a very sick and troubled man begged me to find his missing daughter. At the time I didn't understand. His daughter's name is Marsha Kline. I'll give you any odds you want you've just found her."

Pieces were falling into place faster than I had time to catalogue them but this wasn't the time to stop and sort them out. I handed Dana the club, positioned her at the ideal spot, and told her to do her level best to pound the first man who came through the door right into the ground like a tent peg. She accepted it, hefted it, selected a workmanlike grip I approved of, and gave me a nod with fire in her eyes. This was no frail wallflower; I'd seen her put more than one man to shame changing sails in a fresh breeze, or winching in a stubborn sheet. There wasn't a racing crew around that wouldn't have welcomed her aboard. The next guy to pull bed check was in a lot of trouble.

Now able to forget the door, I stepped up on the iron head frame of the nearest bed on the right and felt all along the top of the wall. Ours was the last building in line and that was the blind side. It was there I had to find a way out.

The rough-grained, weathered boards felt like iron. I pressed my nails in at various spots, in the classic test for dry rot. There wasn't any. I repeated the procedure above the second bed. There was a narrow strip of rot right along the top, but nowhere near enough to help.

As I headed for the third bunk, I noticed Marsha Kline pulling away, even as she stared at me with a fixed look of complete loathing. It was going to be a very long time before she'd be comfortable again in the presence of any man, perhaps even including her father. Now I knew the terrible hold Roscoe held over Tina Kline. The one thing the unforgettable sight of her did for me was dispel any misgivings I might have had about running over any of the locals who might get in my way. In spite of all evidence to the contrary, I'd never really believed Tina—incredibly beautiful and talented and dynamic Tina—guilty of involvement in this rotten mess. Oh, she was involved all right—the facts proclaimed it loud and clear—but guilty? Not in my book. If that were Dana lying there instead of Marsha Kline, I'd probably do any damn dance they wanted me to. I knew Win had Tina pegged as a villain, but this time he was dead wrong.

We were running low on options. The wood above the third bed emitted a trace of the sickly sweet, pungent odor of rot, but it was by no means ready to fall apart. There was no use stalling—it would start getting light in another forty-five minutes. I grasped the uppermost plank and pulled it toward me with an even pressure. It would have been easier to push outward, but I knew there was a good chance that might spring a nail loose, followed by the tell-tale screech of protest. A six-inch section broke off neatly at the upright frames on either side. No sharp crack of healthy wood, just the punky sound of soft planks. There was no point in waiting to see whether or not the slight noise was going to summon anyone, so I grabbed another handful and pulled.

The next section came harder and noisier. Coupled with the original six-inch gap, I now had nearly eighteen inches. Nice, but not quite enough, so I took a couple of deep breaths and grasped the heavy siding one more time.

I pulled with everything I could muster; fortunately, the angle of pull had improved, so my arms were nearly parallel to the floor. I'd never have overcome the power of healthy planks otherwise. When the final section did give, I nearly toppled from the bed frame. I was shocked by the sharp report from the fracturing boards. It seemed to fill the eerie silence of the predawn darkness.

Without waiting for repercussions, I pinch-gripped the two roof joists above me and swung my feet through the ragged gap. My prime objective was a limited one—I refused to die inside that crummy room. I worked my way out until my butt rested on the broken siding, turned onto my belly, and transferred my grip to the wall joists. With a powerful shove, I propelled myself up and out, blissfully free of the fetid shack.

Halfway to the ground I began thinking of the lay of the land below. All I needed was to sprain an ankle landing on a stone or an unexpected incline.

I hit flat-footed, knees well bent, ready to tuck and roll as my momentum dictated. But the ground was flat. I made it to the front corner of the building almost without a pause. Risking one wary eye, I quickly surveyed the drab and dusty compound. The harsh lights made the setting even uglier. The Chrysler was still

parked right out front. The sight of it made my skin crawl. Roscoe
and the boys were still around. This confirmed the theory I'd believed from the very beginning. There was no doubt in my mind,
Dana and I had been scheduled for a brisk trek back into the
arid, empty country to the east. It would be a short stroll and we
wouldn't have to worry about tiring on the return trip—we
wouldn't be coming back.

But the most interesting thing I spotted was our guard. At
some point during the night his chin had hit his knees and remained there. He sat with his back to the shack door—hunched
forward—sound asleep. Half a dozen options raced through my
mind, being weighed for risk versus reward. An elfin light of false
dawn was already promising to outline the low hills less than half
a mile east of the plant. I would have opted to take out the guard,
if only he'd been armed. I'd have taken a considerable risk right
then for a decent weapon, but apparently Roscoe didn't believe in
arming the local talent. Voices coming from somewhere inside
one of the other shacks made me flinch.

I had a sudden, dark wish that they'd all gather together in
one building so I could lob in my nasty little watch and solve a lot
of problems quickly. But massacres really aren't my long suit.
And I doubted Roscoe and Sons would join the Mexican workers
in a communal breakfast anyway.

It was time to face the fact that my options were severely
limited. It boiled down to putting distance between us and them.
The flood of light flowing around the corner made me vulnerable,
but I had to risk another glance to verify that all four doors of the
Chrysler were locked. I silently cursed the cautious bastards. If
only one were open I'd have put it all on the line: taken out the
guard, bundled Dana and Marsha into the car, wired the ignition
if necessary, and dared them to try and catch me in any of the
other junkers on the premises. But the combined obstacles of
locked car doors, no ignition key, and the padlock on the shed
door, made such a plan topple of its own weight. I gave one
longing glance at a big delivery truck backed against a loading
dock at the rear of the factory. A filthy-looking old Ford pickup

and a seven-year-old Chevy sedan were parked on the opposite side of the compound. So many variables beyond my control. I could have been wrong about the Mexicans not being armed. My worst enemy now was time—it was a friend soon to turn foe. In about ten or fifteen minutes the flat plain beyond would be light enough to betray anyone crossing it.

I didn't like the situation, but I accepted it. Running back to my exit hole, I leaped up, grabbed the lip, and pulled my chin up over the edge. "*Psst!* Dana?"

She was there within seconds, looking up at me with that special face with far too much strength and character to ever be called beautiful. "Front door's out," I told her softly. "It's got to be here. Pile as many mattresses as you need onto the bunk. Just work your way out and let go—I'll do the rest. And find something to lay over this edge or you'll end up with a bellyful of splinters. Hurry! We're cutting it very close."

I dropped to the ground, and amused myself by picking some of the larger splinters out of my hands. It seemed like ages before Dana's head appeared at the hole. She draped something over the lip, then slid over and down so quickly I nearly missed catching her. It was a difficult save—she was coming head first—but fortunately she didn't have much momentum. We fumbled desperately to catch each other's arms, then I stepped back and let her drop slowly to the ground in a controlled, head-first slide. To her everlasting credit, she never uttered a sound.

I'd planned to head off into the deserted back country—covering the first few hundred yards at a diagonal—to take full advantage of the shed's protection. We'd be without it soon enough. Dana moved in silent competence at my side. I took a look at her feet, pleased to find she was wearing her usual deck shoes—Sperry Topsiders. My own were rubber-soled—the only kind surgeons and detectives ever wear. So at least we had the right footwear for the rocky terrain ahead. Our feet would soon be battered and bruised because of the scant protection of the non-skid rubber soles, but at least we wouldn't be slipping and sliding all over the landscape. And an injury from the waist down would be fatal.

Every five or ten seconds I couldn't help glancing back. Before we were much over two hundred yards away, two men came from one of the small houses opposite our shack. I squeezed Dana's hand and we froze. The sound of their raucous barks shattered the preternatural stillness. One of them pointed at what could only have been our snoozing guard. We couldn't see the front of the shed but certainly he was wide awake and alert by now. Then the two men's backs were turned, and they sauntered toward the factory. Both continued gesturing wildly—shouting and laughing. I clearly caught the words: "*Vamonos, hombres,*" apparently an attempt to rouse any slug-a-beds.

The sudden increase in activity caused us to step up our pace to a quick dogtrot. Within a few minutes we reached the first of the low foothills and gratefully rounded it, passing from sight of the sinister complex for the first time. We both relaxed. Our path was now up a gentle incline. We slowed to a brisk walk.

"I trust you remembered to bring the picnic lunch—I'm starving," I said.

Dana gave me an apologetic look. "Oh, I am sorry. In all the rush to get off before checkout time I forgot. We could always go back and dine with your friends; I'm certain we'd be welcomed. Probably having mountains of huevos rancheros and those wonderful homemade—"

"Shut up and walk."

Morning was coming with a vengeance now. Soft gray light painted the harsh land in subtle sepia tones. The sweet and slightly cloying scent of sage and manzanita lay heavily on the still night-damp air. I knew we were seeing the severe countryside at its best; later in the day it would hold few attractions for the traveler. We were ascending by way of a ravine of rocks and gravel. The hills on either side of us were mantled with coarse grass. The route was noisy, and the footing was sometimes tricky, but we weren't likely to leave a useful trail.

"Matt, I realize we had absolutely no choice, but I still feel terrible about deserting that woman back there."

"You're right about that—we certainly had no choice. But I don't think you have to worry too much about Marsha Kline.

They've kept her alive for a long time; they must have good reason. I think I know what it is. It looks as though Roscoe's using her as a hostage to insure the cooperation of her sister, Tina. She had control of the land he needed to put up his phony construction site for one thing. She may have been forced to put up all the money as well. It's complicated. She's also depositing huge amounts in one of her corporate accounts under the guise that it's profits from a movie her sister—the poor soul back there in the shack—made a couple of years ago. Except the movie never made a dime, so my guess is Roscoe is using Tina and the account to launder his profits from a drug pipeline he's established."

"I see—the same way he tried to use us. As a gun to Mr. Winfield's head to hold up your investigation for two weeks."

"Not quite! Roscoe Blaise is a lying sack of shit. You can bet your next big commission you and I were scheduled to become a part of the local flora just about now. That's why I was so frantic to get us the hell out of there." If I was expecting some big emotional reaction, I was disappointed.

"Then they'll be coming after us, won't they?" she stated matter-of-factly.

"Count on it, Dana."

"But they must be about done with whatever it is they're up to. It doesn't make sense otherwise. After two weeks—if we didn't show up—your boss would know Roscoe lied and he'd raise all kinds of hell, wouldn't he?"

"Not if he were dead," I said flatly. "Look, Dana, what Roscoe's up to is very large and complicated and profitable. It must have taken plenty of time and money to set it up, but it's as slick as they come, and I guarantee they're not going to walk away just because a few people have begun to slightly annoy them. Killing is nothing new to them. You already know about Dirk's stepmother, which is how Win and I were involved in the first place. You can bet the plan was to kill Win too—sometime within the next two weeks. With me out of the way and Dirk in jail there wouldn't be much to stop them."

The ravine was leading us north of east. As we breasted a hill I caught sight of a small airstrip well off on my right. It lay about a half mile almost due east of the compound. There was a red wind sock at one end—it was little more than a narrow track threading a narrow valley. A barely discernible trail led between the foothills, connecting it with the plant. Without being consciously aware of it, I'd been watching for an airstrip. The way the odd bits and pieces were falling into place, it figured to be there. I turned and led the way along the crest right into the wedge of rising sun now visible from our prominence. We'd have to abandon the crests soon or we'd risk being spotted, but I felt it was safe for a while yet, and the going was easier.

Dana had obviously been considering my words carefully. "If you're right, then they really do have to find us, don't they? I mean they'll pull out all the stops, won't they, Matt?"

"True, but I haven't told you the good news. I told Win where we were last night on the phone."

She flashed me a puzzled stare. She was going over the exchange between Win and me in her mind. "Okay, Slick—you got it past those three men, so obviously it was good. I'll admit I missed it, too. What'd you do—use telepathy?"

"It was simple enough and I'm almost sure he got it. Win doesn't miss much, and he'd have been keyed up to listen for clues. Remember when I told him how great we were being treated? That was so obviously inappropriate he had to know it was a prelude to a subtle hint. Next I said we'd had eastern lobster and Seagram's Seven. Well, it so happens we're about seven miles east of the Su Casa restaurant—my favorite spot in the whole entire world for lobster. And Win knows it. I was hoping you'd picked up on it too, since you share most of my lobster rations. And the hotel and restaurant are clearly visible from that old overpass where they turned east from the coast road."

"Not to me. Maybe you got the scenic tour, but I arrived bound and gagged in the trunk of a car with no shocks and holes in the exhaust. They taped my mouth shut and even tied my hands and feet together behind me. I assume that was so I couldn't kick and alert anyone if we stopped."

"Damn! If I'd ever dreamed you could get drawn into—"

"You'd have what? Don't be dreary, Matt. Things happen; you don't make the rules. Actually, the worst part was when they removed the adhesive tape. I was convinced most of the lower half of my face had come off with it."

I stopped in front of her and examined that so-precious face. The quiet strength and ever-present humor in her eyes renewed me. "Good God, Gertie—your mustache is gone. I do believe we've discovered the perfect depilatory."

Laughing now, we hurried on, maintaining the brisk pace. In the distance I could make out a small, wooded area. It lay more northerly. We started down the far side of the modest chain of hills, heading for it. Time to leave the skyline behind, and the thought of some cover appealed. It might ease that prickly sensation I'd begun noticing at the back of my neck.

CHAPTER 16

*I*t was a good three hours later before we reached the protective embrace of the copse and enjoyed our first real rest break. We must have covered more than fifteen miles; distances were deceiving in the shifting lights and shadows of the Baja day. Dana had matched me stride for stride. Though I would have set a far brisker pace alone, my admiration for her had jumped another notch. Now seated a few feet apart on a fallen tree, I watched Dana doing interesting things to the shape of her shirt as she engaged in some serious deep breathing.

She noticed and made a face at me. "Don't you believe in lungs?"

"Too inefficient; had mine replaced with a battery pack."

"I believe you—would it kill you to take a deep breath once in a while, just to make me feel less like an anchor? How long do you think it will take Mr. Winfield to get someone down here?"

"Depends on when Win was able to reach a certain Chief Inspector Fogarty in Los Angeles, who in turn would have had to go through channels. You can't just lead a squad across an international border and start shooting. It would have to call for some pretty high-ranking authorizations. But those two will handle that part of it in record time. With any luck at all, I'd hope to see some signs of activity by late this afternoon."

"Then why are we running from civilization? I'd think you'd want to give the place a wide berth—then circle back to the Baja Highway. We could be home an hour after we hit the toll road."

"I know it sounds great, but there's a problem. Between the compound and the highway there are people. Goat ranches, tiny farms—and you have to figure those people are either friends or family of the factory workers. That plant probably represents a level of financial security that's rare around these parts. We have to consider all those people as part of the guard force."

She simply nodded, accepting the sad logic. She didn't always act that way. Dana could be a very independent lady. She was one of the most successful yacht brokers on the West Coast, and justifiably proud of it.

Though the sun was fast approaching its zenith, the late winter sun was tepid; it felt good to leave the shade of the trees behind. I set a course of due north, figuring to cut back west for the Baja Highway after all, when we were about ten miles above the factory.

Ten minutes out, I suddenly clutched Dana's hand and we stopped. The unmistakable *whackety-whack* of a helicopter rode the crisp, still air. There wasn't even a shrub in sight except for the small wooded area we'd just vacated. The land was gently rolling and sparsely covered; the patches of brown grass and small boulders offered no hope of protection.

"Back into the trees, Dana—make like a track star."

She was away before I finished, running well, getting her knees up, and pumping with her arms. I caught up and paced myself beside her, but not too close. It wasn't necessary for me to gear back much to just stay even with her.

The irritating sound increased until it seemed I could actually feel it. Then I could see it approaching from the southeast, as if circling the area. As I looked I saw its course roughly paralleled ours—but it was headed in the opposite direction, maybe a third of a mile away. Even as I watched, though, the ship nosed over and pointed directly toward us. Not pessimistic by nature, I still had every hope it was help arriving, but the only sane thing to do was streak for cover until we knew for sure. Either way, we were going to get a good look at them long before we reached the tiny forest.

The nearest tree cover was still a couple of hundred yards away. The final hundred yards was definitely going to be dicey. Dana glanced over her left shoulder at the oncoming aircraft and shifted into high gear. "Good girl!" I called over in appreciation. I don't think she heard me.

The chopper hovered in our path, blocking our route into the woods. It was swaying excessively with a pendulum-like motion. The ideal position would have been behind us—our target areas would have actually increased rather than foreshortened, as they were now. And distance could have been maintained easily at a constant for increased accuracy. At first I thought it meant friendlies attempting to reassure us. That dream went down in flames as I recognized Roscoe's fat red face. But the real shocker was the familiar-looking woman beside him at the controls—it was Tina! The girl was full of surprises. Two guns sprouted from the open side panels and the fun began in earnest. I profoundly regretted not lingering in the woods an additional fifteen minutes. We'd have gotten away clean and been appraised of the new danger. Being caught out in the open was the worst of all possible breaks, but the truth was we'd been vulnerable ever since breaking out of the shack, except for the brief respite within those same trees.

At sight of the guns, Dana broke off and began to zigzag back and forth. I intercepted her, screaming: "Run in a straight line—all you're doing is prolonging your exposure time. They can't hit the broad side of a barn, the way that thing is jumping."

I quickly pulled away again, reluctant to give them the increased odds of the two of us as a single target. The racket was horrible now, and I was afraid she might not have heard me until she resumed running in a beeline for the sanctuary ahead. It's by no means the easiest thing to do—race right toward someone who's shooting at you. It usually isn't very bright either, but I knew very well firing from one of those vibrating, yawing crafts was like trying to shoot from the back of a running horse—it only works in the movies. Unless of course, one or more of them were properly equipped with a machine pistol or other automatic weapon. All I could see was a handgun along each side of the ship; it was obvious they were being fired, though the reports of the small-calibre weapons were lost amid the incredible clatter of the monstrous blades.

If Tina'd really known what she was doing she'd have set the whirlybird down right between us and the woods, but apparently she wasn't up to any fancy maneuvering. Fortunately for us, the ship continued yawing violently, and she seemed to be having trouble maintaining a constant altitude. Maybe Roscoe's sword over her head was slipping. It looked to me as if she were doing what she could to help us without being too overt about it. Either that or she was merely a lousy pilot.

Dana and I charged directly beneath the shuddering ship, scooting to cover the last thirty yards to the oasis of trees. It wasn't nearly as foolhardy as it sounds. We afforded very small moving targets because of extreme foreshortening, and the motion of the ship provided first one and then the other gunman only passing glimpses of us.

To show how wrong you can be, I felt a sharp tug on the sleeve of my jacket. It worried me some—but the one that scared the hell out of me never even touched me. I heard the *phut* in my left ear and knew that bullet had—if not my name on it—at least my initials. It's a sound you only hear when a muzzle is pointed directly at you and fired.

Those final few yards could have been very bad. I could tell they were finding our range—probably getting used to the awkward shooting angle. And now we were growing targets, even though we were moving away. But then Tina—or whoever was giving the orders—probably saved us by electing to turn the chopper around to face us again, a very stupid maneuver. It shut out one gunman entirely and fouled up the other's chances because she experienced stabilizing problems after completing her hundred-and-eighty-degree swing. It served to reinforce my theory that she was resisting the reins as far as she was able.

We hit the edge of the woods and kept right on moving for another twenty yards. Suddenly I found what I'd been looking for and stopped. There was a four-foot-long limb about the circumference of my wrist. I ran over and snatched it up, as if it were an Uzi automatic weapon. Panting, I stood there, feeling the hair rising on my neck and arms. Primitive beast preparing for battle, making himself appear bigger and meaner in the hope of frightening off his attackers. Not much help, I'll admit, but probably it was more effective a million years ago when all any of us had were sticks. And there I was—a thousand millennia out of date—still armed with just a lousy stick.

"Go to the far side and find yourself a deadfall to burrow into, or climb the biggest tree you can find," I rasped at Dana. She was gasping like a beached whale. For a few seconds she thought she might want to debate the issue but—noting the look on my face—she wisely opted to comply. Assuming I looked anything like I felt, I didn't blame her a bit.

"Good luck, Matt," she wheezed, taking off in the general direction I'd indicated.

I moved diagonally away from our entry point, then worked back to within a dozen feet of the outer edge of the trees. The entire copse was only about twice the area of a football field and not terribly dense, so a game of hide-and-seek didn't figure to last all day—not with one side armed with guns and the other with a stick.

The copter had settled to earth fifty yards away and two men were climbing down. I recognized my escorts of the prior evening—Danny and Joe. The engines were still idling, so I didn't get to hear what they were saying—they were no doubt discussing tactics and didn't appear to be in any hurry. No reason they should be. Dana and I were no better off than a couple of fat bugs on a small table.

I studied my immediate surroundings, searching frantically for an angle. Most of the trees were a stunted variety of field oak, barren of all but a few dessicated leaves. The idea of disappearing Tarzan-like overhead was ludicrous. There was a six-inch carpet of dead leaves overlying a soft bed of humus underfoot. I remembered a popular cliché used in war films and westerns: The good guy covers himself with leaves—or snow or sand or whatever—and after the bad guys pass him by, he pops up and plugs 'em. I couldn't think of a better way to commit suicide. Any movement on the ground was tantamount to leading a brass band. The helicopter's idling engines were a mere insect hum within the sound-absorbing baffles of the woods. Every step taken could be heard dozens of yards away.

It was this fact that ultimately dictated my plan. I left my club braced against a tree and raced about twenty-five yards into the heart of the copse. Selecting a thick oak clearly visible from our point of entry, I removed my jacket and hung it at the right height, using a bark end for a hook. After some fiddling around I was satisfied. I retraced my steps before I turned and checked my handiwork. There was a four-inch swatch of my light gray coat clearly visible—the effect was everything I'd hoped for. It might well be me, hiding behind a tree. I knew it wouldn't fool them long, but the question of "long" never entered into it in any case. A very few minutes from the time those two entered the woods it would all be over—one way or another.

After rubbernecking a while, I selected an oak about ten yards inside the tree line. It featured a substantial limb, nearly parallel with the ground and about eighteen feet high. Before climbing, I fished around beneath the ground cover for a pair of fist-sized rocks. After stuffing one in each side pocket, I made my ascent.

It shaped up very tricky. I would have to lay face down on the limb, leap to my feet, and fall upon a pair of very substantial guys who would be intently alert with guns drawn. If I got lucky and took one out, it left the second man free to plug me at his leisure. Recovery time after the long drop was going to be two or three seconds, at the very least. Worse, I was anything but invisible from the moment they entered the woods. If either happened to look up just right, it was all over but the shooting. But Dirk had told me never to hide at eye level, or behind anything. People looking for something will naturally search down and all around, but will seldom look upward unless something attracts their attention. Everything depended on one of them spotting the coat right away. Now that I was hopelessly committed to the plan, it struck me as flimsy as hell.

My cheek pressed against the hard, rough surface of the big limb—I did my best to think small. I felt incredibly vulnerable. I couldn't see the ship, except for a spot of white here and there through the maze of branches. I did have a fair view of the last five yards of open ground bordering the copse. Clutching my crude cudgel in my right hand, I concentrated on breathing slow and deep. It was one of so many things I'd learned from Dirk. I thought of what would happen to Dana and Win and Dirk if I lost. And I waited.

At last they came. It was the pair I'd expected; I hadn't pictured Roscoe charging around the forest waving a gun. Neither could he, apparently. He may also have had good reason for not wanting to leave Tina alone with the aircraft.

They both entered the woods right where I'd wanted them to. There was the semblance of a trail where we'd disturbed the leaves, exposing the humus as we'd run in. It gave them a focus. They came single file, about six feet apart. Silently I willed them to close ranks. My only workable plan called for them to be no more than an arm's length apart.

"What makes you so sure they didn't keep right on going on out the other side?" Joe spoke in a loud stage whisper; it wouldn't surprise me if Dana heard it at the other end of the woods.

"He isn't that dumb," Danny replied in his normal, challenging tone. "The only chance he's got is right here, and don't think he doesn't know it. Now shut up and watch your ass—he'll try something."

"If that little cunt knew how to fly worth a damn, we'd never have had to come in here," Joe observed with disgust.

"Ain't that the truth. Now I really want you to shut up. . . . Hold it!" Danny was still a dozen feet short of my tree, with Joe back even farther. I was locating them by sound. I could picture Danny squinting, then staring intently at the portion of my coat he'd just spotted.

"You see it?" Danny demanded. I imagined him pointing and Joe peering in the indicated direction, hopefully closing the gap to see better. If only they'd both come forward another four or five steps it would be perfect. As it was, they may as well have been fifty feet away. I gritted my teeth, and concentrated on becoming part of the tree.

"I see it!" Joe replied. "So—what do you make of it? You're the one who said he wasn't dumb."

"Damn right he's not! He's made monkeys out of us twice already—in my opinion it stinks. If all he could think of was to hide behind a tree, I believe he'd do a little better job of it than that." Now both men were speaking in quiet tones.

So it wasn't going to fly—it was all coming undone. A reputation can sure trip a guy up.

"Well, now; shows how wrong you can be, doesn't it, Joe?" Danny sounded smug. His remark made no sense to me.

"Yeah, it's her all right. I seen her too. What're they figuring to do, heave rocks at us?"

"If all you got is rocks, I guess you throw rocks," Danny observed sagely. They still hadn't moved an inch. "Let's go gather them up. We don't want to kill either one," he told Joe softly. "First we walk them back to the chopper. Wing the guy if you have to—and you probably will—but if you drop him you can bet your ass you're going to be the one to carry the big bastard."

"I still don't see why we can't just leave 'em here. Shit! It ain't as if this was a busy street."

"Because the boss is careful, and there's a hell of a lot at stake, that's why. If the boss wants them stashed in the gravel bed with the secretary—that's the way it is. Besides, I think the boss likes doing it. Remember how high things got after the secretary? I never saw anybody who likes it more."

My jaw muscles ached from strain; I was raining sweat. They were on the move now. I listened intently to the crunch of each footstep, estimating carefully. I had no notion of what their respective positions were but—whatever—I was about to launch an airborne strike. Transferring the club to my left hand with infinite caution, I reached into my right-hand pocket and removed the rock.

Danny passed beneath me, walking upright, staring fixedly ahead. After seeing Dana, he was satisfied. Dana's presence behind an adjacent tree—her true presence—sold a premise he would never have taken as a gift otherwise. Once more, I recognized the magnitude of my debt to her—it was one I'd be hard-pressed to ever repay.

I rose up from the tree, every muscle humming in tune. I wanted to take Danny out first, but it would have been lousy tactics. At least this way, Danny had to make a half turn before he could even begin to react. It wasn't much, but I'd take every fraction of a second I could get. There was always an off chance the rock would prove more than just distracting.

Poised on my knees, I threw the big stone at Danny's head with a great deal of enthusiasm. At the end of the throw, I allowed the momentum to pull me over. I had no way of knowing how accurate my pitch had been as I dove, grasping the long club in both hands, arms straight in front of me.

Joe never saw me coming. The pole hit him in the back, just below the shoulder blades, driving him into the ground. After riding him down, I slipped the staff under his face, pressed it into his neck, brought my right knee high behind, and gave one quick, powerful jerk. The entire sequence took less than two seconds, and Joe was no longer a source of concern.

Even before I'd broken his neck my eyes were scanning, searching in desperation for Joe's gun. Everything depended on recovering the first man's weapon. It was nowhere to be seen; the deep mulch had swallowed my only chance.

"Not bad! I warned him you were cute. Too damn cute—I'm not going to fool with you. I think you already busted my fucking shoulder. They can either leave you lay or Roscoe can work off some of that blubber lugging you back." Danny spoke too loudly—like someone who'd just had a bad fright and was over-compensating.

Still on hands and knees, I lifted my head and looked at him. His right arm hung useless at his side—broken collar bone in all probability.

Unfortunately, he had managed to shift his .45 automatic to his left hand. Its monstrous-looking muzzle was staring me right in the eye. He wasn't a southpaw, but surely he was ambidextrous enough to pull the trigger. The look on his face told me he was savoring the moment, but the tensing hand tendons told me he was about to fire.

My club was still pinned under Joe's neck. There was no chance I could free it before he placed a bullet in my head. But it was something to do instead of kneeling there feeling foolish, frustrated, angry, and helpless.

The muzzle blast and thunder of the big gun assaulted my ears, but not before I saw a surprised look in Danny's eyes, and thought I heard him grunt. The blinding impact freed me from my paralysis. I sprang to my feet, pulled the staff free, and tried to drive it right through Danny's midsection. I may not have succeeded, but did note a satisfying mask of anguish on his face, and a pronounced inclination to bend forward at the waist. Nevertheless, he managed to hang onto his gun, and was quickly bringing it to bear on me again. I figured he was only entitled to one chance at that range, so I went into a full backswing, broke my wrists just right, and didn't neglect to follow through. The heavy club caught him on the nape of the neck, and he went down with bone-crunching finality. I bent over him hastily and relieved him of the awful weapon still clutched stubbornly in his left hand.

Dana stood twenty feet away with a dazed look on her face. Her lips were trembling. "It's going to be fine now," I told her. "We got lucky." I walked over to hold her to make the shakes go away.

"That man . . . was going to . . . I couldn't find . . . one
. . . was so afraid . . . I'd miss . . ."

I gathered her into my arms. She was shaking violently.
"You couldn't find one what?"

She drew one deep, shuddering breath and looked up at me.
"A rock, you idiot! I could see him pulling the trigger just as I
threw. It hit him on the back somewhere, I think. But it made
him miss, didn't it?" The familiar husky voice filtered through
quaking lips lent her a vulnerable quality I'd never seen in her
before.

I hugged all hundred and thirty-five pounds of her and lifted
her off the ground. "Kid, you are really something," I told her in
complete sincerity. "From now on, I don't go anywhere without
you. I do not cross on the green without you."

She ventured a tremulous grin. "Steady, Matt; a designing
woman might take that as a commitment."

"Some might, but it sure as hell wouldn't be you." I put her
down and turned back to the scene of the carnage. On my hands
and knees one more time, I started raking through the leaves,
determined to find the second gun. Perhaps it was an overreaction
to having felt so deprived a few minutes earlier. "Go over and
take a look at those two in the helicopter, Dana. But be careful—
just make sure Roscoe isn't on his way in here."

Finally, I found it several feet to one side of the path. It was
a twin to Danny's. Checking Joe's pockets, I came up with two
extra clips. I crawled over to Danny and felt for a pulse. I didn't
expect to find one, and that's what I found. His pockets contributed another full clip to our swelling armory. They would come in
handy, in case I was attacked by the Mexican Army next.

I joined Dana halfway to the edge of the trees. "They're just
sitting there watching, Matt. I don't think they have any intention
of coming in here after us."

"I didn't expect them to. My guess is, Roscoe has a real
problem now. You saw the way Tina was flying that chopper when
they were trying to shoot at us? I think she did that on purpose.
Danny and Joe were even complaining about how impossible she
made it for them to hit anything. They've still got her sister back

there, but what would happen if she found out these two were dead, and I could get the drop on Roscoe? Right now I have to get out there and make my move, before he forces her to get airborne. Once that he realizes his team came in second, he'll know we're armed and he'll be out of here."

"That girl who's flying, she's the sister of the woman we left behind? How are you going to get to Roscoe without endangering her?"

I shrugged. "What I hope to do is disable the aircraft—after that we'll hold most of the marbles. Roscoe wouldn't have a thing to gain by harming Tina once we cut off his escape route."

"Makes sense," she reluctantly agreed. "Why not just go to the edge, but stay in safe cover, and blast a hole in that thing where it'll do the most good? You're supposed to be pretty good with those disgusting things, aren't you?" She nodded grimly at the pair of automatics stuck in my waistband. I must have looked like a very drab pirate.

"Honey, I'd be better off throwing these guns than firing them from that range. The chopper is maybe fifty yards from the nearest trees. These 'things' are moderately accurate at up to twenty yards. At anything over that, the slugs tend to tumble. Even when they don't, it's strictly a matter of luck after that. If it weren't for the girl, I might risk rushing out there, guns blazing, and we'd see; but as it is, I'm going to have to find a way to get within at least twenty yards of that ship."

The distant clatter of the idling blades hadn't changed volume or cadence since the sound of Danny's gunshot. It was remotely possible they hadn't heard it—the racket would still be considerable inside the machine. "I'll try approaching from an unexpected direction, Dana. Once that flying Mixmaster is disabled, we'll have him. Even if it's a standoff—at least he'll be pinned down until the cavalry arrives. Sit tight; I'm going to work my way to the north end of this cabbage patch. Odds are he's fixated on the point where everybody entered the woods, so I should be able to get close enough."

"Is it really necessary, Matt?" She held my arm lightly—not

as if to restrain me, but just to get my full attention. "If you get close enough to hit what you have to, what's to stop him from hitting you?"

"Don't worry; I plan to hit the deck at the first sign of trouble. And we know all he has is a handgun and—since he let Danny and Joe handle the duty before—he probably isn't any great shakes with one. Besides, he'll find it's a whole other ball game shooting at someone who's shooting back. I know what you're thinking, honey—why not just let him go on his merry way, and concentrate on getting out of here alive? I can't risk it. One of those two dead men there on the ground probably killed Dirk's stepmother. There is a third possibility—Tommy—but who knows where he is? My only chance of getting Dirk free of this whole mess is sitting out there in that helicopter. If I let him fly free we may never see him again, and without him Dirk could very likely rot right where he is. I can't risk it—I won't risk it!" I gave her one last hug for luck—though I didn't expect to need much—apologized for the painful jabs inflicted on her by my twin gun butts, and began picking my way north.

The course I was forced to follow was made erratic by deadfalls and occasional clumps of some wicked breed of bramble that liked to eat legs. Once clear of the woods, I followed the perimeter around, waiting until the craft was in sight to abandon the comforting shelter of the tree line.

It took much longer than I'd expected to raise the helicopter. When it finally came into sight, I left my sanctuary behind and moved diagonally away, directly toward the ship. A gun in each hand, I had closed to within thirty yards without seeing a soul aboard, when I suddenly caught sight of movement out of the corner of my right eye.

Roscoe and I discovered each other's presence simultaneously. We both stood stock still. He looked even more squat, lumbering from the woods, knees bent, laboring beneath his great burden. Though her face hung hidden behind his back, I recognized Dana. She was draped over his right shoulder, lifeless as a sack of grain.

"Well there you are," he grunted. "What a relief! The thought of you . . . running around loose with . . . the boys' guns was . . . giving me the fidgits." Fatty was almost as short on breath as he was on scruples.

I gripped the handles of the guns with all my strength— anger and frustration threatened to rob me of my fragile hold on reason. All I wanted in the world was to give a primal scream and charge him. But the gun he held buried deep in Dana's belly stopped me. Not only because it threatened her life—it also told me she was still alive. "If she's hurt, Roscoe, old son, you've bought a one-way ticket to hell."

"Now, don't you worry. I only gave her . . . a little tap to encourage cooperation. It was self-defense . . . if you want to know the truth. She's . . . quite a tiger, Matt."

Roscoe resumed his clumsy shuffle toward the ship. "Big girl!" he commented conversationally, watching me approach. When I was within twenty yards, he ordered me to drop the useless weapons and keep coming. I obeyed without breaking stride. Tina's face appeared at the starboard cockpit window. I switched my gaze to her, attempting to communicate my thoughts to her. Roscoe must have tied her somehow, but the odds were three-to-one now. If only Roscoe let me live long enough to get airborne, surely Tina would realize we had him cold. But Roscoe wasn't that stupid—I would have to make my move on the ground.

I timed my pace so I'd reach the ship a few steps ahead of him. He seemed unconcerned about me, but obviously near exhaustion from his long trek carrying Dana. I looked back at Tina, and had to struggle to keep my eyes from popping. There she sat at the controls, nonchalantly waving around a petite automatic as if it were a pom-pom. She was smiling—it was all quite chummy. It looked like a .25-calibre something or other, but I couldn't wait to get my hands on it. There weren't many places you could plant a small-bore slug like that and be absolutely certain of stopping a man before he could pull the trigger on his own gun. It was risky as hell, but it was a chance and I gave it a lot of thought. I actually believed Roscoe's instinct would be to turn the gun on me in self-defense and not take time to shoot Dana, but it was a theory I hoped we wouldn't be testing. The gun dropped out of sight, below the cockpit door, for which I was grateful. I certainly didn't want Roscoe to spot what was going on now.

I reached the side of the ship while he was still five yards away. "Nice to see you, Matt." Tina smiled that great smile of hers, as I held out my hand to receive the gun. That's when she negligently lifted the little automatic, and shot me in the face. It all happened in Super Slo-Mo. I could almost see the bullet leaving the gun. And I had more than adequate time to experience the searing, white-hot sensation of the slug tearing off the top of my head.

CHAPTER 17

I swam blind, deep down in a coal black sea of sludge. Progress was impossible—the surface was too far away, and I had no notion of which direction it lay. And besides, there was nothing I wanted up there. I went deeper.

Eons later, I inadvertently broke the surface. I'd been right—it was a big mistake. My body had disseminated; no two cells were cooperating. And worse, every one vibrated horribly—several billion tiny tuning forks. Someone was certainly going to hear about it. The Hereafter was shaping up as a major disappointment to me. I'd never really bought all that sugar about harps and angels, but this was ridiculous.

A sea of sound cast me onto a beach of rough stones. The deafening volume of noise was incredible. Still, I was freed from the black, viscous sea. Furry images dissolved in and out, rarely holding steady for longer than a second or two.

I must have stared blankly at the vinyl-covered overhead for a long time before I recognized it for what it was. From that meager beginning the data began pouring in. I was lying on the lower deck of a boat. In a stateroom. The boat was underway—explaining the terrible noise level and the devastating vibration. I decided the boat could use a new stern bearing or two. If not for the bunks and the rich decor around me, I'd have sworn I was lying right on top of the engine housing.

My shifting vision showed signs of stabilizing, fading out on me only every minute or two. Still, things remained fuzzy around the edges at best. I sent out messages to all the troops—all leaves were canceled. Fingers move, toes wiggle, arms lift. Discipline was very sloppy in the ranks, but eventually most reported for limited duty.

After a few false starts, I managed to roll over onto my right side. It was a huge relief to lift my head off the throbbing deck. Getting from horizontal to vertical was a long, complicated procedure, involving miles of curiously attenuated limbs. My feet weren't even in the same county. On my knees at last, I clutched the sideboard of a bunk, shoved, braced, and eventually pulled myself erect.

My body was a fragile, delicate thing, apparently made of tissue paper and library paste. Compared to me, soap bubbles were tough as nails. I hung onto the mahogany bunk for dear life, willing the dizziness to clear. My worst problem remained an inability to distinguish between the true sea motion of the boat and the imagined ebb and flow of my own frangible world.

I slowly turned and surveyed the small cabin. The totally unexpected sight of Dana lying with her back to me on the opposite bunk a few short feet away jump-started my brain. I stilt-walked across to her on spaghetti legs, thrilled to see she was bound—it meant she was still alive.

"Dana, are you okay?" I touched her shoulder tentatively.

She went rigid as an oak board, then bucked high off the bunk. She turned to stare at me with saucer-shaped eyes void of all recognition. Huge with total terror, they were. Her mouth was taped; still she began making ugly sounds, bestial groans. I waited, caressing her cheek with a trembling hand, and slowly the terror was flooded away in a torrent of tears.

"Sorry, Sweets, but there's still only one right way to do this." My numb fingers fumbled to start a tag end of tape. It felt as if I were wearing heavy mittens. At last I got a corner free and yanked the damnable muzzle away.

Dana inhaled sharply, choking on the involuntary spasms of her sobs. I reached for her wrists and began worrying at the knots. "Ever get that weird feeling this has all happened to you before?"

Her sense of humor was temporarily AWOL. I didn't blame her a bit. "Matt, you were dead; I even heard them say so. I saw you myself, and *you were dead!* God, you should see yourself. Your head . . ."

"Think I'll pass, thanks just the same—if it looks like it feels, I don't want to know. Now, where the hell are we, and what's going on?"

"We're on Roscoe's boat. Left San Diego Harbor less than an hour ago. They brought us aboard last night sometime."

I removed the last of the line from her hands and started on her ankles. The bonds were snug; it was no way to treat one of the world's truly great pairs of ankles. "Why the boat ride?"

"They're leaving the country, Matt. Yesterday afternoon— after they caught us—they flew back to the compound. I was conscious by then. It was crawling with police, so they kept right on going. The two of them sat up all night making plans; I could hear almost every word. They had to wait until the bank opened this morning. Tina left to make a bank run—the second she got back we pulled out. You were wrong about her, Matt. *She's the boss!* Roscoe is the puppet and she's definitely the puppet master. He's so hot for her, when she says 'jump,' all he does is ask, 'How high?' It was pitiful last night—with all that was happening, and you lying there supposedly dead, all he could think of was to keep begging her to go to bed with him."

Her ankles were free. I straightened up and made the mistake of running my right hand over my head. It felt all crusty and dead, and the shape was all wrong. It was like running your hand over the rusted-out rocker panel of an old car. I jerked my hand back in disgust. "Nice of them to invite us along." I remembered Danny's description of the boss's love of killing ruefully—it honestly hadn't occurred to me he was talking about Tina. As Jimmy Durante was often heard to say, "I was mortified."

"We're only invited for part of the honeymoon," Dana informed me bitterly. "I had the dubious pleasure of lying here listening to them hashing it out. In the end, they decided to play it safe and deep-six us well out to sea. This way, should they ever get picked up in Brazil—which is where they're ultimately headed—they won't be extradited. If the police could pin our murders on them, they'd be in jeopardy, but this way the most anyone could ever prove is drug smuggling, and Brazil doesn't extradite for that."

"So we're scheduled to go swimming, are we? I wish I knew how much time we've got—it would sure help."

"None, I'm afraid. They decided as soon as we were well clear of the Los Coronados Islands in Mexican waters—that's it. We've been in Mexico for the last five or ten minutes, Matt. I'm an expert at dead reckoning and I've been keeping track—it's automatic with me. And I've run this same model of boat over this same course more than once."

"Is that what you were doing? Lying there, ticking off the miles, and waiting for them to come for you?"

She stood up now. Taking a closer look at my head, she winced, shook her head in wonder, and came into my arms. "No. As I said, it's just automatic. I was trying to get into a trance— the very deepest I could manage. Even cease breathing altogether if I could swing it. I didn't want to know when they came for . . ."

Her fine, dusky voice began to break. I pulled her tight as my feeble arms were able. "I don't know about you, honey, but personally I'm tired of our new friends."

"Mostly what I want is a drink," she told me wistfully.

"Done! Let's hie for the nearest bar. I believe I'll even join you. We may have several."

She pushed off, just far enough to look at me in mock disbelief. "You? Several? I can hardly believe my ears."

"What can I say? Tina and Roscoe have left a bad taste in my mouth. Bring on the wassail."

"Just like that, huh?"

"All we can do is try, kid. I've got an idea—nothing complicated. I'm not up to any fancy gambits. Things are all furry looking, and they want to fade in and out at times. So here's what I suggest we do . . ."

She was less thrilled with my plan than I am over brussels sprouts, but had to admit she didn't have any alternatives. We left the small guest cabin—which was aft starboard—and crept forward along the narrow passage. The first of the sticky parts came as we mounted the four steps to the salon deck. At the port corner aft was the companionway leading outside. Tina and Roscoe were probably at the lower helm station just beyond that hatch, but not within view of the salon, unless one of them happened to be over on the port side of the bridge deck. It would be a real bonus if they were clear up on the flying bridge, but that was unlikely, since it wasn't warm enough at sea this time of year. Besides, they had a chore to perform below decks any minute.

We scuttled unchallenged across the tiny living area and down another four steps into the galley. All the way forward from there, we squeezed into the cramped nose of the ship and closed the forepeak door. Two separate chain rodes lay gathered in bins, both leading up through the deck where they were presumably attached to anchors.

I reached up to make sure the brass dogs securing the forehatch weren't seized. They turned, reluctantly, but quickly freed up. "All set?" I asked Dana, lifting the unsecured hatch an eighth of an inch to be certain it wasn't blocked from above.

"Don't worry about me. But I still can't see the point to plan B. I can't swim fifty miles and that's what it would take, allowing for the strong southeast currents along here. Wouldn't it make more sense if I were to go back with you, and we put all our chips on plan A?"

"Thanks for the offer, but no, it wouldn't. If it doesn't fly, they'd have us right where they had us before—twice! And I for one am getting a little tired of that. Trust me, Dana, there really is a method to my madness."

She managed to conjure up a smile—guaranteed to curl any man's toes—though it was in sharp contrast to the frightened look in her eyes. Then kissing me fiercely, she whispered, "I know you can't be careful, so be lucky, Matt."

I nodded, opened the narrow door a crack, then made my way aft quickly. As I scanned the galley and salon for any makeshift weapon, the feel and the sound of the ship changed. The noise level dropped off considerably, and her bow settled as she lost way. I knew exactly what that meant. Roscoe had shut down one of the engines. It was common practice on the Baja run. Fuel supplies tended to be unreliable along that desolate coast. Yachtsmen often ran on one engine, thus achieving about two-thirds the speed and distance for only half the fuel. The usual system was to alternate engines every twenty-four hours, in order to burn fuel evenly from port and starboard tanks to keep the ship in trim. It also meant he'd plotted his course—probably set the auto pilot—and was now free to come below and discharge any excess baggage. Namely Dana and me.

I was rummaging through galley drawers with my back to the hatch when the ominous sound of heavy footsteps on the teak deck aft reached me. Settling for the nearest carving knife, I turned and raced for the stairs. By the time I'd mounted the four shallow steps to the salon deck, Roscoe was right there, staring wide-eyed at me from the companionway. I gave him a dirty look and undertook three actions simultaneously: heaved the feeble blade in his general direction, spun and dove down the steps forward, and screamed: "Dive, dive," like some lunatic submarine skipper.

If the thrown knife accomplished anything, it certainly was nothing significant. The flimsy blade was a poor excuse for a weapon. The boom of Roscoe's gun overfilled the below decks, and a chunk of mahogany molding disintegrated from the passage as I raced along it.

Dana'd had the good sense to leave the forepeak door open,

which may well have made the difference. She was gone, and the foredeck hatch was flung wide. The door behind me exploded, spitting splinters at my legs as I mounted the fo'c'sle bunk and crawled out of the hatch.

Poised on the coaming, I glanced aft. Tina smiled at me gaily as a child from behind the helm. It still startled me to see again how stunningly beautiful she was. Then she darted quickly around the port side of the wheelhouse clutching her deadly little gun in both hands, apparently determined to be more accurate this time. Suddenly I knew why she was smiling so happily: I was alive—an unexpected bonus. She was going to have the pleasure of killing me again. I hastily shucked the ugly timepiece from my wrist, pulled the stem free of the housing, dropped it back down the hatch, and made a flat Indian dive over the port rail.

The frigid Pacific was a shock. I ignored its numbing threat and fought for depth. Kicking and clawing my way down, I devoted some time to hoping Randy had known what he was doing. When my momentum was soon spent, it was all I could do to keep from popping right back up to the surface. Suddenly I felt as if an elephant were stepping on me. Water can't be compressed, so everything within it has to take the beating. My chest ached—I could sense a great sound, but I couldn't hear a thing. I hung in liquid space—stunned and unable to function, yet entirely aware. Time stopped flowing. I remembered a childhood fantasy—Kingsley's *Water Babies*—and idly wondered why I too couldn't exist under water. And where in the hell were those damn sea faeries when you needed them?

A pleasant reverie was shot to hell as I broke surface and swallowed a mouthful of sea water and diesel oil. My violent reaction to the noxious draft at least served to bring me back from the brink of oxygen starvation.

Treading water gently, I gazed around at the debris. It struck me as incongruous to see material burning on the sea, but smoke and even a few small flames dotted the seascape. The largest single intact piece was a four- by six-foot section of the coach roof floating inverted some ten yards away. I was thinking it had definite possibilities as a lifeboat, when I heard a saucy cry: "Hey, sailor; want a good time?"

There was Dana—far off behind me—perched high and dry in an Avon Redcrest inflatable dingy. I must have swallowed something besides sea water. It was about the size of a softball, and I had a lot of trouble getting it down. "You going to just sit there, wanton lady, or are you going to come over here and snatch me from the jaws of death?"

She giggled. Now—please understand—Dana is not a giggler. It's one of the approximately two thousand four hundred and seventy-six things I like best about her. Still, I admit she giggled. Maybe it was her way of swallowing softballs. "Sorry, sailor; I forgot to order paddles."

Renewed by the glorious sight of her, I crawled the thirty yards to the craft. After I wriggled aboard, we sat and compared notes. Finding we were both reasonably intact, we began using our hands to maneuver over to likely looking flotsam we thought might serve as paddles. After upgrading our mobility by means of a pair of suitable strakes of planking, we set out on a serious salvage expedition. We both knew we might be faced with a prolonged sea interlude: the Mexican coast lay due east, but our glorified inner tube would only go southeast—inflatables minus engines don't go to windward very well. We weren't too particular, retrieving anything that struck us as even remotely useful. Our wealth of booty included such riches as sodden bedding and choice delicacies highlighted by waterlogged crackers. There was no sign of our would-be executioners, for which we were both enormously grateful.

"See—plan B wasn't so bad, was it?" I remarked smugly.

"I don't think you'd have been too thrilled with it if I hadn't had the good sense to take this Avon over the side with me."

So much for smug. "Where did you find it?" I asked, chastened.

"Right there in the forepeak. You left me with nothing else to do, so I dug around after you left." She grinned innocently—after planting the hook she'd given me an out.

Dana took command, since she was the pro when it came to things afloat. She suggested a schedule. It didn't amount to much, since the current would bring us ashore well down the Baja coast in its own good time regardless of anything we did or didn't do. Mostly we were to alternate watches—to look out for shipping—and man the trolling fish line. Neither of us was dumb enough to want to discuss what we were supposed to do if we found ourselves under the oncoming bow of a freighter. We'd come up with some gear from a floating plastic tackle box and Dana seemed anxious to test some weird theory about pressing moisture from fish to take the place of fresh water—said it was something Thor Heyerdahl and others had found useful. I told her in no uncertain terms I found the idea repulsive in the extreme. She assured me my views would be subject to review if we were still adrift in four days. The one priceless commodity we hadn't been able to salvage was fresh water.

When the timid sun finished immersing itself into the western sea, we each sought the warmth of the other's body. Stretched out in the bottom of the tiny boat—with heads propped against comfortable rubber gunnels—we covered ourselves with a damp blanket.

"Is the nightmare really over, Matt?"

The raft flexed beneath us as a thing alive, reacting to the gentle undulations of the restless sea. The realization that the motion had never ceased since the beginning of time inevitably made you feel a part of the whole—an integral piece of the continuum of time and space—at peace with yourself and the world around you.

"Yeah, it really is—honest."

"Thank God for small favors. I enjoy your company, Matt; you know I do. But these last forty-eight hours have been an utter bitch. I've never in my worst nightmare dreamed I'd have so many people trying to do so many nasty things to me. Does this sort of thing happen to you often?"

"Um," I mumbled fatuously.

The last thing I remember, the admiral was calling for a vote on who was to stand the first watch. I left it to her to decide, and tumbled into a bottomless pit.

CHAPTER 18

*I*t felt absolutely fine to be back in my favorite room in the world. A full week had gone by since Danny's phone call had driven me racing into the night. It was my first meeting with Win since my Prodigal Son act. I leaned well back, head against the rest, the back of my lap balanced on the edge of my chair, and my feet propped on my middle desk drawer. The position annoyed him something terrible but there wasn't much he could say at the moment—the timing for chewing me out would have been all wrong.

He looked at me and frowned, though he didn't think he did. His words and tone of voice told me he thought he was smiling. "Remarkable!" he stated. "In spite of your frightening head wound—and several days at sea to boot—Randy declares you to be quite fit."

"So he tells me. No little splinters of bone doing nasty things to my brain—no bleeders leaking vital fluids anywhere. My vision has stopped fading out on me. All I've got left to complain about is one whale of a bone bruise." I couldn't control the reflex that made me reach up and touch the bandaged area where my hair had been shaved away. At least it felt more or less the right shape again.

"It's fortunate Miss Kline wasn't a more accurate markswoman."

"At a range of three feet, it's hardly a question of marksmanship. Much as she loved the concept, she'd probably never really learned how to fire a handgun. Made the usual amateur's mistake of pulling her shot. The bullet struck at sufficient angle to deflect and follow the skull. I guess it tunneled beneath my scalp and exited near the crown without penetrating. Call it a combination of bad shooting, too-small calibre a bullet, and a thick skull. Randy says the saltwater rinses and sun made a fair disinfectant, and I shouldn't even show a scar after the hair grows back. Until it does, I'm afraid you'll have to put up with me around the house a lot. I don't want to run around frightening kids and little old ladies into fits." I was ready for a change of subject matter. The vivid image of Tina's gun blowing up in my face and the certainty my head had been split wide open was with me day and night.

"Pity, in a way. A Heidelberg scar would have added character. Supposed to appeal to women as well." The subject of women depressed him as always, and triggered an additional comment. "It would seem your lady friend—Miss Marsh—proved a boon companion." He said it dubiously, no doubt thinking I'd padded her part to make her look good. That would threaten him because then he'd have to wonder why. But it was the sort of thing he expected of me—which is eminently fair, because I expect the opposite of him.

"You'd better believe it—if not for Dana, I think it's safe to assume I wouldn't have made it."

"On the contrary: If not for her you would never have had to place yourself at such terrible risk in the first place," Win corrected me.

Our eyes clashed like drawn swords. I gave as good as I got, then passed it off with a negligent wave of my hand. "We're never going to work that one out, so we'd better let it lie." He had this theory we should both live like monks, to avoid being vulnerable to exactly the sort of extortion Dana had just been used to accomplish. Easy for him to say at his stage of the game. From what I'd heard, at my age he cut a wide swath through the ladies.

"Miss Marsh emerged in good health and spirits?" he asked solicitously. His way of yielding the point and healing the breach.

"We came ashore right in the middle of this little shark-hunting village, sixty miles south of Ensenada. Should have seen those guys' faces when Dana stepped out of the raft. I think they elected her queen, or something roughly equivalent by the time we left the next day. As for spirits, they make their own cactus juice down there, and we made a serious dent in their supply. Those people are having it rough—most of the tonics and other products they once used sharks' oil for are now being synthesized chemically. There are certain things they are desperate for; Dana and I are getting a load together and running it down to them sometime next week."

"I congratulate you upon the cogency of your cryptographic telephone message; it was enough to allow me to pinpoint your location."

"We'll split that one. Afterward, I realized what an esoteric reference it really was—chalk it up to that leakproof mind of yours that it worked." It was a rare day when we exchanged compliments verbally. I knew this would fulfill our quota for the duration.

"When will you be fit to resume your regimen with Dirk?" Another of his obsessive hangups was making certain I exercised constantly. For him, a rough day meant having to walk from his bedroom back to the office at night because he forgot his book. At my age he was far from a teetotaler, but it damn near killed him to think of me taking a drink. It had been an adolescent fillip to mention it, and I was already beginning to regret it.

"Whenever he's ready. I've been giving Dirk lots of space since I got back—he's wound up pretty tight. Right now he's taking it out on the grounds, catching up on all those things that didn't get done while he was caged."

"*Caged* is apt, Matt. He was almost like a wild animal by the time I secured his release. Get him back into the routine as soon as possible—tell him you require it as a result of your ordeal. It's what he needs most in his life right now."

"Sure, Boss—I just hope he doesn't tear my head off the first time we work out on the mat. I take it there are no loose ends left in the case? I understand Roscoe's third Musketeer—Tommy—was nailed at the tile factory and sang like a nightingale."

"In the usual manner such birds usually sing," Win nodded. "He indicts everyone, while assuring the authorities he's innocent of all save the most venial of sins. Yet we should be grateful—he did lead Chief Inspector Fogarty to Marlee Reynaud's body, thus paving the way for Dirk's release. The Inspector—you were correct, he's an able man—is currently occupied running to earth and arresting your fellow players. If they're poor thespians it's not surprising—their primary function was the disbursement of high-grade Colombian cocaine throughout Los Angeles. Alas, I fear your debut on the boards will never be released. The film, of course, was a ruse to justify the daily gathering of her army of 'retailers,' just as Sea View was nothing more than a shell game to disguise the 'wholesale' end of the horrid business. In the beginning—oddly enough—it was the film that was important to Tina Kline; the money was merely to support it."

"It's the world's loss my picture won't be released to a panting public," I told him loftily. "What exactly was the gimmick used to get the nose candy into the country?"

"Simple, yet ingenious: A portion of each shipment of the blue roofing tiles was being drilled out and filled with a plastic bag of cocaine. The opening was then cemented over. It never occurred to anyone that the site of Sea View was taking delivery of an excessive number of roofing tiles."

"It occurred to Barney Clyde." I had to chuckle at the thought of the turkey-necked old geezer, sitting watching one of the biggest drug pipelines in the country. But to his everlasting credit, at least he knew lousy condo builders when he saw them.

"It may interest you to know, Mr. Clyde will be coming out of retirement. In my most recent conversation with Mr. Kline I put forth Mr. Clyde's name as job foreman to oversee the completion of the project at Sea View. As compensation I suggested he be given his choice of units and might thus be enjoined to remain as manager/custodian. So, as a satisfying side effect we've managed to return Mr. Clyde's ocean view to him." It was just the kind of quid pro quo that appealed to Win. It was all he could do to keep from simpering.

I was beginning to get an idea. "So you've been in touch with Reuben Kline a number of times? He must have come out of his so-called stroke okay."

"Considering he's been confined to his bed for the better part of a year, he's doing remarkably well. There has been a good bit of muscle atrophy—to be expected—but he enjoys daily improvement. His mental acuity seems unimpaired. He sends you his very best regards, by the way."

"Of course. And how about poor Marsha?"

"His elder daughter is currently undergoing treatment in a private sanitarium near her home in Newport Beach. She's been tentatively diagnosed as suffering from a schizoid-type state that effectively prevents her from interfacing with her fellow beings. Naturally, she is severely depressed as well. The prognosis is good—so I've been told—but only to a point."

"In other words, Marsha Kline is never likely to be the life of the party."

"Parties for her are unlikely in any event. At best, it is to be hoped she might one day function within the confines of her own home, and be maintained on an outpatient basis."

"Does anyone even know why Tina did all this? Didn't her father realize what a sicko he had on his hands?"

"No! Neither did you, apparently. And you didn't even have the excuse of parental nearsightedness," he added with surprising vehemence. "He tells me the situation developed gradually, as a result of Tina's own increasing use of cocaine. It often works that way. Bright, creative, hard-driving individuals on cocaine may become amoral villains, convinced of personal invulnerability because they perceive themselves as so much quicker and brighter than those around them. We'll never know exactly how Tina and Roscoe Blaise came to join forces; probably he contacted her concerning an honest desire to build upon her father's land. It's clear she completely controlled him in the traditional way in which women control men." He gave me a meaningful look—to make sure I got the moral. "We do know there shortly followed an incredibly violent and tragic week within the Kline household, beginning with the murder of Deborah Kline."

I just sat there for a few seconds waiting for the name to register—nothing! Maybe Randy was wrong, and Tina's bullet had erased some of my memory tapes. "Who's Deborah Kline?" I finally broke down and asked.

"It never occurred to you—I thought not," he said, very condescendingly. "Deborah Kline was Tina's mother, the first casualty of her mad rampage. According to our 'songbird,' Tommy, Tina once boasted over the fact that she'd laced her mother's nightly vodka tonic with half a dozen Valiums, then forced another several dozen down the numbed but living victim's throat with a straw, and by massaging the swallowing reflex under the jaw—the same way one gives capsules to a domestic cat. You grimace at the vision—I don't blame you. Reuben Kline was highly suspicious because his wife was very cautious about never combining alcohol and her Valium. Of course, his fate had been decreed whether or not he was suspicious. The only thing that kept him alive was the knowledge that his death would result in an audit of the estate for purposes of probate. Tina could ill afford that.

"Her elder sister's confinement was originally to force Mr. Kline to execute a proper power of attorney in Tina's favor. But then—in the throes of her mounting conviction concerning her own omnipotence—it became necessary to degrade the elder sister who'd always been the ideal against whom she'd been measured and found wanting all of her life. Marsha Kline was a graduate of UCLA with a degree in cinematographic arts. Her father indulged her by backing a film she did. Tina's request for the same privilege was refused. It's a mistake too many parents make, but seldom has it reaped a sorrier reward. How it must have tickled her sick fancy to know this paragon was suffering the most sordid of degradations imaginable."

I pictured Marsha Kline—lying curled into the fetal position—staring at me with a look of terror and disgust in her huge eyes. I remembered the stink. . . . Unwilling to summon up that particular demon at the moment, I changed the subject. "One thing I still can't figure. Which one of the boys stayed home and helped Tina dispose of Marlee's body? I realize we'll only have Tommy's word for it, but I'm curious what he says."

"The answer—and I'm certain it's the truth—is none of them. They were all aboard, even as Mr. Blaise avowed. No one saw Tommy aboard because he was indeed *hors de combat* due to *mal de mer*. It's also why he was elected to stay behind when Tina brought in the rental helicopter to facilitate the search for you— motion sickness would have rendered him a liability in the air as well."

"I can't see crazy, beautiful Tina managing to lug the body from that apartment alone. Somebody had to lend a hand."

"Not at all," Win proclaimed smugly. I could almost see the hat where the rabbit was about to pop out. "Mrs. Reynaud left with Miss Kline voluntarily—alive!"

"What? Good God, why?"

"Because she'd quite foolishly elected to blackmail her employers with her discovery of their transgressions. We may presume she only knew that drugs were being channeled through the ersatz construction site; had she known the range and depth of Tina's growing penchant for violence, she would scarcely have structured her plan as she did. Yes, it was Mrs. Reynaud who dictated that all four men be isolated at sea, in a naive assumption she would be safe enough dealing directly with the disarming Ms. Tina Kline. When I said she left with Tina, I didn't mean from her apartment. Tina would never have gone near that apartment for obvious reasons. But they rendezvoused somewhere, and Mrs. Reynaud was actually given the hundred thousand dollars she'd demanded. Her fears apparently allayed, she agreed to accompany Tina to the airfield in Mexico. It was also part of the agreement she leave the country immediately so there was nothing suspicious about the trip south. We have this much information courtesy of Tommy, but we know at least this portion of his tale is true. And we also know Tina was totally unaware of the contrived murder scene that awaited all of us back at Mrs. Reynaud's apartment."

"But why dinner with Dirk the very night she was blowing the country? His prints carefully preserved on a bloody knife—more blood everywhere?" The implications were clear, even as I spoke. *"She set Dirk up?"*

"The facts speak for themselves. She sought to kill two birds with a single stone. No one would search for her if she were presumed dead. Apparently the second dead bird was to be Dirk," he added dryly.

"Sweet Jesus!" I muttered in disbelief.

"Perhaps she somehow still blamed Dirk for the death of his father. Distance lends enchantment—she may have recalled him as a paragon among men, difficult as that may be to imagine. More likely she felt nothing for Dirk, and he was merely selected for convenience and credibility. No doubt it was a simple matter to find a way to hold the knife bearing Dirk's prints—perhaps with some tool such as a padded pliers—and open a vein. She bears such a wound high on her left arm, a convenient location, easily covered with sleeved dresses. The amount of blood donated to a blood bank would be enough to paint the scene of several massacres and yet not noticeably weaken the donor. And there you have the essence of the entire, sordid tale."

"You aren't planning to tell Dirk, are you?"

"I don't respond to fatuous questions, even from you," he replied frostily.

I'd asked for it, and I'd gotten it. It was definitely time to change the subject. "I still think Roscoe missed his calling—he should have been the actor. I'd have sworn he was telling us the truth when he gave us that blank look the day I thanked him for the candy."

"You overestimate him. He had no idea what you were talking about. Tina Kline sent that horrid box of candy, after hearing about your late-night visit to Sea View. As I've said before, she suffered no ambivalence when it came to making violent decisions."

"What a girl!" I shook my head in sad disbelief. "But I still haven't actually figured out how you knew it was Roscoe and Tina. I remember you got a gleam in your eye after my report on my visit with the realtor who leased Danny and the boys their house."

"Merely attention to detail," he purred. "Mr. Benchly told you he'd received a call from one of his tenants stating their intention to leave. The call came two days earlier, he said. That means he was given notice one full day before Roscoe Blaise claimed to have fired them and sent them away. And Miss Burman's tedious recital was also instructive. Her description of Marlee Reynaud's inexplicable habit of accosting people at her door and talking interminably in a loud voice was suggestive. People seldom behave unaccountably in real life, therefore such an inconsistency was suggestive."

He sat there—bolt upright in his chair—grinning at me. There was nothing I could do but take it. If I'd had a hat on, I would have taken it off to him. He'd earned it. Now there was only one area he hadn't brought me up to date on. He'd walked all around it, but left it up to me to ask. Typical! "Would it kill you to tell me? Other than his best regards, did Reuben Kline happen to send anything else? Something a bit more tangible, perhaps?"

Win's lean, elegant face affected a look of surprise. "Oh, did I neglect to mention it? Yes, he did. I took the liberty of reminding him when he made his dramatic appeal to you to find his daughter—Marsha—it constituted a contract for our services. He is a gracious man. Most generous, in actual fact."

I sat upright, waiting for him to go on. He waited for me to beg. He's a better waiter than I am. I don't really mind. He doesn't get out much—baiting me is about the only real fun he has. He was having a great time right now. "Has the amount slipped your mind? Or are you waiting for me to get down on my knees?"

Win grinned hugely. "That I would pay to see. The amount of our fee was seventy-five thousand dollars. I realize it is ordinarily your province to handle financial arrangements, but you were occupied at the time, floating about at sea with a comely lass, or perhaps attending a drunken revelry," he told me airily.

I grinned right back—things were back to normal. While I was quietly savoring the notion of a longer trip back to Mexico with Dana than originally planned, Louis appeared through a crack in the office door. "Yes, Louis?" Win inquired grandly.

"That terrible policeman is here," he said, allowing the resentment to show on his normally placid face. "You know—the one who drops lighted cigarettes all over the porch." Louis usually liked everybody, but he had a very proprietary attitude toward the house. Dixon was on his shit list—the same as he was on ours, only for different reasons.

"That's because you never invite him in," I explained. "It upsets him; he thinks you don't like him."

Louis wrinkled his face in thought, then said: "If I let him in, he'd drop them on the floor inside. I don't think he's a very nice man, Matt." Louis may be slow, but he gets there. I couldn't have summed it up better myself.

"Thank you, Louis," Win said, dismissing him. He turned to me and told me icily, "Mr. Doyle, please tell Inspector Dixon I do not wish to see him."

"You can call me Matt. He's only on the porch—he can't hear you. Don't you think we ought to find out what the man wants first?"

"I know full well what he wants. He wishes to berate me for

extending the full cooperation of this office to Chief Inspector Fogarty to the exclusion of him. This—mind you—from the very man who took inordinate delight in arresting Dirk before my very eyes as I sat dining at my own table in my own home. This from the man who vandalized my house and grounds. This from the man who . . . never mind! The man is a dolt. Send him away. Inform him I have attained an age whereupon I no longer suffer fools gladly."

I was up and on my way, pleased at the prospect of my task. "Can I quote you?"

"Please do!"